"HELL'S CARGO"

A SPLATTER WESTERN

MICHELLE GARZA & MELISSA LASON

DEATH'S HEAD PRESS

Paperback ISBN: 9781639511709
eBook ISBN: 9781639511716

Published by Death's Head Press,
an imprint of Dead Sky Publishing, LLC
Miami Beach, Florida
www.deadskypublishing.com

Cover by Luke Spooner
Illustration by Mike Fiorentino, Jr.
Edited by Anna Kubik
Copyedited by Deanna Destito

To our families—Ricardo, Kiki, Bobby, Kahlan, and Chris—Thanks for always supporting us and our love for all the spooky things!

WHERE NO WIND BLOWS

THE HORSE, LATHERED WITH sweat, had been pushed to its limits. Its breathing was labored but still Henry spurred it onward. Henry's vision blurred around the edges, a constant halo around everything he looked at. He could hardly see at night anymore; it was the reason he made damn sure to leave just before the sun rose.

He had to make it far, far away before his eyes gave out on him or he fell over dead.

He coughed, wet and painful, and spat blood down his shirt and onto the back of the horse. Thick crimson mucus hung in slimy strings from its mane. Henry tasted blood day and night now. His lungs were turning to red custard in his aching chest. Consumption was a nasty way to go.

Henry was a dead man already, that's why he took the box. There was no sense in having one of the younger men at the T.B. home do away with it. They were sentenced to die like him, but they had what he didn't anymore, time, even if it was only days or weeks.

When he crawled from his deathbed, he planned to just ride the cursed thing out as far as his body would allow and bury it somewhere in the endless desert, somewhere no human could open it again, and then lay himself down to die. His only regret would be pushing Star too hard and taking her with him. She was a good old horse and didn't deserve for him to run her into the ground. He eased up on her a bit, hoping she could carry him farther into no man's land, someplace fitting to bury a box full of the demonic.

The thing inside the box, tied in a gunny sack spoke, its incessant gurgling voice sounded like it came through sludge. He wanted to ask it if it had also contracted tuberculosis.

Henry first heard it talking through Gabriella. The poor young woman, the thing crept inside of her, and ate her up like a maggot. By the time it was done with her, only a matter of days, it opened her right up and crawled from her hollow shell like a crimson slug back to its box, leaving a trail of her blood behind it.

Henry always liked Gabriella. She was the only nurse back at the house of the walking dead, the consumption hospital, he actually liked. The others were callous, soulless, exhausted things draped in dingy white dresses. The worst of them was a nun Henry called old Sour Puss because her face always looked like she had just sniffed the turd shoot of a pack mule. She sure touted God's word but was an evil cunt that enjoyed the suffering of others. He could see it in her eyes because he was a mean motherfucker most of his life and a wolf could always recognize other wolves.

After the thing burst from Gabriella's belly, the old nun chased it down the hallway with her crucifix. It laughed at her as she tied the box in a gunny sack and prayed over it, confirming to Henry that Sour Puss wasn't any closer to God than a snake's asshole. Her words didn't even phase the damn thing. If anything, they entertained it.

The box came in a trunk with a foreign man. Henry thought he was Russian: he wasn't too sure because the man died within days of coming to the consumption hospital, coughing and gagging up what was left of his ravaged lungs. The foreigner either didn't have the breath to warn them about the box or didn't give a shit who found out what was inside. It was old Sour Puss who went rummaging through his belongings.

"It states he has no family, like the rest of you. It would be a waste to let this get burned," Sour Puss said carrying the ornately carved box and placing it up on the mantle above the fireplace she refused to light. She was too lazy to clean the ashes from it, even when dying men were cold down to their bones.

Gabriella opened the fancy box, though. Poor young thing, curiosity got the best of her. He couldn't blame her. The box looked so beautiful on the outside she decided she needed to see the inside, too. She cracked it open, only for a second, and her eyes rolled back in her head, a stream of piss ran down her legs.

It took her over fast. She was under its control in a matter of minutes, and it ate her up like a greedy sow, stomping its own young to get to the slop, and then gorging until its gut ruptured.

Henry spoke from experience because he'd seen the sin of gluttony in every form from a barnyard to a dope den with velvet cushions to fall into. His eyes were keen to it.

After Gabriella collapsed and soiled herself, Sour Puss helped her clean up, unaware something was hitching a ride inside her beautiful flesh. The nun blamed the dizzy spell on the humidity and sent Gabriella back to wiping asses and catching buckets full of bloody lung butter. But, when night fell, and Gabriella shed her nurse's dress to roam the hallways naked as the day she was born and jump into the thin beds of some of the younger patients to ride them harder than he had ever ridden Star, it became obvious she was no longer herself.

The outcome for the patients ended up the same, though, especially for Marty McAllister, a thirty-two-year-old dying man. Gabriella fucked him to death. He came and threw up his lungs at the same time in a bloody explosive cough that flung red chunks up on her face and breasts.

When Sour Puss caught Gabriella, or whatever it was controlling her, covered in infectious secretions and the cum of a dead man running down her thighs, she confronted her.

Gabriella's voice was a throaty gurgle when she told the nun to eat shit. Henry could hear it down the hallway, the whole incident from her naked roaming to the fucking of Marty, to the showdown with Sour Puss. He couldn't believe it and was disgustingly entertained. Gabriella called her an old cunt as the orderlies came to drag the corpse of Marty away, his peter still standing at attention.

They strapped Gabriella down in his stained bed. Henry couldn't see it but he could hear it. Days came and went, and Gabriella wailed and cussed nearly the whole time. She once talked an orderly into sticking his finger in her ass and then in her mouth. He was jerking off with his free hand and didn't even realize she was plotting something until she bit his finger clean off.

Sour Puss not only fired him, but she also beat him across the back of his head with a broom and told him he deserved to live his life missing a finger for being such a fool.

Henry didn't sleep, he just listened, a blind witness to the young nurse's death. It came upon her without mercy, like a sudden attack from a wild animal. Sour Puss came with her cross but couldn't subdue the gelatinous creature or kill it. She couldn't stop it from tearing Gabriella open. It escaped back to its box to hide and wait.

Henry looked like an idiot but wasn't one; he knew that's how it "lived" and for who knows how long. The foreigner had brought the devil with him and didn't lift a finger to stop it from being unleashed before he took a dirt nap. For all Henry knew it was some Russian demon that could never be killed, but he would do his best to hide it.

When he spoke of his plan, no one even tried to stop him. Who would after watching it burst out of Gabriella and crawl down the hall like a gelatinous dwarf-sized humanoid blood clot back to its precious box? They wanted the box gone and they didn't give a shit who took the damn thing. Henry was given his horse and a canteen by Sour Puss and told good luck and go fuck himself all in the same breath.

"Take it someplace where no sun will shine on it, where no wind will blow across it. A place where no humans will find it. And may God travel with you for I know you won't make it back."

They watched him go, more to make sure he didn't come back than to admire his courage. They knew it would be his last ride. He knew it too and accepted it. He just hoped God would forgive his past sins and save him a spot in heaven after his last act of bravery.

Henry's lungs were barely functioning anymore. He was drowning in his own blood. When he coughed, he no longer tried to catch it in a hankie or clean himself up. He wanted to look like a scary motherfucker when Death came, maybe make it think twice about taking him for a minute or two.

His mind was haunted now, just kept remembering the sound of Gabriella's death. Her screams ending in a wet ripping sound was the same kind of pitiful torment audible when he was just a young 'un somewhere between being a boy and a man, and his father insisted on his assistance when one of the sows was having a hard time giving birth. One of the piglets got stuck; it was forced out all the wrong way and obstructed the hole. His father tried saving the mama by yanking it free. It came out, the mama squealing in torment, showering his father in blood and chunky liquids. Henry couldn't bear to watch it all, but he heard it all and when his father called his name he turned around to see him, his face blank. He stood motionless for a moment holding a limp piglet by one leg. He finally snapped out of it and looked to Henry who vomited down onto his boots. He was too young to understand anything about birth, but he was beginning to understand death. It spared nothing no matter how young or how innocent it was.

The sow died three hours later, her belly still twitching with unborn young she didn't have the strength to push out.

Henry never had any children of his own. Somewhere in his mind he always worried whoever he knocked up would end up like that sow, crippled and dying by a mangled birth, succumbing to blood loss with a disfigured babe dangling from her gash.

Star faltered, stumbled, and Henry clung to the saddle. If he fell, he might not get back up and he couldn't let her run off with the box tied to her side. Star's breathing was deep puffs, nostrils flaring as if there wasn't enough air in all of Texas to fill her lungs. He didn't push her to haul ass anymore, but she needed a break, or she'd keel over in the dust and take him with her. He slowed her to a halt even though he knew they didn't have much time. He could feel death crawling up his back.

He climbed down from the saddle and nearly collapsed. He struggled with himself; his mind was still willing, but his body was not> He managed to free his canteen. He dumped a little into his mouth and then went to Star, holding one hand cupped under her mouth as he poured water into it and listened to her gulp it down.

"You can make it a little longer, then you'll be one your own," He whispered.

His guts twisted. The small mouthful of water was already trying to either come back up his throat or blow out his ass. He didn't give a shit anymore; he'd crap right in his pants and still keep riding. The box in the sack echoed with laughter, but he paid it no mind.

Henry crawled back into the saddle, feeling a burning ripple through his chest. He wasn't sure which would give out first, his lungs or his heart. He opened a leather saddle bag. Tucked inside was mercy passed into his palm by an orderly on his way out the door. The cold steel of a pistol with one bullet in the chamber, the last trigger he'd pull.

His journey into death had given him time to look back upon his many fuck ups. He had failed many times in his life, but he couldn't let this be one of them, the turd on the top of the cake. This had to be his redemption after decades of fighting, fucking, drinking, and thieving.

Ever since he ran away at fourteen, the day after watching the sow die, he had been no good. What sense did it make to be a good man when God didn't bother to spare the innocent? Their pureness didn't guard them from death's hands. He figured he'd live however he pleased, doing all he wanted until Hell opened up like the mouth of a catfish to take him.

He had some good days, laid down with some pretty women, and drank all he could, but there were bad days too, evil days. He had robbed and killed to survive, but he never killed a child or a woman; no matter how evil some of them could be only other criminals died by his hands. His days stealing cattle had left him slightly disfigured and not just walking bow-legged. The end of his thumb had been ripped off when he roped a steer with far more heart than him. It went wild and like a dumbass, he didn't let go of the rope. It wrapped around his thumb and pulled the skin and muscle off leaving a mangled thumb bone behind. Henry's partner cut the rest of it off for it to heal completely. His gang called him "Stumpy" after that, a nickname he despised and got into many fistfights over, especially when the prostitutes asked if something else was also stumpy.

Those boys he used to run with, one by one they were either hanged or ended up in jail, breaking rocks with hammers. He was lucky to avoid both the rope and the cell, but he guessed ending up with tuberculosis was just as bad in the end.

His lungs seized up and he gripped his chest. He coughed out mouthfuls of his lungs, dark red, almost black like he had rotted from the inside. It hung from his chin like the beard of a much younger man. His breath returned shakily, weak, and nearly useless.

Henry was no longer Stumpy, couldn't fuck all night and fight all day, but he still held onto life like the stubborn bastard he was born to be. After living in the consumption hospital for a little over a year, he found Henry to be much stronger than Stumpy ever pretended to be.

He found humility there, and for a short time in the care of Gabriella he felt compassion through her selfless caring for other human beings. She was an angel in the flesh. The way she died was not only horrifically painful but also degrading. Henry would do his best to defend her honor by burying the box where no human would ever accidentally open it again.

A mesa loomed in the distance. His tunnel vision focused on it. It looked like a stumpy thumb sticking up out of the sand, stout and flat on top. It was a sign to him in his almost delirious state. At the base of the mesa, he would put the box into the earth and then lay himself down and eat some lead.

He became aware he had pissed himself but didn't let it bother him, dying men did lose control of their bladders and bowels and he was walking corpse. He kept his eyes on the mesa, and thought it had to be the place where no wind blows. He prayed it was. At least if there was wind below the mesa, hopefully it wasn't strong enough to unearth the demon's box he planned to bury as deep as his shaking arms could handle. He was exhausted, ready to die, tired of tasting and smelling blood and the infectious chunks of the insides of his lungs.

"Just a little further, old girl," he said to Star.

She was going at a steady pace, and he urged her to move a little faster. He still didn't want her to keel over in the dirt because he knew he'd never make it to the stumpy mesa on his own. They crested a small hill and looked out on a series of narrow canyons at the foot of the mesa, winding like snakes.

He felt the wind blow across his face, fresh and cool, heavy with the scent of rain. His tired eyes realized above his destination hung dark clouds. He grinned; dying in the rain would do his desert-born soul some good. He'd always enjoyed the storms that swept across Texas. He'd dance in the rain when he was a child. He didn't have the strength to dance anymore, but his soul would celebrate when it left his body. Thunder rolled through the sky above him. The storm clouds were like a welcoming party to the dying man.

The scent and cool breeze seemed to liven up Star, too. He patted her neck, noticing she wasn't sweating anymore. She wouldn't have made it much longer if it hadn't been for the gathering rain clouds. No sweat was a sign of hyperthermia, and Henry hoped it poured enough to provide her with more water to cool and hydrate her insides.

"You can make it," he said to Star.

Laughter from the sack reminded him of what failure might bring. If a nun as stone cold as Sour Puss with a crucifix didn't scare it, he didn't know who or what could. He didn't have time to find out. His only option was to hide it.

"You'll never make it, Stumpy. You'll fail like you always have," The voice gurgled, sounding worse than a consumption-stricken Henry.

"Shut up, you sumbitch!"

"No man can get rid of me. I'm ageless. I know all and cannot die!"

"Listen, you piece of hog shit, I'm gonna put you in a place where no one will ever find you!"

"Foolish old man," it laughed. "I am everything, flies, maggots, vultures, and coyotes ready to feast on your innards. You're a dead man...but I can make you live longer, give you all that you desire."

"What I desire is to die a decent man, you fuck!"

Henry coughed and gagged. Bloody snot shot from his nostrils.

"Horse shit! You want to be whole again. You want to drink and fuck and ride the night down. I can give that to you."

"You really are a terrible liar because I know I don't want any of that anymore. I want to die."

Lightning streaked the sky like flaming spider webs. The black clouds rumbled angrily.

"I can never be destroyed, Henry. I will never stay hidden long. Parts of me die while others drift on the wind like swarms of flies looking for carrion. Set me free and reap my rewards."

"And yet you're trapped in a box. Can't you just open it if you're so damn strong?" Henry said with a weak laugh.

"Done talking, huh?" he asked.

He figured Star had enough strength built up to hurry her along again. He spurred her into a gallop as they came to the canyons at the base of stumpy mesa.

"You can't open it. You need a human to do it for you and to live inside of like a worm, like Gabriella. Without a body, you're just a pile of snot! I won't let you take over another person again."

The system of narrow canyons had been etched into the red stone by the millennia of erosion. Lifetimes of precipitation and wind molded it like clay into something majestic. Henry entered the canyon mouth closest to him. He rode down the center of it as rain began to fall steadily onto him and his horse. Winds howled into his face, cold and loud, deafening him to anything else. The canyon walls were sheer cliffs rising up on each side, and ahead he could see them slowly inching inward. There would be a point where he couldn't ride Star anymore, and when it came he decided he'd set her free to race back the way they came and leave him to his fate.

"Almost there," he told her.

The sound of Star's hooves on the stones and the wind blowing his hair back filled his ears. He was grateful the voice from the box couldn't be heard even if it howled. Its promises were tempting, but he wasn't so foolish to believe it wouldn't use his body long enough to get to a fresh, healthy person to inhabit. He refused to be a vessel for it to continue its reign of chaos.

The rain came down harder, drenching Henry. He'd set out before sunrise wearing a pair of pants cinched to his skeletal frame with a belt, his old boots, and a thin button-down shirt. The wind chilled him to his bones and left his hands numb. Little waterfalls from the cliff tops soaked him further, but he wouldn't stop. His chest hurt so badly he could barely stay seated in the saddle. His time was nigh; he resigned himself to it. This canyon at the base of stumpy mesa, as he named it, would be his tomb.

Up ahead, the canyon grew too narrow. He would have to squeeze through it on his own. He stopped Star beneath the cascading rainwater and climbed down from her back. His hands struggled to unbuckle her saddle. She spun to face him, and he kissed her on the white star between her eyes. He untied the sack, put the pistol in the waist of his pants, and pulled a shovel free.

"Go on. Live free, old girl," he said and slapped her on the ass.

Star hurried back the way they came with rain washing away the sweat from her hide. He watched her go, his eyes struggling to see her running back to the land of the living. He listened to the sound of her hoof beats until they were swallowed in the storm. He let the rainwater run over his face, washing away some of the blood staining his stubble lined face.

"Wash away my sins and give me strength to finish my task."

He stepped forward and fell against the canyon wall, his legs feeling like jelly. He righted himself and picked up the sack and shovel, determined to see it through.

He headed forward; his lungs were on fire. He could barely breathe, and the fear of failure swept through him. He gulped air, mouth opening and closing like a fish suffocating on dry land. His head swam as his vision darkened. He fell to his knees. He thought back on the hard ride, how it was a miracle his body endured it. He would force one more miracle and get to his feet.

He rose and struggled forward, turning to squeeze through the narrow canyon walls. Beyond the tight spot it opened a bit and ended in a circular space. His eyes fell on a dark spot in canyon wall, a hole shaped like the eye of a serpent. It would be the perfect place to shove the box into. He would seal it off with rocks and mud, and no one would ever get their hands on it again.

It would rot there until the end of time in a hole where no sun would shine on it and no wind would blow across it again. Henry smiled and waded into knee deep water, vision going black, hands ready to do their last work.

Night was falling and the storm was raging around him, drowning him as he inched closer and closer to the hole in the canyon wall. He lifted the sack and jammed it with the box into the hole. It got stuck. Even laying his meager body weight against it wouldn't force the box inside. It wasn't big enough to accommodate both the rough sack and box.

His hand trembled so bad he almost dropped the box twice as he took it out of the sack. He caught it before it could be carried away in the rising flood. Touching its surface sent a shock up his arms, and he could hear the voice inside shouting, but his mind was slipping. He couldn't understand a word it shrieked. He lifted it, but movement inside the hole caught his attention and the sound of hissing registered in his mind. A snake den. Rattlers poured out of the hole, pushed out by a surge of flood water. Henry fell backward and the box tumbled from his hands.

"You failed again, Stubby!" the box cackled.

The rattlesnakes glided on the surface of the flood and encircled Henry who was leaning against the canyon wall, watching helplessly as the box floated away. They crawled up his body and wound around his neck and arms. Henry cried out as they sank their fangs into him. His heart seized in his chest. A booming crack of thunder was followed by lightning snaking through the sky. Water crashed down on Henry from above like a dirty brown wall, but he was already a dead man.

THE GIRL AFRAID OF STORMS

EVER SINCE SHE WAS a child, Eve was afraid of storms.

More than a decade of living in Louisiana didn't help. The wind and rain howled like lost spirits in the night. Maybe it wasn't just the storms but what was in them, and the fact she never had anyone to ease her fears of them, no one to soothe her when the walls shook and the windows rattled. When the roof wept cold tears down on her trembling body, she was always alone.

She prayed nightly but she prayed harder when the storms came rolling through the dark skies, almost demanding God to stop them, but he didn't hear her. Maybe he was deafened by the thunder, too? She was now a woman but still cowered in fear when the rain came down hard.

For too many years she had no mama to wrap her in a warm embrace and chase her terror away with promises of fighting away all the haints on the wind. Her parents had died when she was little, and she was left in the orphanage at the church ran by the stone-faced nuns.

Eve tried making the other little girls and boys her family, but none of them understood her. None of them were afraid of storms like she was.

But there was one who at least didn't laugh at her. His name was Peter. They grew up together, never finding any other home.

Peter's parents died when he was only a baby. Eve's was taken by influenza, but she at least had them for eight years. She missed her mama everyday as a child, but she couldn't say the same about her daddy. He was a mean man, especially when he drank.

Peter had come to the orphanage when he could barely walk. The nuns refused to care for him until he was older, but the kitchen lady took him in. She died when he was seven, a year before Eve arrived.

What a life, being an orphan twice. Eve never saw him cry, though. She would sometimes imagine she was Peter when she was afraid. He was brave; she always told herself she needed to be like him.

The others, children and adults, didn't understand her. They didn't know why she was a skittish child and always afraid of the howling winds. She could never explain to them she heard voices in them, and they said things that came true. It was usually terrible things like when the garden cat, Mr. Puff, died. What made it worse was the voices revealed it was Mother Marie, the Superior, who killed the cat because she was tired of it shitting in the rose beds. When the children found him lying stiff beneath a tree Eve couldn't tell them the storms told her it would happen and how she felt a twisting pain in her neck as if she was being choked. When she saw Mother Marie approaching the poor dead cat and the crying children, she had to force herself to look away, to not meet the Mother Superior's gaze, for fear the old nun would know she knew the truth.

And when the novice priest, Anthony, hung himself in his dormitory, the voices told Eve he'd be found the next morning. He was, with piss staining the floor beneath him and his eyes open and bulging like a toad. The entire churchyard erupted in screams and crying from Anthony's colleagues and friends; they had no idea he planned to take his own life. But the voices did, and they told Eve all about it in horrific detail, right down to him regretting his decision but it being too late for him to get the noose untied from his neck. How he dangled from the rope and his feet kicked wildly only inches from touching the ground. How he reached out to the door but knew no one would come to discover him; how his last thoughts were riddled with fear of damnation. Eve was still a young girl then and sat up wide eyed in her bed, weeping and waiting for the sun to rise and for the shouting to begin when Anthony would be found suspended from the beam. The voices didn't tell her in time to save his life. No, they informed her only after Anthony had met his pitiful end so she couldn't even awaken Sister Abbie or anyone else to help him. Eve was forced to sit and count the hours and minutes down by watching the light slowly eating the darkness with the rising sun and letting someone else bear witness to his corpse.

She had already opened her mouth too many times about voices and was looked at like a freak or a lunatic by the others, which made her laugh bitterly at Mother Marie since she knew damn well the old nun was a cat killer. And she had the nerve to insinuate there was something wrong with Eve?

No, the girl couldn't perpetuate those rumors. She had to be "normal" if she wished to be accepted. Each time, she pretended to be surprised like the rest of them, but inside her stomach turned into a knot; the voices had been right again. They were always stronger during storms, as if the great supernatural power of the heavens thinned the veil between the world of the living and that of the dead and amplified their cries. She remembered hearing the whispering her whole life,but as she grew older she began to listen to what they said. She was unwilling to admit to anyone there was something God could not protect her from. A nun knowing there were things you can't pray away, that wouldn't look very faithful, would it?

Tonight, the storm was wild, violent, whipping the trees around in the courtyard. They raked across her window like slashing claws, and amid the turmoil of rain and thunder she heard the whispering.

Peter.

Eve pulled her blankets up over her head and felt beneath her thin pillow with a trembling hand. The paper, thin and crinkled, the letter from Peter stating they had made it to California. It gave her an ounce of comfort. She prayed he would come back alive before drifting off.

When the storms were particularly bad, they manifested into vivid nightmares once Eve was finally too exhausted to keep her eyes open.

She still hadn't decided if it terrified her more to stay awake and listen to the voices or to fall asleep and be tossed into dreamscapes of pure horror. This night would be no different.

She is walking the desert cloaked in rainclouds, a baby is crying somewhere in the distance. Pain, a sudden burning burst lit the inside of her head on fire. She brings her hand up to feel the wound where her eye once was. She's blinded on one side, but still able to see that her fingers are not her fingers, dirty and bloody, long and gnarled. Seeing them makes her heart jump, They're not right; they're not human.

She stumbles back. She is wailing and then falling, her blood dancing in the wind as she descends. She is swallowed by water, muddy, filthy. It invades her nostrils and sears the hole where her eye once was. She feels like she's being carried away. Her nose stings; her lungs burn. She lets her arms fall limp at her sides. She can't control her legs. She's like a rag doll, soaking up the river around her. Her thoughts split in two; one side is a frantic, terrified mind, and the other is a gravelly voice, a monster housed inside her skull. The human side is wishing death would just take her quickly while the beast is screaming to live and to seek retribution. Her chest hurts too much; she inhales a lungful of the murky water.

She can't breathe, she can't scream. The skeletal arms of a submerged tree reach out for her. She is forced into them by the current where the blood from the hole in her face seeps out and is carried away from her. As she dies, the two sides of her mind separate, one birthing into the universe as a spirit, filled with sadness. The other flees her body like a serpent and snakes its way along with the flow of the racing water, seeking refuge in either another human body or the peaceful darkness of the black box, its home.

She awakened in a sweat, muttering and crying, unsure if she was alive or dead. A knock on the wall brought her back to reality, and Abbie's voice soothed Eve a bit. She knew it must have been bad if the nun took pity on her and attempted to settle her down. Her heart rate was beginning to return to a somewhat normal pace when she heard the whispering in the storm again.

Peter.

SISTER ABBIE

ABBIE COULDN'T GET COMFORTABLE. She knew the storm would keep the girl awake, but Eve needed to learn to overcome her fears.

Abbie didn't sleep during storms for her own reasons. Memories flooded her mind with pictures of years before, of when she found God through nearly dying, and meeting the devil face to face.

In 1842 Abbie was living in Texas, not yet a bride of Christ, and using her knowledge of a midwife to assist a small church render aid to the unfortunate. She had learned her trade from her mother and her grandmother. They were what some would call granny women, trained through experience mostly in delivering children. Over time they learned more about healing and treating the sick and injured, and it became their trade, a way to make a living.

Abbie was the last of her line. Being a woman of forty years, her mother had passed on fifteen years before in a horse riding accident and took a lot of the granny woman's knowledge to her grave before she could impart it to Abbie.

Abbie was never a mother of her own children and never married, so settling in at the church provided her something to do and somewhere safe to live. After surviving the Comanche raid of Linnville just a few years before, it showed her how dangerous the territory could be. Father Connor's offer was a godsend. She intended to seek out a protégé and teach them all she knew of healing, but it wasn't long before her life took a turn, one leading her closer to being a soldier than a midwife.

The rain started one Thursday afternoon, falling from a gray Texas sky down onto the dusty streets of the small town of Piedra, and didn't stop for seven days. The washes filled with muddy rivers and overflowed, flooding the tiny town. People of the desert never expected such a storm when the town was built.

She remembered the line of people making their way up the hill to the church and Father Connor ringing his bell to call them all to safety. The hilltop church was an island in the storm waters, a beacon to all the sodden people looking for refuge. She came to the gate and welcomed them in; one by one they thanked her and hurried into the safety and warmth of the sanctuary.

The community wasn't very large so she recognized every face passing her, the men, women, and children she tended to regularly. At the end of the line, lagging far behind the rest of the group, came a man and a woman. He had on a black, flat-brimmed hat and a child in a sling across his chest, a baby of no more than a year. The woman came painfully slowly up behind him.

Abbie protected herself with an umbrella, but its thin material couldn't stand up against the heavy drops falling continuously from above. She squinted and didn't think she recognized the last family until they came closer. They lived on a ranch a good distance from Piedra and only came to town to get a few supplies now and then. She didn't even know their names, only that the ranch was named Bauman after the old man who built it, but he had died a few years back. She wasn't sure if they were kin to him or just hired hands looking after the place for Mr. Bauman's family.

"Come on. There's plenty of room," she hailed them over the rainfall.

They were about forty feet away when they stopped beneath a tree just below the crest of the hill.

"No, we just needed high ground," the man in a black hat called back.

"But you're welcome inside. You don't have to be a member."

"No. Thank you."

His reply was short, but she didn't pay it any attention. The rain was bothersome, and he probably didn't want to get roped into converting to Catholicism. She understood; she was once an outsider too, and when it came to being a believer she was still mostly on the outside.

She retreated to the church door and paid them no mind for quite a while. When the sun began to set and the rain hadn't ceased, she walked back to the gate. The man in the black hat sheltered beneath the arms of the tree. He seemed to be rocking the child, but the woman stood out in the rain. She was completely drenched, her dark hair hanging in her face. The girl had always seemed quite proper and intelligent, not someone to stand out and catch her death in the rain.

"Mister, why don't you come inside before it gets dark?"

"Are you deaf? I told you we're fine."

Abbie hadn't taken any sort of vows yet. She was just an ordinary woman, so she almost opened her mouth and told him to get bent, but she restrained herself when Father Connor joined her.

"Tell them to come in. They'll be soaked!"

"I tried, Father. The man said they are fine, but something seems funny about that woman."

"Maybe they've been drinking and don't want me to preach to them?"

"Naw, I've been around plenty drunks. There's something else wrong with her."

Abbie felt a weird energy coming from the couple and not like the woman being mad, something else. After the rude way the man in the black hat spoke to her, she had to admit to herself if it wasn't for the child, she wouldn't give a damn if they froze or got washed away in the hellacious storm.

"You can lead a horse to water, but you can't make it drink. Come on inside and we'll see about our other guests."

"Yes, Father."

The folks gathered inside were a small enough group; there would be plenty of room for them all to get comfortable and warm. There were many smiles, many jokes, and the time slid by.

The hill on which the church sat grew dark as night fell. The sky, still filled with rumbling clouds, was like a charcoal blanket stretched out over the desert.

Abbie kept glancing out the window, each time looking at the tree down the hill and the man standing under its branches. She thought every now and then she could hear the child crying in the storm.

The tiny church held a group of maybe twenty people. The rest of Piedra was holed up in their attics, barns, or the top floor of Rocky's Saloon, drinking, gambling, and whoring their way through the storm.

Only the family men, women, elderly, and children huddled in the pews, watching the rain beat against the windows. Abbie made them coffee and shared a pot of beans and a loaf of bread she baked a few days before.

"I'm sorry we don't have much right now."

"This is all a blessing," Ms. Hutchins said and ate like a horse while her daughter blushed with embarrassment.

There were a few children happily chatting and playing with the few wooden toys Abbie managed to find tucked away in a storage closet. Her heart broke for the baby out in the rain in the company of some asshole and a weird woman. Even if he kept it wrapped up and stood beneath the tree, there was no way it could stay dry.

Lightning split the sky beyond the window, but most of those gathered were in good spirits. They prayed the storm would end so they could get back to their homes and assess the damage left behind. It had been six days of nonstop rain, a feat Abbie hadn't seen in her time in Texas. It seemed so unnatural in the desert to see water rushing waist-high for days on end, but she wasn't a native. It may have happened once or twice years before she rolled through.

"We were survivin' but the rain hasn't stopped long enough for it dry up, even a day or so would have spared our house...but that wasn't the case," Old Mr. Darby sighed. "My son went to Rocky's but that ain't no place for an old man like me."

The group giggled, agreeing he was in better company in the hilltop church.

Abbie wandered to the window again. The night beyond the pane was a fearful plain, sodden and black; no place for a child.

"You're worried about the others, aren't you?" Father Connor asked and came close to gaze out at the storm.

"More for the baby."

"Maybe they'd agree if someone else tried? That we don't want to convert them, just keep them warm and dry."

Abbie nodded and looked back over her shoulder to the group and to Mr. Darby. He looked far too warm to agree to trudge out into the rain. Beside him was Mr. Wiley, a shop owner with a kindly smile, a man known for being able to convince the drunkards in the streets to stop their fighting and put their guns away.

"There's Mr. Wiley. He's an ordinary sort of fella. They have shopped his place a few times. Maybe they'll listen to him?"

Abbie made her way over to him. He was leaned against a wall, wrapped in a blanket. His hair had gone white, but he still had strength in his muscles, not someone she would consider being frail or over the hill.

"Mr. Wiley."

"Hello, Abbie. Thanks for taking me in. I'm afraid I'm far too old to seek refuge in Rocky's too."

"You're always welcome here. Can you lend me a hand?"

"Of course, what do you need?"

"There's a man and a woman outside, a little on down the hill. I have seen them comin' out of your store once or twice. They didn't want to come inside. They must think we're all in here preachin' and they aren't interested."

"Can't say I blame em'," he teased.

"They have a baby with them, and I'm worried it'll catch its death out there. Can you go see if you can convince them to come inside?"

"Well, sure. Especially if it helps the little one."

"Oh. Thank you, Mr. Wiley. Thank you so much."

Abbie was flooded with relief, sure the older man could talk them into coming in out of the rain.

"You're a good man," Father Connor said, walking Mr. Wiley to the door.

"Make sure you tell the man upstairs that. When it's my time to go I want it to be quick!" he laughed as he buttoned his coat and grabbed the lantern and umbrella.

Abbie sat down at the bench by the window and watched the rain racing down the blurry pane of glass. Her breath left a fog on it, and she wiped it away as she watched the orb of lantern light cross before the window and out to the gate. Its light buffeted and bounced off the underside of the umbrella, and for a heartbeat she could almost see his face.

Cold crept up her back just from the door being open for a few minutes while Father Connor sent Mr. Wiley on his way. The baby could freeze or get pneumonia in such weather. She hoped it wasn't too late for the little thing. She had seen adults die rather quickly from exposure and children fared far worse.

The glowing light grew smaller as Mr. Wiley made his way to the path leading down the hill and the tree. It was like a tiny beacon, a distant lighthouse warning ships of impending doom. It traveled farther until it looked almost like a firefly, farther still until it was even smaller. Then, it halted, and she knew the good Mr. Wiley must be within feet of the tree and the man in the black hat cradling the baby away from the rain.

"Do you think he'll be successful?" Father Connor's voice startled her.

"I hope so!"

She pressed her forehead against the cold window and kept her eyes on the light. It was stationary for a long while, suspended in the darkness. She felt her stomach knot with anticipation. If the man refused to bring the baby inside she was ready to stomp out there and slap him right across his face. In her mind she called him every dirty word in the book, but she didn't let them pass her lips. She promised Father Connor she would clean up her language when he allowed her to become an assistant to the church, and that she would join the church in a formal way...but she hadn't yet. She wiped the window to get a better view and lost sight of the light; it had disappeared.

"Father."

"I saw it. Do you think he dropped the lantern or the storm blew it out?"

"Somethin' ain't right."

"No, don't panic. I'm sure he just dropped the lantern. The wind out there is powerful tonight."

Abbie ran to the door. She could feel the eyes of the group on her. She threw the door open and stepped out into the storm. She was met by darkness and pouring rain. A handful of the group came to stand in the doorway, knowing something wasn't right.

"Where'd Wiley go?" Ms. Hutchins yelled over the wind.

"I can't see him!" Abbie said.

"Get back in here outta the rain!"

Abbie knew Ms. Hutchins was just trying to be kind, but she almost told the old woman to shut the fuck up. She held words in and remained standing there while her hair and clothes got soaked through. She hurried to the gate and searched the descending path but saw nothing.

"Mr. Wiley!"

There was no reply, only the steady pelting of rain against her head.

"Mr. Wiley, are you okay?"

Abbie put her hand on the gate latch, determined to go and find the old man but stumbled backward at the snarling of some animal out in the rain soaked night. Her heart lurched, her instincts carrying her back to the safety of the group waiting for her.

The people crowding the door drew away quickly, making way for Abbie as she retreated back into the church.

"What happened?" Mr. Darby asked, catching her before she could collapse.

"Somethin's out there."

"Where's Mr. Wiley, and the man and his family?"

"I didn't see them, just heard somethin' growling."

"It could be a mountain cat. They're quite elusive and very dangerous," Ms. Hutchins said.

"Wouldn't doubt it. One of them would surely attack. Probably got washed out in all this rain and can't find anything to..." Mr. Darby shook his head, unable to finish his sentence.

"To eat," Abbie said.

"Yes," the old man said and helped her to sit down.

"What are we gonna do?"

Abbie's gut sank when Father Connor said, "If anyone survived such an attack, they'd be calling for help."

Abbie was speechless. Had she sent Mr. Wiley out to a horrible death and failed the baby of the strange couple by not insisting they bring it inside? She felt a wave of nauseous grief hit her stomach, regret to such a magnitude she couldn't contain the tears streaming from her eyes. Waves of frustration, helplessness, and despair hit her all at once.

She got to her feet and hurried to the small kitchen where she vomited into an empty bucket she kept for cleaning the floors.

"Are you alright?" Father Connor asked, following close behind her.

"No."

"This is not your fault."

"Why did I ask him to go out in this shit storm?" She stared at the vomit in the bucket refusing to look up.

"Now, now, how could you have known what would happen?"

"I should have gone myself."

"We don't even know if he was attacked. Why do you assume the worst? They could have seen the mountain cat or whatever it is and found shelter somewhere else."

"You're right, Father. I just got frightened by the sound of that thing growling..." Abbie said, thankful the priest was keeping a level head in the situation.

"We should go in a group, find Wiley and the family, and bring them back. I've always heard animals are afraid of big groups of people."

She rushed back to the doorway, resolved to go back out into the storm to find Mr. Wiley.

1861, New Orleans

Abbie drew a deep breath, stood, and walked to her window. The memories flooded her mind worse than the rain flooded the garden, forcing things she tried to bury back up to the surface. It had been nearly twenty years, and still they kept surfacing.

"Shit always floats," she said to the foggy reflection of herself.

She usually reprimanded herself for using such language now, but Abbie couldn't help it tonight. Her heart felt exceptionally raw. The storm felt all too familiar to her.

She slid her hand up one arm and let her fingers trace the scars stretching up her forearm from her wrist to her elbow. They were jagged, lightning bolts etched into her flesh, made by the claws of the beast. It was the one time in her life she knew she saw the devil.

"The rain needs to stop soon, can't take it much longer. I'm tired of remembering."

She picked up a pitcher of water and filled a glass on the table by the window. She sipped it and continued to stare out the window, rain tracing down its pane, hypnotizing her into remembering more to exorcise it from her mind.

"Why did I settle here? I should have ran the opposite way, farther into the desert. It rains too much here. Fuckin' Louisiana."

Her breath caught in her throat at the sight of two yellow orbs in the courtyard, eyes in the darkness. She gripped her chest, her finger fighting to find her rosary.

"No, not here."

When the pair of lights separated, she realized it was time for the brothers to make their rounds to check on the property before retiring for the night. Father Connor always made them do it whether it was raining or not, and with the storm they needed to check on the sandbags they stationed around to halt all flooding they could. They were nearly useless tonight.

The lights made her think of Father Connor and his trip to California. He took Peter with him. There was urgent work there he needed the young priest to assist in then he was sending Peter back to Louisiana.

Father Connor offered a spot to Abbie in their coach but she declined it, feeling a calling in her heart to stay and look after the young women who were ready to take their vows. One in particular required a lot of attention ever since she was a girl.

A thump against the wall was like confirmation Abbie couldn't leave Eve, not yet. It made her jump and drew her away from the window, holding in any vulgarities the old Abbie would have unleashed. She tapped on the wall and spoke softly to the girl like she was still a child, "It's alright, Evey Bee. Get some rest."

She felt silly after nearly scaring herself to death at the sight of two lanterns in the dark. It taught her not to be so hard on Eve and her fear of rain. She listened closely, but there was no tapping in reply. She prayed Eve was sleeping now and the rain would blow over by morning.

She climbed into bed but knew she wouldn't sleep, not when the memories were so vivid in her mind.

She would weather them like any storm and assess the damage by the light of day, praying it wouldn't be too bad. Abbie's fingertips found the scar once more, and she let her mind drift back in time again.

1842, Texas

The volunteers for the search party were Abbie, Mr. Darby, a young rancher named Richard West, Father Connor, the Furman brothers who ran the depot Christopher and Allan, a cattle hand named Jose Valencia and his two sons, Aurelio and Ramiro, and Ada Alleman, a hardy woman and daughter of a rancher who refused to let her elderly father go.

"If there's a mountain cat out there, I'll kill that sumbitch," Ada said, patting the pistol on her hip.

"Now, I know you're tough but be careful. I never had a son to leave the ranch to," her father teased and handed her his pistol. "Take this too; you can never have too many bullets."

She smiled, "Just leave it all to Jenny." She spoke of her sister who was in Arkansas.

"She married her a rich'un. She don't want all those acres of dust and cow shit."

"Then she's crazy." Ada's smile never left her lips but her eyes were sad.

The group stepped out into the storm, wind and rain hitting them in their faces. As if in response to their presence, a snarling growl cut through the sound of the downpour.

"Fuck," Abbie cursed and Father Connor shushed her.

"The bastard is still hungry!" Ada said.

"Then feed it some lead," her father yelled from the door of the church.

Abbie would never forget the grin on Ada's face, her thin lips and pale blue eyes, a brave woman through and through. It was the first time Abbie could recall seeing someone's soul. In the storm which stripped away the outward beauty of anyone, in the darkness which obscured any features, Ada was as close to an angel as Abbie could imagine.

The beast claimed her first in a flash of pistol fire and blood.

They had only made it part of the way to the trees downhill from the church when a flash of lightning illuminated the silhouette of a man in a flat-brimmed hat for a second. Their lanterns hardly did any good against the dark and the storm, but they did enough to spotlight the ground where Mr. Wiley laid, his face white as bone and his neck a raw, red hole.

Another crack of thunder preceded by a flash of lightning shook them. Its bright flash revealed a twisted shadow drawing near. Ada had pulled Abbie close to her and drew her pistol. A hero at heart, right until the end when the shadow came to swallow them up in the strobe of lightning and blackness.

Darkness, light, darkness, light, a blast of gun fire, the group ran in separate directions. An elongated face, black hair with white streaks at the temples, a maw full of razors. The mouth of the devil ripped through the side of Ada's neck. She fell to the ground, her shirt soaking up blood and rain.

There was shouting, of Spanish and English; nothing made any sense to Abbie who fell to her knees to press her hands against the gaping wound in Ada's throat.

Mr. Darby cried, running for the bushes. The thing that followed him, it wore a torn dress. Its black hair streamed behind its head in the winds like the great black sails of a death ship. Mr. Darby was taken down, his legs knocked from under him in a swipe of its clawed hands. His screaming cut off by a wet crunch.

Abbie's breath caught in her throat. She was unaware of how long she held it in, but as the Mexican cattle hand and his son chased after the beast, blasting bullets at its back, she finally exhaled. A weak grip on her hand got her attention. She turned to the dying Ada who placed a pistol in Abbie's shaking hands and mouthed "Go."

The creature's growls and shrieks filled up her mind and her ears, but her eyes were focused on the man beneath the tree. He was motionless, uncaring to what the beast was doing to the people who only offered him help.

Abbie was fixed on him. Her mind was screaming for her to put a bullet in his head. He knew what was going to happen. He knew it and didn't stop it. The beast was the woman he was traveling with. Abbie ran to him and raised the gun,

"You knew! You brought her here to kill!"

"She's hungry and can't nurse the boy if she don't feed."

Abbie's arm trembled, not with fear but the urge to blow a hole through his flat-brimmed hat and into his brain.

"She'll kill you too," he said.

The sounds of screaming tore through Abbie: the father and his sons were getting torn to pieces.

"Abbie!" A familiar voice yelled, Father Connor.

He was approaching but was not close enough to stop her.

"Give me the baby!" she commanded.

"No!"

"I'm gonna shoot yer ass and I don't' want to hit it! Give me the baby!"

"You'll be dead before you get two feet away. She'll knock your head clean off!"

A snarling to her left rattled the rain drenched brush. Abbie's skin rose in goosebumps and a hole of terror opened up inside her heart.

"My sister won't let you take her son."

Abbie lowered the gun. In her peripheral vision glowed two yellow eyes. She could smell blood on the wind; a prayer passed through her mind. She'd be dead before she could aim and pull the trigger.

A sound, louder than thunder chasing the storm across the night, deafened her. A gun shot. Animalistic cries erupted from the brush followed by crashing of distant trees as the beast retreated.

Father Connor knew about more than the Bible. She brought the gun up and fired at the hat on the top of the man's head. His body lurched backwards and bounced off the tree behind him. He fell to his knees.

The startled baby screamed, and with shaking hands Abbie pulled it from his arms. She wrenched the blanket sling free and wrapped the boy in it. She brought it to her chest and held it tight.

She spun around to see Father Connor behind her, his black vestments sodden and fluttering in the strong winds, a gun in his hand. She admired him then, understood his daily battle against evil. It wasn't always tangible, but it was always waiting. Kneeling beside him, clutching his wrist was Ada, still refusing to die until the mission was complete. She let her hand fall from the open hole in the side of her neck and settled back on the muddy ground. Father Connor bent down and performed the last rites over her eyes that were already staring into the afterlife.

Abbie ran toward Father Connor. The child in her arms made her feel so vulnerable, so helpless. The beast, its mother, was still out in the darkness. She could feel its eyes, its murderous rage focused on her. The church and what safety it provided felt a thousand miles away. It would run her down before she made it to the door. Father Connor was her only protection.

"Get back to the church. It didn't come inside because it couldn't. That's the house of the Lord and the devil can't step foot there," he urged.

"I'll never make it."

She was suddenly aware of hot breath bearing down on her. The beast spun her around and slashed her arms with its claws. The baby wailed, just inches from being sliced open by its own mother.

It pushed her back as Father Connor blasted a hole in its side. The gun fell from her hand. The beast wouldn't have cared if she still held it. If she fired a few rounds in its guts, it wouldn't give up. It clawed at Abbie's skin, shredded her shirt until it was nothing but bloody rags, but she refused to release the screaming baby. Its twisted face, half woman, half beast, lowered to within inches of her own, its breath reeked of death. It growled and spoke in a garbled language Abbie didn't understand, but she felt its intent clearly.

It wanted its son and it wanted to bite her face off.

The rain didn't abate; it fell into her eyes blinding her mercifully for a moment to the sight of the beast. She remembered the priest's teachings, that God's name chased evil away.

"In the name of God, leave me be!" she shouted.

The beast hesitated. Its lips curled back into a grin.

"No God." It barked, with laughter.

"I command you in the name of God to be gone!"

This time the creature just grew agitated and raked its claws across her arms again. The baby had fallen too close to Abbie's neck, or she knew the creature would have slashed her throat open and ran off with the child.

"Release her, demon! In the name of God, and of the Son, and of the Holy Spirit!" Father Connor cried, running to the fray. He pulled a cross from his coat pocket and pressed it into the back of the creature's head. Its skin sizzled, and it shrieked and clawed at the smoking wound.

The creature rolled off Abbie and retreated for the cold darkness surrounding them, rain beating down on the bubbling crucifix shaped blister rising on the back of its head. Its path was straight down the muddy road leading away from the church.

The priest helped Abbie to her feet and grabbed her gun, Ada's gun, from the mud and put it in her hand. He then turned around to pursue the beast.

"Take the child to the church!"

"Father! You can't go alone!"

"This is what I do," he said and turned towards the endless rain and darkness.

She watched him halt to kneel next to the man under the tree, unafraid to step away from the path leading back to the church, to warmth, to safety. He chose to head in the direction of darkness, to put an end to it.

It was at that moment Abbie knew she too would devote her life to the Lord. She ran to the church, her lungs burning by the time she reached the door. She handed the baby to Ms. Hutchins.

"All of you stay in here. Do not leave the church for any reason."

"They're all dead, aren't they?" Ada's father asked.

"I won't let it be in vain," Abbie said.

She gripped the pistol, cold and heavy in her hand, and ran in the direction of gun fire.

Father Connor had cornered the beast at the edge of a cliff, below it a rushing river created by flood waters barreled down a dry wash. The rain soaked holy man held a crucifix in one hand and a gun in the other. He meant business.

It was a side Abbie had never seen. He was always a kind man, gentle, always nagging at her for using foul language. He wasn't old but he never looked like the type to go face to face with a monster from the pits of Hell. Abbie came to his side, and he looked at her in surprise.

"I couldn't leave you alone in this."

"Watch it. Demons are tricksters."

Abbie raised her pistol, "It's hard to be tricky if you ain't got a head."

"That won't kill it, not completely. I have to perform the rites of exorcism and try to save the poor woman it took over."

"Do what you came here for, Father," she said.

He began to speak the words; they filled Abbie with courage, but the beast howled and launched itself at them.

Without hesitation Abbie pulled the trigger. The bullet went through the right eye socket of the beast, knocking it back. It tumbled and rolled. It came to the edge of the cliff. Blood poured from its head; it crawled on shaking limbs to the very edge.

"No!" Father Connor cried.

The beast laughed and lurched over the side of the cliff, sacrificing the human vessel it hid in, unwilling to be banished back to Hell.

"Will it die?" Abbie asked.

"Only the woman. It will hide for a while until it finds a new host; it's a parasite of Lucifer."

"That water leads away from town. Maybe we can warn them to watch out for it."

"It's going back to the black box."

"Black box?"

"The dying man, the one you shot. He said the flood washed up a black box. His sister opened it and that's when it took over her body. Her first victim was her husband, the baby's father."

Abbie felt her heart sink, "So we didn't send it back to Hell?"

"Not this time, but we still have the rest of our lives to keep fighting it and things like it. Don't we?"

The baby boy was cared for by Abbie and a wet nurse until he grew old enough to eat soft foods and she decided to follow Father Connor to Louisiana. The child went with them after they couldn't find a home for him in town. No one wanted the child of the Beast Woman.

They brought him to the new church in a different state. He was nearly sent to a state orphanage, but the kitchen woman took him in as her son and named him Peter. Abbie watched him grow up and loved him dearly, but there were moments when she looked into his eyes and saw the face of his mother, twisting into the snarl of the demon which possessed her.

They had found the woman's lifeless body stuck beneath a dead tree days later. The force of the flood water had nearly buried her in the mud. The black box was never found. Thinking about it kept Abbie awake at night, especially when it rained.

LADY ELIZABETH

"Don't touch it!"

Father Connor gripped Peter's shoulder. The look on the old priest's face rattled Peter for a moment; he had never seen Father Connor look alarmed.

"You recognize this?" Peter asked in a whisper.

"I've never seen it, but I have heard stories of it."

The black box rested on an oak table. It was elaborately carved with geometrical shapes. Peter found himself drawn to it.

"Where did you get it, Mr. Willard?" Father Connor asked the exhausted older man.

"An antiques dealer. She thought it was a jewelry box," he answered.

"When did she purchase the box?"

"Nearly three weeks ago, but she only unpacked it two weeks ago. After that she...changed."

"How?" Father Connor asked.

"At first she just seemed distant, as if her thoughts were somewhere else. Then, she started speaking to someone I couldn't see. The night before I had to restrain her, she, her face, it changed into a beast. I found her eating my horse." Willard was nearly weeping.

"What is it?" Peter asked his mentor.

"A burial box, an urn, a prison…the final resting place of something…"

Peter nodded but had to restrain himself from touching the box. Even after learning its morbid purpose, he felt the need to run his fingers over the intricate designs cut into it.

"Will you destroy it?" Mr. Willard asked.

"Of course."

"I tried that, couldn't throw it away, it came right back. And when I tried to burn it a storm came and put the fire out."

"Mr. Willard, we have to destroy the link the thing in the box has to your wife before we can destroy it and the box."

"I was told Father Glover would be joining you."

"He's my mentor. Unfortunately, he's too ill to be here."

"I see, then let's get this over with." As if to punctuate how badly he needed to be rid of the box, a scream from down the hall cut their conversation in two.

"Please hurry. Save my wife!"

Father Connor nodded and then looked to Peter, "It's time to go to work."

"I'm ready."

"You have no other choice. This is what you wanted and this is why I trained you. This will be unlike all the others. Those were child's play compared to this…because this is real!"

"I have witnessed strange things in our time together, Father."

"Nothing like this," Father Connor said.

Elizabeth's bedroom with all its thick velvet curtains, dark wood vanity and armoire, and the shelves with porcelain dolls glaring down at them looked the part of the boudoir of an aristocrat's spoiled wife.

The woman on the bed was little more than a ragged skeleton, her blond hair in knots, and going white at her temples. She was Mr. Willard's wife, a much younger woman, but now she looked aged prematurely, emaciated. She wore a dingy nightgown, and her arms were bound to the bedposts with thick leather straps.

"She's been very ill. I couldn't stop her from leaving the house, so I had to tie her down." Mr. Willard's voice is filled with shame.

Father Connor nodded to Peter, "Get prepared."

"Hello, Father," rasped a voice from inside the woman on the bed.

"That will be all, Mr. Willard. You may leave us with her."

The older man looked to his wife, hesitated, but then nodded and left the room.

"Do you remember me?"

Father Connor ignored the voice coming from Elizabeth. Instead he turned to Peter who was quickly unpacking a black leather bag.

"I remember you," it said.

"All demons are deceivers, Peter. Remember that well, especially tonight."

"Yes, Father."

Peter handed him his stole. He kissed it and draped it around his neck.

"I remember the rain, don't you?" she rasped.

Father Connor halted. His hand trembled, but he took a deep breath to steady himself.

"Would you like me to help you remember?" the demon laughed, and a boom of thunder rattled the window.

A storm gathered in the sky outside; Peter's mouth went dry. He had assisted in a few cleansings, saw the existence of darkness, but he already felt the difference being in Elizabeth's presence. The malevolence was suffocating.

"Oh, yes, you remember."

"Peter, my prayer book."

Peter placed the book in Father Connor's hand and tried to prepare mentally for what he knew was going to be spiritual warfare.

"Look at me, Father," the demon said.

The priest opened the book and began reading the prayer to St. Michael.

"Look at me!"

Peter glanced at Elizabeth, her pale face ran red with blood and one of her eyes was missing, just an empty hole remained. Her blond hair was now black and wild.

"That bitch shot me in the eye!"

Peter lurched backward, but in a flash of lightning beyond the window Elizabeth's face was once more her own.

"Peter."

He looked to Father Connor.

"I said do not listen to it."

"Yes, Father."

The priest began the prayer. His eyes were emotionless as the demon laughed and spewed vulgar obscenities.

"You and the nun...she confessed to you, didn't she? Got down on her knees for you!"

Father Connor dowsed Elizabeth with holy water. Her skin sizzled and blistered.

"And you baptized her in your holier-than-thou seed!"

Father Connor didn't relent in reciting the rites of exorcism, but the beast kept trying to stir anger in him.

"No, you fucked this one here, the young priest! He opened his ass for you, didn't he?"

Father Connor pulled a silver crucifix from his coat pocket, never missing a single word from the prayers. He placed it against Elizabeth's forehead, and she screamed, two voices in unison, one of the demon invader and the other her own weak, pitiful cry.

He was slowly breaking down the beast inside of her, separating them, cutting the invisible thread it used to bind itself to her. The wind and rain outside battered the window, howling like a legion of ghosts.

"Peter, Peter, you were such a tiny thing." Elizabeth's face stretched into a wide grin. "I wanted to eat you, but your uncle wouldn't let me. He promised me a church full of people if I kept my paws off you. But your mama didn't fight too hard, only when I demanded your flesh. She would cry and say how much she loved you. Boo hoo hoo."

Father Connor said nothing, refusing to break his rhythm of reciting the rites and throwing holy water.

"Oh, Father. Don't lie to him. You remember Texas and the flood. That's where you found this little boy here. You orphaned him! You killed his mother!"

"Be silent, Demon!" Father Connor commanded and pressed his crucifix roughly against its cheek.

Elizabeth's mouth gaped open; she screamed, sounding more like a woman.

Lightning lit the window, bright even behind the thick curtains, and all the dolls flew from their shelves. In a crack of thunder, they all stood up, their lifeless eyes fixated on Peter.

"Peter!" they said in unison.

He leapt away from them and ran to the door. He grabbed the door knob and froze, knowing he couldn't leave Father Connor, but over his shoulder he could hear the dolls laughing. He stole a quick glance at them. They were toddling toward him on their stiff legs, falling and pushing themselves back up onto their small feet. Their eyes, too large for their faces, dark and unblinking, saw right into him. Their smooth porcelain surface began to crack at the corners of their lips, and their mouths yawned open, revealing tiny sharp teeth like the maws of rats. Peter fell to his knees screaming.

"Peter! Come play with us!" the dolls teased in a voice of an old man pretending to be a child.

The dolls rapped their teeth together, chomping and giggling at the terror they filled Peter with. They hunched over, and the soft, handsewn bodies and dresses bulged like their was something nesting inside them. They began to split, and clawed feet protruded from holes in their clothing. Paws pushed aside the shattered faces like party masks. Plague rats emerged from the ruined dolls. They were the size of small dogs with oily fur and eyeing Peter hungrily.

"Oh, Lord, help me!" he shouted.

A rain of holy water from Father Connor sent them shrieking and squirming and then lifeless to the floor, nothing more than dolls once more. Peter stayed there on his knees, feeling like a coward.

The old priest didn't stop. His voice droned the hallowed words, and his hand sprinkled holy water on Elizabeth again, a divine machine in motion. She wailed and fought against her restraints, her breathing labored.

"Please help me," she wept, and her head slumped to the side.

"We're almost there," Father Connor said. "In the name of God, I command you to leave this woman! Go back to your box!"

"No!" the demon shouted, and its voice sounded distant.

Elizabeth's face was terrified, as if she had just awakened momentarily to find she was not in control of herself. She cried out, pitiful and weak. Father Connor pressed the crucifix to her forehead again;it burnt her skin, and she screamed in agony.

"BEGONE, DEMON!"

Elizabeth opened her mouth to scream, but her voice was silenced by a swarm of flies. The black mass darted to the ceiling and then flew for the door. Peter scooted across the floor frantically and like smoke it escaped through a crack between the top of the door and the seal.

"Watch her," Father Connor said, pointing to Elizabeth before giving chase to the demonic swarm.

Peter did as he was told but didn't leave his spot on the floor. From the other room, he could hear Father Connor fighting the evil entity back into the black box.

"Is it done?" Mr. Willard's voice asked after a long silent pause.

"Yes, our part here is complete," Father Connor answered.

"Honey?" A hoarse whisper from the bed drew Peter's attention. Elizabeth was awake and exhausted. Mr. Willard came running down the hallway and fell onto the bed to hug his wife.

Father Connor returned holding a black sack. It was heavy in his hand.

"Let's go, Peter."

Peter rushed to gather their things, carefully avoiding the broken dolls for fear they might rise up again.

"Thank you, Father!" Mr. Willard wept.

"As soon as she is a little stronger, take her to church. She needs to remain in the holy presence until she has fully recuperated. I already arranged for Father Daniel to see you."

"Yes, anything to keep her safe."

The storm outside died; the howling wind and rain settled to nothing but a light drizzle and the sun began to break through the clouds. It beamed through a crack in the curtains.

"Leave it in the bag. We will perform the rites on the box and then cremate it. Don't look inside."

Peter waited in the cold morgue office. Father Connor told him the diener, Mr. Blevin, would allow him to cremate items on occasion if the priest thought they had been used in black magic rituals and such. Mr. Blevin was a drunkard and hard to awaken so Peter would be in charge of the box momentarily while Father Connor roused him.

"I would have you do it, but if he doesn't recognize you then he might shoot you and we can't have that."

"Shoot me?" Peter asked.

"You'd be surprised how many necrophiliacs are in these parts," Father Connor said.

***

Peter found himself alone with the box. He found it odd the demon mentioned Texas. How did it know Father Connor had found him there? He had so many unanswered questions about his childhood, things that plagued his dreams for years.

When Peter was a boy, from the moment he could remember his dreams at night upon waking in the morning, he would have a recurring nightmare of looking into a mirror and watching his face change from his own childish reflection to a woman. He could never clearly recall her face, just the shape of her and her hair. It was damp, wild, and ragged like she had been running through a thunderstorm. Her countenance was always obscured by a thick fog and dewy perspiration raced down the mirror's face.

In that dream world, he would bring his small hand up to touch the area of her cheek, his cheek. His dream self would know she was a motherly figure, but as soon as his heart would swell with love and longing for her, the mirror would shatter and through it would jump a wolf. He was left unsure who she represented, his birth mother or the kitchen woman, Sarah, who was the only mother he remembered to the age of seven. He would always awaken when the beast had his neck in its jaws. His other dreams weren't as terrifying as they were heartbreaking, scenes of him on a small circle of land in the middle of black water, or crying alone in a cold dark landscape, or digging with his hands deep into the Texas sand, searching desperately for something and never finding it.

He discovered his only comfort was talking with Eve about his dreams, and she would nod as if she fully understood and tell him she too experienced nightmares all the time. He learned Eve was afraid of everything all the time, something which annoyed the other children and most of the nuns, but Peter treated her gently and never mocked her or called her a chicken. They were the freaks of the orphanage, a place filled with children without families who were able to shake free of the tragedies of their lives, unlike he and Eve. She, the girl who ran away from the smallest clap of thunder and cried over the tiniest thing, and Peter, the clumsy, twice-orphaned boy, became each others only families.

It wasn't until he was older and his dreams began revolving around Eve that he forgot the nightmare of the wolf in the mirror and only recalled it when he was truly afraid. He buried it under memories of watching Eve garden and thoughts of the way her hair always smelled like the flowers she loved so much. Those things pushed aside the fear of the beast.

The apprehension of knowing he was falling in love with Eve one tiny moment at a time, like helping her pick leaves from her hair in fall and making wooden animals as Christmas gifts for her and her laughter at his lamest attempts at jokes, overshadowed his other fears. She never made him feel stupid for tripping over his own feet and for being the mess that he was.

But the exorcism, the dolls, the box...they all brought up the memory of a darkness that seemed to follow Peter from the moment he was born and the questions as to who he was.

Slowly Peter reached out and placed his fingertips on the black box. They hummed softly, and he pulled his hand away.

"I can tell you everything, Peter."

Peter backed away.

"He lied to you when he said he didn't know your mother. He killed her."

"Liar!" Peter shouted and put his hands over his ears.

"I know the whole truth. I can show it to you."

"No!"

There was a silent moment before a woman's voice came from the box.

"Peter, is that you? Is that my baby?"

Her words tugged at Peter's heart. Tears stung his eyes. He hadn't cried for his mother in years, but now he felt anguish welling up in his heart. The need to know who he was bit into his soul again and refused to let go.

"No, you're lying!"

Peter stepped closer, feeling the pull of the box calling to him. There was only one thing he could think of that tempted him more, and it was Eve. He tried to remember her face, the way she laughed, anything to break the spell the box was trying to cast on him.

"You look just like me. What a handsome boy."

He closed his eyes; his hands shook. He felt weak, unable to withstand its call.

"Go on. Open it up."

Peter's eyes fell on the elaborate box he felt his heart swell. It was more tempting than Eve now, more alluring than when she let him brush her long hair.

"You love that girl?"

Peter ran his hands over the box. A tingle shot up his arms. It was exhilarating.

"I see her as you do, through your mind. The beautiful girl, the forbidden one. She can be yours. Just let me in."

Peter cracked the lid, and his vision went black for a heartbeat. His eyes saw something his memory would soon wipe away because it was replaced by a vision so sweet, yet his mind couldn't fully grasp onto it. He was holding Eve as a man would hold his wife and kissing her sweetly, running his hands through her hair. It lasted seconds but felt like an eternity.

"She is special. She could see me! She has a gift for seeing beyond the human realm. I could convince her of your love. I could make her yours."

Peter felt a wind blow his hair back; it smelled like Eve. Sweet and pure, like summer rain on the wild roses behind the church.

"Peter!"

Father Connor forced him away and slammed the box shut. He shoved Peter down in a chair and carried the box away. After what felt like hours, he returned to inspect Peter.

"Why did you open it? I said not to open it!" The old priest yelled. He never yelled.

"It was only for a second. It felt like it was telling me the truth, that it could show me my mother. I've asked you about her, about who I am...but you can't or won't tell me."

Father Connor shook his head and squeezed Peter's shoulder. His grip was rough and angry, and his eyes screamed disappointment. For a moment, Peter thought he might strike him.

"I will tell the truth, if you want to know so badly," Father Connor sighed, releasing Peter.

Father Connor put Peter on the Butterfield stagecoach. It would be almost three weeks before he got home, but it would give him time to clear away any frustration he harbored for Father Connor and Sister Abbie for not telling him the truth about his mother years ago.

He had lost count of the times Peter had asked about his mother over the years, who she was, what town she came from, if it was possible he had other siblings or relatives in Texas. These were all understandable questions of an orphaned boy, but neither he nor Abbie could produce any answers that seemed to quell Peter's curiosity or quench his thirst for answers. That is, after all, the root of most orphaned children's questions...who are they? They seek their identity through who their ancestors were.

Father Connor had promised to tell him everything but still tiptoed around pieces of it like a coward. He knew Peter could feel it, and it left him feeling guilty. He told Peter his mother had been possessed and died when he and Abbie attempted to help her. He didn't go into great detail, and he was sure Peter noticed his hesitancy to do so. He was thankful the young man didn't press him any further or he might have broken down. The ordeal with his mother was far worse than what Peter witnessed in the bedroom of Lady Elizabeth.

"I'm sorry, Peter. One day we will tell you the whole story," Father Connor said, watching the coach depart.

The truth was they saw something in Peter, a weakness, a flaw they desperately wanted to correct. Father Connor wasn't exactly sure what it was. Perhaps it was how much he resembled his mother sometimes or the way he smiled too broadly at Eve. But he and Abbie had made it their mission in life to guide Peter to the service of God, maybe as a form of penance.

He became Father Connor's protégé, his shadow, and watched him as he performed not only religious rites but also did service within the community. They nurtured Peter's spiritual body and showed him what it meant to help his fellow man. Abbie also accompanied them into the city around the church to give medical aid to those in need. She taught him ways to comfort those who were on death's door. They both tried to show him how to be a good man and priest for when he finally earned his collar.

Father Connor made his way to the first barroom he could find. He was accustomed to the odd looks he got when he ordered whiskey and didn't blink an eye when the bartender sniggered, "Sure thing, Padre!"

Father Connor stared into the amber liquid in his glass, and his mind wandered down the old roads he usually fought to forget. He recalled Peter's mother's demise and the years following it. He marveled at how Abbie had cared for the boy and made sure he had a home at the church in New Orleans with Sarah. It even made him admire her more than he already did.

If he only had the balls to admit to her he loved her and not allude to it and evade it in favor of his books and promises he already made to God.

Peter grew up surrounded by the church and its teachings, but something always felt off about him. He was awkward and skittish, asked too many questions, and was more than just a little clumsy. Calamity seemed to hang around him; bad luck was a well-worn coat, oversized and far too familiar, always on his shoulders. Father Connor often felt pity for Peter, not just for being responsible for Peter becoming an orphan, but for the boy in general.

Only two years before, Peter was on an errand in the neighborhood surrounding the church and he was robbed of everything he had, even his shoes. When he hobbled back into the church with his cobble-bruised soles and black eye, Father Connor nearly forsook his vows of forgoing vengeance just to teach the thief a lesson. Before he could, Peter admitted he got rolled by a ten year old girl who feigned hunger pangs and when Peter knelt beside her, walloped him over the head with a stick and didn't stop beating him until he had relinquished all his valuables. He could see Abbie was both concerned and a little embarrassed for him when she cleaned his wounds. Eve was beside herself with anger.

When Peter was a child, he discovered Sarah's body. She died in her tiny bed behind the kitchen in the staff quarters. Father Connor was quite sure the boy had spent more than an hour with the dead woman before he even alerted anyone to the corpse. Father Connor didn't feel it was for any malicious or unnatural reason, just that the boy couldn't bear to admit to himself she was gone. Peter seemed constantly starved for affection, for acceptance, for someone to care for him. Father Connor could understand; life was cold and hard, and everyone needed at least one person to love them. He wondered if Peter's endless need for a mother or someone to care for him lead to him becoming inseparable from Eve.

He also noticed how Peter and the young Eve looked at one another, and it twisted his heart into a knot. He sighed and drained his cup. He knew getting drunk wouldn't change a damn thing, but it did serve to dull the worry in his gut and the doubt he felt gnawing at him in his quest to turn Peter into the greatest exorcist in the Americas. He laughed to himself and tapped the bar, "Another one!"

"Take it easy there, Father," the bartender said.

"I've seen worse than a few drinks...just pour it and leave me be."

The bartender nodded and filled Father Connor's glass. He turned and left him to his thoughts, his worries that Peter couldn't be all Father Connor hoped he could be. The boy was so much like a blood son, shattering his parent's dreams for him, and for better or worse becoming his own person.

Peter was getting too close to Eve. He had nearly botched the exorcism, and now he had opened the black box even when Father Connor told him not to. Two whiskeys wouldn't be enough for Father Connor. Before he paid for a whole bottle, he reached into his pocket and pulled out his notebook and pencil and began writing a letter to Abbie to let her know he had to reveal parts of the truth, and in Father Connor's roundabout way, tell her how desperately he missed her.

***

Peter couldn't lie to himself, Eve was taking up his thoughts both while he was awake and when he slept. His soul and heart being pulled in two different directions at times.

Did Father Connor and Sister Abbie see it? He thought he saw looks of disapproval, especially from Abbie, when he sought Eve out to talk with her in the garden. The nun would always smile at him, but her eyes told him something else when she found them sitting together.

He couldn't quite recall when her eyes changed when she looked at them. Was it when Peter and Eve were caught sneaking out to look at the wild roses, or when Peter saved Eve from a swarm of bees that grew to the size of a bull's head and hung balled up in a tree outside the church kitchen doors? Both of those instances happened when they were still just children, far too young for her to look at them with suspicion behind her eyes. Maybe it was just a few years prior when Peter picked her flowers for her sixteenth birthday and sung to her as he presented them.

Or were the looks directed at Eve? It was said women are things of sin; they are the true temptation of man. Would Sister Abbie believe Eve was trying to seduce Peter when she brought him warm bread from the kitchen or blotted his bruised eye with a cold towel when he walked into the low hanging branch of the leaf-bare trees last winter?

Whatever the looks were about, or if they were even real and not a figment of his guilty mind, he couldn't deny they had merit. He was feeling things for Eve he should not feel if he was sworn to be a priest.

Was he failing them by letting his heart yearn for Eve? He sighed and laid his head against the side of the stagecoach.

"Father, what church do you belong to?" an old woman asked.

"St. Louis Cathedral."

She grinned, her mouth stretching until it nearly split her face in two. Peter blinked and rubbed his eyes.

"Are you feeling ill, Father?"

He looked back and her face was ordinary, kindly, there was no monstrously stretched smile.

"Yes, I have just had a very long journey."

"Oh, you get some rest. I'll wake you at the next stop."

"Thank you."

He needed to shut his eyes and forget about the horrible experience with Lady Elizabeth and the truth he learned about his blood mother.

"Wake up, Father."

Peter opened his eyes to darkness, the coach bumping and jumping. The old woman was snoring loudly.

He shook what he believed was the remnants of a dream away. There was a shade drawn down over the coach window, but he could see beyond it was nighttime. He pushed it up to look at the dark desert. He had no idea where they were, but he guessed somewhere between Stockton and Los Angeles.

He was never woken up at the last stop. He felt a bit of irritation with the old woman who promised she would. His stomach felt empty, so he opened the leather bag at his feet. Father Connor had sent him a few apples in case he needed something light to eat on his travels. He pulled one out and rubbed it against his shirt. His eyes were still staring out at the shadows of the cacti in the night. In the distance a pack of coyotes started yelping, their cries breaking the stillness.

He brought the apple to his mouth and sunk his teeth into it. Instead of the crisp sweetness he expected, it was too soft and tasted foul. He spat it out and examined it to see its flesh was brown and something squirmed inside of it. Disgusted, he cracked the coach window and threw it out into the dirt.

"Father."

Peter turned quickly to see the old woman still asleep. Another passenger had joined them. The man wrapped in a thick ankle-length duster coat, its collar pulled up around the sides of his head, but he too appeared to be sleeping.

"Excuse me?" Peter said, thinking maybe since he just couldn't see the gentleman very well in the dark coach that he was actually awake. "Did you say something?"

He was met with silence. He could see the gentle rise and fall of the abdomen beneath the coat.

Something writhed in his mouth. Panic rose, and he tried spitting it out. It tickled the back of his tongue, and he gagged. He jammed his finger into his mouth trying to fish out the squirming intrusion. The tip of it raked across something, and he dragged it out.

Nearly vomiting he stared down at a small ball of black hair. He threw it out the coach window and sat back against his seat, breaking out in a cold sweat. His stomach turned and knotted violently. He pulled a hankie from his pocket and began wiping the sweat away.

"Feelin' ill?"

He looked to the stranger on the other seat, "Yeah, just a little."

"Why don't you pray it away, Peter?" the stranger laughed.

Peter opened his mouth to give the man a piece of his mind when his stomach lurched into the back of his throat. He beat the thin wall behind him, "Driver, stop!"

He didn't have the time to argue with the passenger or to ask how he knew his name. He couldn't even spare another moment to beg the coachman to stop. He got to his feet, flung the coach door open, and vomited out onto the dusty road. The coach came to a halt.

"Are you alright, sir?"

"I'll... I'll be fine," Peter said and climbed down carefully avoiding the vomit.

The wind felt cool against the perspiration on his face; it eased his stomach a bit.

"Here, let me fetch some of my stomach tonic. My doctor fixed it up for me because I get sick on coaches," the old woman said from the door of the couch.

She disappeared back into the coach and returned with a vial of bitter liquid. After tasting it, Peter worried it would only make him vomit again, but in a few minutes his stomach relaxed and he felt like he could continue.

"Come along now. It ain't safe to stop on the road at night."

To punctuate the driver's meaning Peter could hear the yelping of coyotes in the darkness again.

Peter nodded and climbed back into his seat beside her. The coach lurched and started to head onward, but Peter glanced at the seat across from him.

The stranger in the coat was not in his seat.

"Wait, we can't leave. There was another man. We can't leave him behind."

"What? There was no one else, Father. Only you and I are in this coach."

Peter stammered but couldn't say a word.

"You must be running a temperature, probably had a fever dream. Come on, lay across this seat and I will sit on the other one. You really need to rest."

Peter didn't argue. He was stricken with confusion. The old woman helped him lay down.

"There, now those stomach drops will help you sleep. In the morning we should be at the next stop, and we can have some breakfast."

"Thank you," Peter said, feeling the medication taking hold of him.

He closed his eyes, his mind puzzling over the man in the coat. A chill of fear raised the hair on the back of his neck. He pulled his collar up around his head and let himself drift off.

The morning light settled in the coach, and they came to a stop in Fort Yuma. He could hear the voices of men as they hurried to secure another team of horses.

To Peter's amazement, he did feel better. His stomach no longer hurt, and soon the odd stranger in the coat was pushed to the back of his mind. He chalked it all up to being sick, just as the old woman suggested.

He sat at a small table by a window looking out over the coach and the men exchanging the horses. The driver was a hardy man with a black mustache. Beside him riding shotgun was a potbellied old man with a thousand-yard stare for everyone passing by him. Across his arms lay the tool of his trade, a rifle ready to kill anyone looking to rob the stagecoach.

Saloon girls whistled at Peter from a balcony across the street, and when he looked in their direction, they pulled their breasts out of their bodices and laughed at his red face.

"Hey, Sin Buster, come up here and exorcise our demons!" one girl yelled at him.

"And I thought the men around here were rough," Peter said as he retreated into the coach.

Peter settled in opposite the old woman and looked out the window as they departed, unable to pull his eyes away from the three saloon girls. One of them blew him a kiss. The sun shining in her hair reminded him of Eve, and for just a moment he almost blew her one right back.

"These kinds of places just aren't for me," The old woman sighed.

Her comment drew his attention away and sent a rush of embarrassment through him. He hoped she didn't see him staring at the prostitutes on full display.

"It is a quite different to what I am accustomed to," Peter agreed.

Their course took them onward through vast expanses of desert.

He had never seen such bright sun and knew Eve would be delighted with it. She had always been afraid of the stormy weather they endured in Louisiana. The summers there were extremely humid; he didn't think he stopped sweating from the moment he woke up to the second he fell asleep at night.

He knew it would be different in the country passing by the coach window. They could live in such a place, he and Eve.

He saw a church in the desert sitting at the top of a hill. There was a small town below the church with a handful of loyal parishioners who would ascend the hill every Sunday. Eve would stand beside a small gate and welcome them inside while he waited by the door to shake their hands and ruffle their children's hair as they went to take their seats. His daydream drew on as he went to stand at Eve's side, her eyes turned up to the sky, her smile fading at the sight of storm clouds gathering over them.

"Don't you worry," his dream self tells Eve.

"But the others..."

His eyes follow where her arm is outstretched and her finger is pointing.

He sees the silhouette of two people at the bottom of the hill. On the growing winds of the approaching storm, he can hear a baby crying.

"We need to bring them inside," she said.

Thunder rolls, and lightning streaks across the sky. Peter's heart beats wildly, and he knows in his dream these people are not right.

"The driver said we only have a few minutes at the next stop, unless you wanna sleep there for the night," his companion's voice brought him back to reality.

"Oh no. I plan on riding on through. I have to get back as soon as possible," he said.

Peter made small talk, but his mind couldn't let the image of the two silhouettes at the bottom of the hill fade from his mind.

It was the story Father Connor told him about his mother. He felt a pang of sadness hit his gut. He had been on the verge of tears when Father Connor finally told him the truth, or as much as he would reveal. His mother, the poor woman, had housed an evil spirit just as Lady Elizabeth had; only Elizabeth had been lucky enough to survive.

"I never wanted to make you feel so distraught with sadness or fill you with fear, but that is the truth, Peter. That is what happened to your mother," Father Connor's voice echoed in his mind.

Peter thought it all happened for a reason, that God didn't want Peter to know the truth until he was ready. If he had been told as a child, then he would have grown into a completely different man, one who didn't have the bravery to become an exorcist. It was all God's plan. He would not fail Father Connor;he would return to Eve a better man.

The stagecoach came to a jarring stop. Peter fell forward against the old woman's seat.

"My goodness!" she shouted.

Sudden yips and yelps cut through the quiet day.

"What's that?" she whispered.

"GET OUTTA THE WAY!"

"Coyotes," Peter said, confused because he had never heard of coyotes surrounding a stagecoach. They were known to be frightened of horses and men. The driver shouted, and the horses stomped and neighed fearfully. 11111

"Give'em what for!" the driver yelled.

He was talking to his gunman. Peter covered his ears, but the booming of the rifle still rattled his brain. Screaming from the old woman mixed in with a crying yelp echoed from a dying coyote.

"I caught him in the gut!"

"Nice shot!"

The Coyotes ran for their lives because the coach jumped and powered down the trail.

Peter stuck his head out the window as they passed the carcass of a bleeding coyote. He fixated on its eyes. They were wide and its tongue hung out of its mouth, but he swore the paws were oddly shaped, its toes far too long and thin, almost like fingers. But the coach took off and moved too quickly for Peter to really get a good look at the dying thing. Running along the roadside were a handful of other coyotes, their hides mottled and ragged. Something in their eyes looked desperate.

The rabid coyotes would definitely be something he could tell Eve all about. He wasn't so sure if he would tell her about Lady Elizabeth; he wouldn't want to frighten her. Eve had always scared so easily.

The creature chased along behind the stagecoach, jumping between the coyotes until it found the strongest among them.

The demon passenger wouldn't be content running in the body of a mangy coyote for long. Any living thing could not house it forever; corporeal bodies began to rot after it took up residence inside it, especially animals, and they festered much faster. The need to jump hosts was a constant necessity, especially now that the box was burned.

It had been carved centuries before as a prison for the demon, but its maker seemed to forget he was not immortal, and when he died the true nature of it was forgotten with time. So, the box was passed along between human beings in all sorts of transactions, being opened hundreds of times and unleashing the demon on humanity.

The ornate box traveled the world, leaving suffering and death in its path. The evil inside it had been fought and nearly defeated countless times but if even a piece of the creature, something as small as a fly escaped, it would just hide until it grew strong again in the body of a man or woman. It could cause hallucinations, project spectral visions, inflict illness and pain, and those were just its parlor tricks. The demon could do so much more, but not for long if it didn't find a living body to dwell in.

It was never human, never meant to walk the world of man. Suffering of the soul was its nourishment, and it needed a human's body and spirit to feed on. Without those it was nothing but a small mass of malevolence waiting for a home, a demonic parasite that's state of being was more like a crawling blood clot as the old cowboy Henry had described it. But, men were weak, easily persuaded and dazzled. The thing usually didn't go without a host for long, and besides, time was irrelevant to a thing that never aged. A year, a week, a millennium, it was all a blink of an eye to the beast. It was always waiting.

It enjoyed tormenting Peter very much; it could feel a weakness inside of him, a soft spot to manipulate. Sure he was a tool to get revenge on the priest, but the young man also possessed the potential to bring light to so many lives. If the demon corrupted him, it would be like destroying all those souls Peter could have saved. It could only read pieces of his thoughts and most of them centered on a young woman, a love he couldn't confess. The fragment of it that slipped out of the box would seek the thing Peter treasured the most.

The girl, Eve, she would help it gain its strength again. It prickled when Peter thought of her. The fragile thread it kept attached to him wouldn't be strong enough, but Eve had an opening in her mind, one that left her responsive to the voices of things beyond death and it would exploit it. The demon would use it as a doorway into Eve's physical form, and the suffering it would cause her through her gift would sustain it, give it such strength it hadn't obtained in centuries. She would be one of its greatest conquests.

Except maybe Gabriella, she was a healer, and just like Peter, held the possibility of saving so many humans or redeeming them on their death beds with her mercy and compassion. She was trained to restore a man's body, his temple, but the young nurse's curiosity got her killed. Her wasted potential was sweet like honey on the demon's tongue. The demon ate her up greedily after being locked away for years by a Russian holy man.

But Eve... it would savor her. It would take its horrid time with her, and Peter would be forced to watch it all.

The demonic passenger halted the coyote it hid inside of, and the pack ran out ahead of it; they were afraid of it. Coyotes and other animals could sense its power and usually fled from it, like the surge of fear that kept deer from being devoured by predators. Humans had it but they rarely listened to it. Animals were simple to take over once they were caught. Humans were easily cornered, but their minds made them harder to penetrate, so it had to bide its time with them and win them over.

A black bird landed on the arms of a creosote bush, its feather shining in the sunlight. The passenger could feel the strength in its heart and wings. It leapt from the coyote, leaving it lifeless in the sand and swarmed over the bird like flies until it found its way down the poor thing's throat. The bird fell from the branches and lay on the ground. It struggled only a little bit before the demon took control. It hadn't been a bird in centuries;flying felt better than running.

It beat the bird's wings and leapt into the desert sky. The demon followed in the path of the stagecoach, but it knew it would soon leave Peter behind and seek Eve. It always preferred demeaning women and Eve would be its greatest corruption. She was what it desired the most. So pure, so sweet, she was virginal. It would destroy both Eve and Peter all at once, a priest and a nun. It shivered with the thoughts of it.

WILD ROSES

ABBIE WANDERED HER WAY to the garden. She enjoyed the warmth of the sunshine on her cheeks though there was the bite of approaching winter on the breeze.

Eve was tending the flower beds. Her favorite roses needed pruning before the frosts came. Abbie always saw Eve talking to the flowers as she worked, or maybe to herself, to work out her anxieties. Either way, Abbie was happy to let Eve sit among the roses for hours.

Today, Eve seemed happier than usual and the fact that Peter would be back soon didn't slip by Abbie. She had spoken to Eve on a few occasions, trying to gauge whether Eve harbored more than sisterly love for Peter, but Eve would never admit it.

Abbie had a life before taking her vows, and she knew the way a woman's eye would shine when she looked on the man she loved. That glimmering was present in Eve's eyes whenever she was near the young student priest. She knew "the look" because she had given it to Father Connor on many occasions though nothing ever blossomed from it. Abbie's heart lurched a few times with familiar pain when she noticed the way Eve would gently touch Peter's arm when they spoke, letting it linger there just a little too long, or the way Eve looked at Peter across the churchyard when she thought no one else was around. There was attraction in her eyes, a blush in her cheeks. More than a few times Abbie could see Eve's face turn red after Peter complimented her. It was more than a crush; Eve was longing for Peter in the way a woman does when she wants to feel a man's skin against hers.

Abbie knew Eve was more than just a child now. Even when she looked quite innocent, she was growing up and nature was a force that is hard to ignore. Forbidden love, she knew from experience, could blossom into great disaster; it could be a splinter in the heart that never heals.

"Enjoying the sunshine?"

"Oh yes. I'm happy the rain has gone," Eve answered, her attention still focused on trimming the rose bushes.

It had been weeks since the last storm, and the nightmare, when Abbie knocked on the wall to calm Eve. Life seemed as normal as it could get. "You really work too hard. Let me help you." Abbie pushed up her sleeves and joined Eve to rake up the fallen leaves and rose trimmings.

Eve kept her focus off the scars on Abbie's arms. When she was little, Eve asked Sister Abbie once what happened to her and she was told a mountain cat had clawed her arms to shreds, but the voices told her Abbie wasn't telling her the truth.

That was the day she realized nuns lie just like everyone else. Eve never held it against Abbie, thinking the real story was much more frightening or too sad to speak of. She let the subject go. Sister Abbie could be like the other nuns, very serious and stern, but there were times when youthful joy shone through her, like when she made up songs for all the children to help them fall asleep, or on Christmas when she read stories in the morning before breakfast, and when she gave sweet nicknames to each of the kids.

Yes, there was a kindness about Abbie, a peaceful warmth of her soul and it soothed Eve. She looked at Abbie like a sister in the true sense of the word.

"Peter will be here any day now," Abbie said. "We'll get to ask him all about his adventures and how Father Connor is doing."

"Eight days," Eve said.

Abbie nodded and finished her raking, "I need to see what the other postulants are working on and look in on the kitchen."

Once Abbie was gone Eve turned her attention back to the voices.

"Will you tend the wild ones beyond the wall?" a voice asked.

Eve hadn't been to the wild roses in more than a year, ever since she stopped sneaking out at night to sit with Peter. They weren't far beyond the churchyard, just on the other side of a hole in the brick wall surrounding the church and all its lands.

She and Peter had discovered them when they were little children, pretending to be explorers looking for cities of gold. It became their secret place from that day on. As they grew older, and she felt the attraction growing between them, it became clear the nightly walk in the roses was only a painful reminder they weren't like average young men and women. They couldn't explore what their hearts and bodies yearned for. She felt guilty for it, but there were times she just wished he would grab her by the hand and take her far away where they could have the freedom to just be two human beings navigating life with all their faults and flaws, a place where they only had to be Peter and Eve.

"You shouldn't let them be neglected," the voice persisted.

"Alright," Eve agreed, mostly to get it to be quiet.

It had been pestering her for a few days, quite unusual for the whisperers. They commented on her daily life or butted in on her conversations, but they usually didn't demand things of her. This one was like a nagging old woman shouting from across a great distance. Eve wished it would find someone else to talk to, but she knew there couldn't be many others like her.

"Do you want to know a secret?"

Eve felt the hair on her arms rise and didn't answer.

"Peter's mother gave Abbie those scars."

"How would you know?"

"Because I am Peter's mother," the voice hissed.

"Why would you hurt sister Abbie?"

"Come out here and I'll tell you."

The voice was suddenly so far away Eve could hardly hear it. She looked around, trying to discern its location. Her eyes fell on the hole in the wall.

"Come tend the wild roses and I will tell you the truth about Abbie," the voice insisted.

Peter had confided in Eve his questions about his mother; she knew this could be important to him. If she discovered the truth of his childhood, he would forever be grateful to her and he would owe her his undying love.

"It's all for Peter, isn't it?" the voice said.

"Yes. I need to know for him," Abbie said.

"I can tell you all the answers to all his questions. I'm sure he'd be forever grateful to you."

Eve found herself crawling through the hole in the brick wall. She struggled a bit to get to the other side. It was once so easy to jump through the hole. The wild roses were growing crazily; it surprised her to see them so bushy and full. She and Peter no longer frequented the place. They weren't trampled down by their small feet any longer.

"They missed you," the voice said.

"I missed them too," Eve said and felt a pang of sadness in her heart.

She went to them, smelling of their small buds. They were still sweet and would bloom in the cold, unlike the others she had just pruned. Her eyes caught the shine of sun on black feathers, a dead bird. She knelt to stroke its small body. It lay just beside the brick wall, and she wondered if it hadn't flown right into it and broke its neck.

"Poor thing."

"Now, do you want to know the truth of your Godly Sister Abbie and of Peter?" the voice was bitter and it jarred Eve from inspecting the body of the bird.

"She is a liar, and she stole my baby!"

"Why would she do that?" Eve asked.

"Because she's a bad woman, a phony, a charlatan. But you'll help me get my baby back, right?"

Clouds built up and slid over the sun. The wind began to pick and blow the wild roses against Eve. She knelt down by the dead bird. But now she struggled to stand against the gusts.

"I don't know what you're talking about!"

"You know him...he's mine! Bring him to me!" the voice demanded.

Eve turned to run, but her foot stepped on the hem of her dress and she fell into the arms of the wild rose bushes. Their thorns bit into her skin, and slowly the branches began to wrap around her wrists.

"Bring me my baby! I want Peter!"

Eve refused to let herself get tangled up and held there. She screamed as she yanked her arms free; the thorns sliced her skin as she pulled herself away. Her heart thundered in her ears and in the sky it rumbled behind the clouds. Light drops of rain fall cold on her cheeks, entwining with hot tears running from her eyes. Winds whipped around her, filled with whispering voices.

"Bring me my baby!"

"Peter!"

"The nuns are liars!"

"The priests are bastards!" it incessantly droned, like a fly buzzing near her ear.

Eve couldn't breathe enough to scream. She ran as fast as she could to the hole in the wall. She lifted one leg and forced it and her upper body through the hole, and as she pulled her other leg through, something caught her by the ankle. She cried out, her voice drowned out in the storm beyond the wall. She fought her foot free and fell through onto the dirt in the churchyard. As soon as she touched that sacred ground all was silent. The voice was gone; there was no sudden storm. She inhaled deeply and wept. Her hands were shaking and her arms were bleeding.

"Eve?"

Sister Abbie hurried to help her to her feet.

"You're bleeding."

Eve nodded and struggled to get control of herself. The old need to hide the voices she heard came screaming in her mind. They would never let her become a nun if she was crazy, and Peter would never look at her the same if he knew she was insane. There would be no love in his eyes, only pity.

"I tripped in the roses, but I'm okay now."

"My poor dear. Let's get you inside and cleaned up," Abbie said.

Eve only nodded, thankful her heart hadn't burst with terror.

Eve didn't feel hungry. She only stared down at her dinner. Her mind was on Peter and the voice claiming to be his mother.

She remembered he came to the orphanage in the church at the same time that Sister Abbie arrived. Could the voice be telling her the dark secret about Peter and Abbie? Or, was it lying to her? She had whispering voices lie to her in the past though they usually told her partial truths instead of outright lying. There was an instance when the voices told Eve that her father was going to die, that he'd drown himself in liquor, but he died of Influenza. Although he certainly would have died from the bottle if he'd only lived a few more years, so they weren't far off the mark, which told her they only spoke those lies to torment her, to hurt her, and it scared her to know they meant her emotional harm.

The scratches on her arms were deep. The thorny branches had gripped her and left holes she tore larger into long scrapes in her frantic escape. They stung and looked more like claw marks.

A voice came to her, softly at first and then growing, filling her with agitated energy, "Look at them...they have no faith. They just have no place to go unless they want to sell their bodies for bread. This is the flock you wish to join? Pathetic. Users. Leeches!"

She couldn't help but agree with the voice. She had seen too many young women come to the church proclaiming they wanted to serve God, only to fill their bellies all winter and warm their skin by the fires and then disappear come spring to run the streets again, all the while those truly devoted had to share their meals and blankets with the bloodsucking users. They could waltz in and use the church as a flop house and leave after they had a hot meal to give their bodies to men in dirty beds, while she couldn't even fall in love with Peter?

She looked around her, counting the faces and wondering who would stay longer than three months. The other young women around her dined in silence, but the sounds of their chewing and their utensils scraping their plates grated against her. The sound ate into her mind. She couldn't sit there any longer. She felt the urge to jump to her feet and scream, "Eat quietly, you fucking cows! You only came here for a free meal and a place to sleep. None of you believe in God!"

Eve rose quickly and excused herself, leaving her dinner untouched. She hurried toward the door, but her legs grew numb and she fell to the stone floor. She laid there; her heartbeat in her ears muffled the shouts for help from the other young women. Her breathing was labored, and her vision went black.

The coach bumped over the cobblestone streets, and the sounds of people filled Peter's heart with excitement. He was almost home, almost to the church, and to Eve. His memory could never erase his first encounters with her when she came to live at the orphanage. She had wild hair and dirty feet but was lucky to find herself in the care of the nuns and not cast to the streets like so many other children. She didn't adapt well at first, many kids didn't welcome her, but Peter didn't want to be like the rest of them.

Peter found her sitting against the trunk of a tree in the courtyard, the bark biting into her back had to be a hundred years old. She looked up at Peter who stood awkwardly attempting to introduce himself.

"Who are you? What do you want?" she blurted out after he had already botched a handshake and all the usual formalities.

"Peter...and I want to be your friend."

Peter nearly wept every time he recalled the change in her face. Her serious, perturbed scowl melted into a bright smile. And in her eyes he swore the sun rose, and it brought light to his heart and his soul. He knew that very instant she was special and she would mark his life forever.

It was one night not long after becoming friends, a storm rolled through, and showed him another side to her. The frightened fragile side. He found her hiding in the kitchen pantry closet with her hands over her ears, humming loudly, trying to drown out the howling winds and driving rain.

"Eve?" a boy's voice echoed in his mind, his own voice.

"I, I'm scared, Peter. The storm..."

"Don't be, come, I'll make sure you're safe," he said, offering her his hand.

"The poor thing fainted and has been sick for more than a week. She still had a fever last night but we managed to break it." Sister Abbie's voice seeped in through Eve's dreams of running to Peter, embracing him, and feeling his lips against hers, before the wind picked up around them and she was suddenly ripped from his arms.

"Will she recover?" the voice of Peter asked, shattering the storm clouds in her dreams, and she was left lying in the golden light. Happiness filled her heart, and her eyes opened slowly.

Her bedroom curtains were pulled aside, and the morning sunlight on Peter's handsome face warmed her heart. He looked like an angel bathed in the glow of heaven.

"Peter?" she asked, her voice weak and hoarse.

"Hush now. You need to rest." He smiled down at her; she could see the love in his eyes.

"You came back."

"Of course, I could never stay away from...all of this." He motioned around him.

"Exactly eight days, Eve, as you guessed," Abbie said. "Now, come on, Peter. You must tell me of your trip. We'll let Eve rest for a while."

"Yes, Sister."

Abbie looked to Eve and patted her hand, "We'll come look in on you later."

"That would be lovely."

Sister Abbie shooed Peter out the door; his eyes never left Eve's until the door was closed behind him.

Eve rose and slowly went to the plate of food left for her. She still didn't feel very hungry, but she knew if she didn't eat she couldn't walk in the garden with Peter.

The scratches on her arms didn't look bad anymore. She hardly remembered Abbie coming twice a day to clean her cuts and apply ointment to them, and of course to pray over Eve, asking God to take away the sickness that overtook her so suddenly.

"What's happening to me?"

She had never experienced a spirit so strong and it left her chilled. Her outburst in the dining hall was embarrassing. She was thankful she didn't curse the sisters around her as her thoughts told her to. Eve just hoped they understood she was ill. She couldn't tell them what she'd heard, how the voice awakened a burning anger in her.

Eve pushed away the memories of the wild roses and ate. She was excited to see Peter and to hear about his trip to California. Eve hadn't left the church grounds much, only a few times a year to assist Abbie and the other sisters with charitable work, feeding and clothing the poor and gathering children to bring to the orphanage. Their superior, Mother Marie, oversaw their trips beyond the church walls, but she was old and didn't approve of them traveling. Instead, she opted to spread the word that folks could come to the church when they were in need.

Eve had never seen the west or any desert, but sometimes Abbie would tell her of Texas though she never went into great detail. Eve longed to see California and all the towns in between. Maybe in those deserts she could be free of the storms and rain. She hoped to travel with Peter, too.

If they ever traveled together, would she still wish to become a nun? She thought she might like to just find a house in all the sand and cacti and make a family with Peter. She stopped chewing and scolded herself for such foolish thoughts. She and Peter's love could never grow beyond a glance, a smile, a kindness toward one another.

They were both devoted to God. From the day they were orphaned, He became their only father and the church their families. Sadness filled her. She tried to push it away, but she just wasn't strong enough to fight it. The sickness had left her too weak, too emotionally fragile to admit she could never be anything more than a nun without crying.

***

"How was Father Connor when you saw him last?" Abbie asked.

"He was well," Peter said, not wanting to speak of his mother yet, "He was ready to take over in San Francisco."

"Was your business in San Francisco?"

"No, actually I stopped in Sacramento with the Father to tend to some business."

"He told me before he left you both were called upon for help..." Abbie said.

"More like he needed me to keep him company," Peter grinned.

"He always hated to travel alone," Abbie smiled knowingly. "Was your business dangerous?"

"Dangerous?"

"You don't have to be coy with me, Peter. I know what business you were on. He took me on a few of the same trips," Abbie said.

"He did?"

"Yes, I have experience with such...things," Abbie said.

"Were you ever afraid?" he whispered.

"Oh yes, but you can never show the devil your fear."

Peter nodded, his mood shifted, "I'd never seen such a thing. I didn't know the true power of evil in this world. Never have I been so scared."

"Yes."

"Was it an exorcism that made you decide to take the vow?" Peter asked.

"Yes, I saw the face of the devil. From that day, I knew what I needed to do."

"Could you tell me about it? Your experience."

"One day."

"Did you have nightmares after what you experienced, during the exorcisms? How long before you didn't dream about them?" he blurted out.

"I had many nightmares, but with prayer they are chased away." She smiled her best reassuring grin. She was lying.

"That's a relief. I mean, I was just so worried that..."

"Go on."

"I worried the evil I witnessed could follow me."

"Now, now, not to this holy place. Come on inside, prayer will do you some good. It will ease you, strengthen you."

She smiled to reassure him, but she knew the fear in his eyes; it would never go away completely. He had been changed by witnessing the truth.

EMBRACE IN MUD AND BLOOD

Eve wandered through the garden. The sun felt good on her skin even though the chill of approaching winter was in the wind. The smell of withering flowers perfumed the air, sweetness and death.

Her body felt weak from being in bed for so many days, but she was happy to be outside.

Peter approached her, "Eve! Are you feeling better?"

"Yes. Come sit over here on the bench."

She took him by the elbow, and they sat on a bench beneath a tree. He smiled, and she could feel contentment radiating off him. Sadly, she knew that shared serenity could only be temporary because she could never lean in and kiss him on the lips as she wished.

She had come so close to professing her feelings to him in the silence but held it in as she always did. There were a few times they breached the subject but always shied away from using the words 'In love' and let it go. They let it hang between them, unspoken love they could never consummate, and a relationship they could never have completely, not as an ordinary man and woman.

"Sister Abbie told me you fainted. You looked very ill earlier," he said. "Are you sure you're okay?"

"I feel much better, especially after seeing you. I feel strong again."

"I'm so relieved to be back here."

"Tell me about your trip. How was it to travel so far west?" Eve asked.

"It was very exciting. There was a stop in a small town in Arizona territory, I don't recall it's name, but I called it Thorn City because the cactus surrounding it seemed to be encroaching on everything. And then in California we saw a traveling band of performers setting up their tent. They were all dressed as animals, but Father Connor refused to watch the show because it looked to be too lewd for men of the church," he said.

"And the coach ride? How was that?" She was desperate for stories, for expeirences. She wanted to know everything.

"It was all like a dream. Imagine looking out the window and watching so many acres of land go by, so many animals and trees. I'll never forget it."

"Where did you end up? What did you assist Father Connor with?" Eve asked.

"Well. That was not so amazing. It was terrifying, actually."

"Oh, tell me about it." She patted the back of his hand softly.

"There was a woman. She was a sick spirit, very sick. We had to help her."

"That's awful."

"We..." He hesitated, knowing how prone to nightmares Eve could be. "We prayed over her and anointed her with holy water."

"Like an exorcism? Tell me more!" Eve said.

He knew she would only press him for details, and what he witnessed was something not even he wanted to remember let alone etch them into her mind. His face betrayed the memories of his mind; all the happy things Peter tried to impart to Eve were overcast by the terror of the exorcism and the crumbs of truth revealed to him of his past.

"You look sad. Did anything else happen?"

"Father Connor told me a bit about my mom's passing...she was sick too, and he and Sister Abbie had to help her," Pete said softly, halting before revealing his true thoughts on his mother's demise.

"Really?" Eve said.

"Let's talk about happy things," he insisted. "Like these flowers and the warm sun on our heads, and the scent of fresh baked bread in the kitchen." He sniffed the air and patted his stomach.

"That does smell good! Remember when we used to save our bread and sneak out at night to see the stars beyond the wall, and we'd share our bread?"

They hadn't done it in years. It was so innocent then, when they were just kids, like a secret adventure. As they grew older, being out in the night together began to feel dangerous in a way, too tempting for the pair of teenagers who were trying to stay chaste.

"Oh, yes. I'll never forget that," he said.

"Now that you're back, we should celebrate by going out to look at the stars," she said, the idea leaping from her mouth before she had the chance to really think about it.

"I'm not sure that's a good idea. If someone caught us they may accuse us of being improper. Besides, you are still recovering."

"You're right," she said, turning her eyes away from him.

"Maybe once you feel better, we can find a way to celebrate my return."

"I already feel better," she said, again letting her inner thoughts escape. Eve scolded herself for sounding so flirtatious but for some reason she couldn't control herself.

"You still look tired. You need some good sleep. We have plenty of time for adventures once you're good as new."

"You promise?" she asked.

"Yes. I promise, Peter said.

Eve smiled, her cheeks turning red.

"Well, I need to speak with Father Joshua. Have a nice day."

Eve watched him go, her heart pounding in her chest. Her attraction to him had multiplied in just the short time since he returned.

Mother Marie's office was always stuffy. Abbie would be relieved to get to San Francisco. Father Connor thought she could become the matron of a new orphanage the church planned to build. She would become Mother Abbie, the matron, but that could be years away.

"The list of postulants looking to become novices, is it complete?" Mother Marie asked.

"Yes, Mother."

"And that girl there, Eve is it? Is she on the list?"

"Yes, she is," Abbie answered.

Mother Marie nodded and narrowed her eyes. She had never really taken to Eve; even when she was just a girl Marie would treat her harshly.

"And what about her imaginary friends?"

"Oh, Mother Marie, she hasn't spoken of them years. They were obviously a figment of her childish imagination."

"Very well, if you think she is committed. But to me, she has other things on her mind than God. She's no fool. At her age she can either stay with us or go to the streets."

Abbie looked out the window to see Eve walking through the garden holding a flower. Her eyes were fixed on Peter who was talking with Father Joshua at the gate to the orphanage dormitories.

"I will speak with her this evening to be certain this is the path she wants to take."

"Agreed. You may go, sister."

Abbie had always felt a wall between her and Mother Marie. She thought it was because she took her vows later in life while Mother Marie had committed to it when she was just a girl.

It took years for her to convince Mother Marie she had left the outside world behind and she didn't desire to marry a man or have children. There were many times the tension between them could have been cut with a knife, but Abbie never gave up; she stayed respectful and worked very hard until Mother Marie abated. She thought maybe the older woman looked at Eve the same way, as a nonbeliever or a freeloader.

Eve's mind fixated on Peter. The spirit, it said it was Peter's mother, but was she sick of mind as Peter told her of the poor woman in California? It would explain her confusion and urgency to have her baby back. It saddened Eve to think of Peter's mother being so disturbed. She decided not to force him to tell her anything unless he was comfortable doing so. She didn't want to hurt him...she wanted to comfort him, to love him.

"Love him." A hushed voice spoke to her. It was not the demented screaming of the voice in the roses claiming Peter was her child; it was assuring and soft.

"Take him like a woman does a man."

Eve didn't bother to shush the voice. It felt like it was the only one she could open her mind to, and admit all the secret things she wanted to do with Peter. It didn't scold her or judge her, only spoke what her heart was feeling. She smiled and ran her fingertips over the petals of the withered flower in her hand.

"He loves me," she said in a hushed voice, plucking a petal free and throwing it to the ground.

"He loves me not," she pulled another petal free and tossed it to the breeze.

"He loves you!" the whisperer said in her ear.

She plucked a petal, brought it to her lips, and kissed it before throwing it.

"He loves me not." The words sent panic through her heart.

"Eve?" Abbie's voice cut her daydreams off.

"Huh?"

"Are you feeling sick again?" Abbie asked.

Eve dropped the flower and ran her hands down her dress, smoothing out any wrinkles and drying her sweaty palms.

"No, sister. Thank you."

"Good, come along with me. We have to go to evening service before dinner, and it's getting cold out here with the clouds rolling in."

Eve hadn't even noticed a storm approaching. A sudden jolt of fear marred the heady feeling she had when staring at Peter.

She nodded and gripped the side of her head, a dizzy spell building with the rising winds.

"Eve?" Abbie said, seeing the change in the young woman's demeanor.

"I feel like the world is spinning."

Eve reached out for Abbie who took her hand before she could fall. A small group was passing by, eyeing.

"Sisters!" Abbie hailed three other nuns. "Help me take Eve to her room."

They took Eve under her arms, and Abbie allowed them to lead her back inside while behind them thunder boomed in the distance. A storm was heading for the church and would be upon them by nightfall.

The church stood at the front of the property and its doors always open to the public. Behind it was the orphanage building attached to it with dorms for the children, a kitchen, and dining room. There were two other buildings beyond that, one on each side of the courtyard and garden areas;one for the young women looking to become nuns, and the other was for the young men studying for priesthood. There were more young women and girls than young men and boys, and even then, the group as a whole was small.

Eve's room was on the far end of the women's dorms. Her window faced the courtyard and from it she could see Peter's window on the other side of the garden on the corner of the men's building. A candle burned in it, a bright yellow glow.

She sat on the edge of her bed with an exhausting headache, wondering if his mind was on her too. Rain pelted the window, and her longing for him began to mix with her fear of storms.

"Peter, I need you," she whispered.

She wore a thin white night dress and the cold seeped through it as if she wore nothing at all, but her face felt flushed.

"Take him like a woman does a man."

She didn't try to fight off the whispering; she wasn't even sure if it wasn't her own voice speaking her desires out loud this time.

"Kiss him, touch him, and feel him."

Eve rolled her head to the side and ran a hand up her neck and into her hair. She gripped a handful of it, silky and soft. Her other hand ventured down her thigh and stopped at her knee. It gathered her night dress up and slowly pulled her undergarments down until her thighs were exposed, along with another part of her.

In her mind it was Peter's hands on her body and wound up in her hair. She could almost feel his breath on her neck, hot and excited. She closed her eyes and he kissed her just below her ear. Eve sighed as a caressing at her thigh sent a rush of excitement through her. She lay back on her bed and her legs spread. Fingers glided up her thigh and stopped when she moaned softly.

"Go look up at the stars and he will follow. I promise to give him to you."

Eve's eyes opened; the rain outside didn't register. Her mind full of Peter, she rose from her bed and kicked her undergarments off. The glow in his window was still bright; she was awake. She was ready to see if the voice was all in her own mind or if it was much more...and if it was, she was willing to find out if it would keep that promise to her.

Eve crept out into the hallway and down to the door leading to the courtyard.

The rain hit her in the face when she stepped outside. Her eyes were focused on the candlelight in his window, even as the rain soaked through her night dress. She would love him like a woman does a man, even if it was only once.

"Go to him; take him to see the stars. He will be yours."

Peter was at his desk reading a letter sent by Father Connor. It was mostly about his first days at the new church and Father Glover's declining health, but Peter knew he wanted to say more and he eventually got to it more than half way through his writing. He was concerned about the way Peter learned the truth about his mother.

Peter felt he still hadn't had the time to truly process it all. He wanted so badly to ask Sister Abbie about her part in the story, but he still didn't know how to approach the subject. Father Connor had probably sent her a letter when he mailed Peter's. The timing made Peter believe Father Connor had written the letter right after his departure from California. It obviously still plagued him, and he didn't know how to fully explain it to Peter. He must have felt strangely guilty even though the priest wasn't to blame for Peter's mother's death.

Peter folded the letter and left it on his desk, his heart heavy and his mind fighting away memories of what he witnessed Lady Elizabeth go through.

Peter stood and looked out his window to see a pale figure in the downpour. His heart thundered in his chest and he threw a coat on and ran from his room when he realized he knew the person getting soaked in the storm.

She was moving too quickly, almost gliding over the ground. He didn't want to cry out to her and awaken the others until he spoke to her. He didn't want her to be reprimanded by Mother Marie. He ran in her direction as she passed through the garden. Rain ran into his eyes, and he stopped momentarily to wipe it away only to see her disappear through the hole in the wall. He rushed forward, puddles soaking his feet and pants. He crouched down and wiggled through the hole in the garden wall.

"Eve!"

She didn't turn around; she just kept walking until she stopped by the wild rose bushes. Peter approached her, slowing down as to not startle her.

"Eve. It's raining. Let's go back inside."

"Look, the clouds are opening up just in time for us to look at the stars," she said and turned to face him.

The rain had died to a drizzle, and the clouds drifted away from the face of the moon. He could see through her soaked night dress, the body of a woman curvy and inviting.

"Let's go back inside."

"Look at the stars with me," she said coming close to him, closer than she ever dared.

Peter fell silent. He couldn't find any words; his mind was conjuring up fantasies no priest should have. In the back of his mind, he knew something was wrong with Eve. She had never been this forward. He could feel something wasn't right, but he didn't pull away...he couldn't stop himself, he didn't want to.

Eve ran her hands up his chest and felt its rise and fall, his breathing deep, his heart racing at her touch.

"Kiss me, Peter."

He leaned in and felt her breath on his lips before succumbing to what he had always ran away from.

He pressed his lips to hers, their mouths opened, their tongues touched. He felt her hand slide down to grip his crotch. She squeezed, and he nearly came. Eve pulled him down in the mud beside the wild roses and shed her night dress. Her skin was as pale as the moon, her nipples small pink like the buds on the vines. He caressed her, let his hands feel the softness of her body. It was obvious her excitement was growing as he touched her.

She pulled his trousers down and straddled him. He closed his eyes and inhaled the scents of night and rain, his ears filled with the pounding of his heartbeat. He felt himself being guided into her, warm and wet. There was tension there, but it broke after a few attempts. She moaned. It was a mixture of pleasure and pain. He opened his eyes. His mind spun, something in him screamed it was wrong, but he couldn't stop. She moved in a way that kept his guilt at bay though it would come roaring back sooner or later.

He rolled her over and got on top of her. He let his body take control until he was deep within her, one hand holding onto her buttocks while the other gripped the muddy earth above her head. He thrust himself into her and slid himself out, over and over, with the stars and moon at his back.

Euphoria swept through him as he came, tears falling from his eyes. He pulled out of her, breathing heavily, and immediately felt shame crawling up his back. He got up on his knees and dusted something sticky from his hand. He wiped it down his thigh and saw blood, Eve's blood, and something else dark from his palm, black feathers. Beside her head was the rumpled corpse of a bird; he had been gripping it the whole time he penetrated her. Disgust filled him. This was blasphemy.

Eve lay before him, her legs still spread. She no longer looked like an angel but an abomination of forbidden lust. She arched her back in the mud and reached out to him, welcoming him to do it again.

"We shouldn't have done this," he said and stood up.

She didn't say a word, the silence between them uncomfortable.

"We know this wasn't right, Eve." He was nearly crying now.

Eve ran her hand between her thighs, gathered blood on her fingertips, and brought it to her chest. In crimson she drew an inverted cross between her breasts.

Peter pulled his clothing on, confused as to what to do. He didn't want Father Joshua or Mother Marie to know what they had done, but it was clear to him something was horribly wrong with Eve.

"It's nice to see you again, Peter. I wonder what Father Connor would think if he saw you now? Fucking like beasts in the fields."

The voice coming from Eve's mouth was the same from his nightmares. It was the beast, the demon who knew the truth about his mother.

THE SPIDER OF HUMAN FLESH

THUNDER RUMBLED OVERHEAD. THE moon disappeared behind rolling clouds. The sky opened up in a sudden downpour. Eve lay in the rain naked, but as the cold drops hit her skin it began to wash away the blood between her breasts. She took a deep breath and shook her head. Her face was pale and confusion filled her eyes. Peter went to her and helped her get dressed. He wrapped his coat around her.

"Peter, what happened?"

His heart broke. He felt like an animal. Eve acted as if she had no idea they had sex. He felt his stomach rise in his throat, and tears stung his eyes.

"I feel sick," she cried.

"Come on, let's get you back inside," he said.

They climbed back through the hole in the wall, and Peter helped her to the entrance to the ladies dorms. She was soaking wet and trembling.

"How did we get out there?"

"Eve, I followed you out there, and..."

"What's going on here?" Sister Abbie's voice felt like a knife in Peter's gut.

He couldn't lie to her; she would see right through it.

"She needs to go back to bed, and I need to speak with you, Sister. It's urgent."

Abbie nodded and hurried Eve into the warmth of the building. Peter followed, feeling hollow inside.

He wasn't sure if God would ever forgive such sin. Eve was covered in mud and leaves hung in her hair. She was now just a young woman who had been ravaged without her consent.

Abbie lit a lantern. She cleaned Eve up and helped her to her bed. Eve climbed into her blankets and looked to Peter who stood in the doorway.

"Thank you for bringing me back inside. I don't know how I got out there. You're my hero, Peter."

Her words, they tore his heart out.

Sister Abbie pushed Peter out the door and shut it behind her.

"What is happening here?"

"Sister, I..."

"Just answer the question."

Peter couldn't bring himself to tell her everything that happened beyond the church wall so he lied. "I found her out there. She was nude and speaking in the voice of a demon...the demon Father Connor and I exorcised."

Sister Abbie's face went white.

"We have to help her!"

Abbie nodded and turned back to the closed door and put her ear against it.

"We have..."

Sister Abbie shushed Peter and listened through the door. She could hear deep breathing, like an animal was on the other side.

"Get Father Joshua right now!"

Abbie put her hand on the doorknob but hesitated at laughter that sounded nothing like Eve, and then a voice spoke.

"Oh, Abbie. Did our meeting push you into becoming a nun? What a waste of a life! What a waste of a cunt!"

Abbie backed away from the door.

"Surprised that I can set foot here, in your holy sanctuary? I didn't go into that shit-hole in Texas because I was having more fun hunting. I go where I please!"

Abbie's heart stuttered in her chest. Pain tore through her left side.

"You still got the scars from the last time we met, don't you?"

Her arms suddenly felt like they were dowsed in kerosene and set afire. She didn't even have to look at them to know her scars had opened back up. She beat the door, her blood raining onto it with each strike.

"You son of a bitch!"

"There's the Abbie I know! Let it out, let the anger vomit from you. I can taste it, like honey on my tongue."

Abbie backed away from the door, unwilling to face what was on the other side again. Somewhere in her heart and in her nightmares, she knew this day would come; the demon was never exorcised from Peter's mother. It was set free when the poor woman drowned in the flood waters.

"Where's good old Father Connor? I asked him the last time we spoke and he never answered me. Did you two fuck?"

"Shut yer damn mouth!" Sister Abbie raged, her anger outweighing her fear.

"Come shut it for me, you cunt!" the demon cackled.

Abbie threw the door open and stepped into Eve's room. She was sitting up in bed. She had removed her clothes, and her eyes were solid black when she turned her head to face Sister Abbie.

"You look old, worn out. What a waste of a woman."

The sounds of footsteps running up the hallway drew the demon's attention.

"We have company!"

Eve's body lurched forward. She got up onto her knees and her arms opened wide.

"I'm ready, Peter! Take me again!" the deep demonic voice teased.

Peter and Father Joshua halted just inside the door.

"We need to restrain her," Father Joshua said, but Peter hesitated.

"Don't be afraid. We have to help her." Father Joshua insisted.

"I'm not afraid," Peter said.

Eve stood up and began jumping on the bed, her breasts bouncing. Peter turned his eyes away. She bent over backward, her spine painfully contorting until she looked like a spider made of human flesh, and crawled to the edge of the bed toward Peter. There were still blood stains on her thighs.

"Look at me, Peter. Don't pretend you don't like it!"

"I said restrain her!" Father Joshua ordered.

"Come have a sniff, have a taste, Peter!" the demon in Eve thrusted her cunt in his direction then righted Eve's body to stand up again. She gripped her breasts and sighed.

Sister Abbie and Peter looked to each other and nodded, but Abbie moved first. She grabbed one of Eve's arms and pulled her downward in an attempt to make her fall on the mattress so they could somehow tie her down. Eve yanked her arm away, spun, and spit in Abbie's face. A thick wad of mucus hung from her eyebrow, and she wiped it away.

"This is no longer the girl you knew. Do not be gentle with it!" Father Joshua said.

Peter grabbed Eve by her wrist and pulled her toward him so he could grab the other one too. Eve tried freeing herself by kicking him, but he refused to let go. He couldn't let Eve get away or hurt herself in the thrall of the demon. He recalled Father Connor saying Elizabeth was lucky to survive her possession, unlike his mother. He couldn't lose Eve to the demon inside of her. He forced her down onto the bed and straddled her.

"Get some rope, Sister!"

Abbie ran from the room.

"You like that, being on top of me. You like being inside of me even more!"

Peter hoped Father Joshua would only think the demon was lying, taunting him with offers of Eve's flesh. Abbie returned quickly with the long cords she used to tie her curtains back. She took Eve's wrists and one by one tied them to the headboard of her bed. Now that she was restrained, they could get to work with the exorcism.

"Father Joshua, is it?" the thing in Eve asked.

The priest didn't answer; he just opened his holy book and began reciting the prayer to Saint Michael.

"This is familiar?" the demon said to Peter. "Only there are no dolls to run from here, coward! No Father Connor to save you!"

Thunder boomed beyond the window, and the winds began to howl. Eve opened her mouth, and a multitude of voices wailed. The skin on her forearms split into long scratches; blood ran down onto the bed. Father Joshua dowsed her with holy water, blistering her skin wherever it landed.

"Oh, Peter." This time it was Eve's voice, pitiful and exhausted. "What did you do to me, Peter? You brought this thing to me."

Peter went to the head of the bed and wiped the sweat from her forehead.

"Peter, you love me don't you?"

Peter didn't say a word, but his heart raced.

"Get between my legs and fuck me again!" the demon's voice screamed.

Peter backed away. He wanted to strangle the demon until it went silent. The thoughts flashed through his mind and before he could stop himself, he fell onto Eve and wrapped his hands around her throat. Abbie slapped him across the face, and he released Eve.

"Stop listening to it, you fool!"

Peter stumbled back and fell against the wall.

His eyes were wide, his mind absorbing every second of Father Joshua doing battle with the demon in Eve. He splashed the holy water down onto her naked skin again, and with a hiss smoke rose from it. The window rattled with hurricane force winds. Beyond the pane Peter thought he could see faces watching Eve. He got to his feet and ran to close the curtains.

"Little Eve's friends came to watch. They don't want me to take her, but I will." The demon's voice grated against every nerve in Peter's body. Eve jerked and fought. Her body rose from the bed, only the restraints kept her from reaching the ceiling. Father Joshua's prayer faltered, and the demon laughed. He gripped his chest.

"You're a weak man. I'll eat you alive!"

Abbie went to Father Joshua's side to stabilize him. His voice grew hoarse, and his breathing labored. He fell to the ground mid sentence and gasped as his chest imploded with a crunch as if an invisible vice had crushed him.

"Looks like you need a new priest!" the demon laughed.

Peter took up the holy water and the prayer book. He took a deep breath and started the rites again. Abbie felt Father Joshua's chest and shook her head. Peter dowsed Eve with holy water, and she screamed. Her body fell back down onto the bed.

"Go get help," he said to Sister Abbie.

She ran out the door agian leaving him to continue the exorcism.

"You're not a priest yet," the demon said through Eve's exhausted body.

"I am enough to drive you back to Hell."

"Why would you drive me away when I gave you what you always dreamed of?"

"Be silent!"

"I gave you Eve, all of her. You're an ungrateful little shit!"

"In the name of the Father, the Son, and of the Holy Spirit, be gone!"

The demon hissed as Peter splashed holy water across Eve's body.

"I command you in the name of God to be gone!"

Eve lurched and gagged; a mouthful of blood misted the air. He faltered. He didn't want to kill Eve in the process of ridding her of the demon.

Abbie returned with two other priests and Mother Marie. The old nun's eyes went wide, and she crossed herself at the sight of Eve and Father Joshua lying on the floor. The group went to Joshua, leaving Peter to continue the rites over Eve.

Abbie worried they were in a losing battle, but she didn't speak her fear aloud. Eve had finally fallen silent. Her eyes were closed.

"Is it gone?" Abbie asked, but she knew the truth.

"No, I can still feel it," Peter said.

"We need Father Connor, Mother Marie said.

"It will take too long to get him here." Peter said.

"What about our other priests?" Sister Abbie asked.

"They're not even as experienced as Peter," Mother Marie said sadly.

"She will die if it stays in her," Peter whispered.

Mother Marie folded her arms over her chest, "What do you suggest?"

"I'm taking her to San Francisco. She has to see Father Connor. There is another priest there, Father Glover; he is Father Connor's mentor. I believe he can save her."

WESTWARD BOUND

"This is a terrible idea," Sister Abbie insisted.

Mother Marie agreed, "You can't handle her on such a trip. Even if she survived it, she could get away from you and we can't afford for it to kill anyone."

"We don't have a choice!" Peter said. "It will take weeks to send a letter or even a telegram and then have him travel here. If I leave tomorrow morning, we can head toward him. We need Father Glover too and he is ill. He can't even leave California and may never be able to again. Let me take her there before Father Glover dies, before her only hope dies!"

"If you insist upon this, I'm going with you," Sister Abbie said.

"Only if you get approval." Mother Marie said.

"I'm not lookin' for a pissing contest, Mother," Abbie said.

Eve was in a deep sleep. Her breathing was labored, and she mumbled in a deep voice. It was obvious their exorcism was a failure.

"Have you sent warning to Father Connor we are heading his way?" Peter asked.

"I did as soon as the sun rose."

Abbie looked out the window to the morning sunlight on the storm ravaged courtyard.

Peter smiled sadly, "I believe with his help and that of Father Glover, we can beat this evil."

"So do I. I'll pack a bag for myself and one for her, too," she said nodding toward Eve.

"We'll leave in a few hours, " Peter said.

Eve coughed and whined. She was lost in her mind, fighting against the demon controlling her body. They went to her side, cautiously watching for signs the demon was awakening.

"Do you think she'll make it?" Peter asked.

Abbie shook her head, "It's hard to say, but we have God on our side."

She looked at the bandages on her arms placed there by the priests who tried in vain to save Father Joshua's life. Fear stole over her but she wouldn't let it show on her face. She just kept wondering about the strength the demon possessed. She knew Eve was in grave danger; a miracle was what she needed. She didn't want to tell Peter about the many people she watched die in the throes of possession. She couldn't bring herself to cut the last strands of hope he clung to.

She had also received a letter from Father Connor who had written of his concern for Peter after he had to reveal a bit of the truth to him about his mother. His final sentence seemed like an omen of doom. He was concerned about Peter because he had opened the box.

Abbie wondered if it wasn't all a test in Connor's eyes, to place Peter before the box that claimed his own mother's soul without realizing it. The young man had failed if it was some kind of trial.

Peter was quiet, and she knew he felt guilty. He had told Abbie he was worried the demon had followed him, and it was obvious to her it had. Eve would pay the price for her connection to Peter, and Abbie worried how dearly the cost would be. Eve could lose more than just her life; her soul was on the line now. The girl had suffered far too much in her short life already, and now physically and spiritually she was being torn to pieces.

Her hands were shaking as she exited the room to pack their bags for the road. She hated knowing the only reason she ever ventured so far west was to stand beside Father Connor while he performed the rites of exorcism. For once she would like to go for a pleasant reason. This time would be no different than all her other trips, but this demon was the most evil and insidious force she had ever encountered, one that had returned after decades to inflict terror on her and those she cared about once again.

***

Eve opened her eyes. They were pale blue again, not black pools of evil. Peter came to her side. Her arms were still bound to the bed.

"My wrists hurt. Untie me, please," she whispered.

"Just a little longer," he promised.

"I'm so thirsty."

Peter went to a desk beside the door and filled a small cup of water from a pitcher the priests brought in after informing them Father Joshua had indeed passed. He brought it to her and held it against her dry cracked lips.

She drank slowly but emptied the cup. She let her head fall back on a sweat stained pillow and closed her eyes.

Peter couldn't imagine the terror she had to feel and the deep exhaustion from her body being contorted and abused. He felt like he might weep. He sat on the edge of the bed and watched her breathing and prayed until Sister Abbie returned with her bag and an empty one for Eve. Peter excused himself.

Sister Abbie watched him running across the courtyard from Eve's window. She could feel his love for Eve and thought back on the days when she and Father Connor shared a secret connection. They severed it willingly before it could blossom into heartache. She hoped Peter and Eve could do the same.

She turned around to watch Eve who slept deeply, occasionally fitfully jerking at the ties at her wrists. She had never seen it so bad, never felt such a force. She prayed God would grant Eve the strength to survive it. A light knock on the door drew her attention to the old nun entering. Mother Marie's face looked sour as it always did, not an ounce of sympathy for the young woman tied to the bed.

"Are you packing her bags?"

"And mine."

"You have always had an attitude, but this is too much. You dedicated your life to the service of the church and at this church, you obey my orders."

"Then I won't come back. When I get to California and this is all over, I will stay there," Abbie said.

"That will be the only way I'll ever approve it because I don't want to see you here again."

A rasping laughter rose from Eve's throat.

"I've always loved a good cat fight. Why don't you take off your clothes and wrestle on the floor where I can see it?"

"I think we have more important things to worry about than whether I obeyed your orders or not," Abbie said.

"Just get her out of here today. I always knew this girl would be trouble, ever since she arrived here with her imaginary friends and talking to flowers. Was it really a surprise to you she ended up this way?"

Abbie didn't respond out loud, but her mind was screaming every foul word she swore she would never speak again.

"Oh, I love what's running through your head, Sister Abbie!" the demon cackled. "She wants to call you a ruthless, sanctimonious, dusty-cunted, old twat! And in little Eve's memories I see you being a naughty old girl...cat killer!"

Mother Marie's eyes went wide. Her lips pressed together in an angry line.

"Just get out of here!"

Sister Abbie waited until she could hear the old nun stomping as she made her way down the hallway before she spoke to the demon.

"Stay outta my head, asshole."

"Oh, I'm so scared. You gonna shoot Eve in the eye, too?" it teased.

Abbie swallowed the venom she wanted to spit at the thing; she took a deep breath instead. It wanted to piss her off. It delighted in it.

"You just want to get to California so you can spread your legs for Father Connor. Well, he's a little past his prime. I'm sure his cock is as limp as a wet noodle now. But Peter is young and his still works fantastically, just ask Eve. He gave it to her good."

Sister Abbie turned her back to it and went back to shoving more things into Eve's bag. She didn't want to make eye contact with it or engage it in any way until she was not alone with it. She knew it could be as dangerous as a serpent, always waiting to strike

"Peter opened the box, got a look inside. You should ask him what it was like."

Abbie felt the hair rise on her arms.

"It was a paradise of fire and blood, and your beloved cock face Father Connor destroyed it. Now my only home is these stinking corpses of the living. Do you know what it is like to live in the body of a coyote and have all your friends sniff your asshole to say hello? Do you know what it's like to fly as a bird over the reeking shitholes humans call their homes? This place is Hell, true Hell!" It spoke, its voice rising in anger.

Abbie's throat went dry, maybe the thing was right. Maybe she was already living in Hell; most of her life certainly felt like it. She took a deep breath and prayed Father Connor and Father Glover really could banish it once and for all. She didn't want to spend what time she had left, whether it was minutes or decades, fighting it.

She searched the table beside the door. Father Joshua's holy water shimmered in the sunlight seeping in through the window. Abbie grabbed it and faced Eve who was thrashing in the restraints on her wrists.

"Untie me, you fucking bitch. I'm gonna open your throat this time."

Abbie could feel it searching her with its power, looking for a way to torture her or even crush her as it did to Father Joshua.

"Be silent!" she screamed and let the holy water fly onto Eve's face.

She shrieked as blisters rose on her cheeks.

"You stupid bitch. You wouldn't be so strong if you didn't have me tied up."

Abbie dowsed Eve again and watched her writhe.

"I'm going to tell Peter the truth. The little shit deserves to know who killed his mother!"

"It was you!" Abbie screamed and grabbed Eve by the jaw. She dumped the holy water into Eve's mouth.

Eve cried out, her voice a high-pitched wailing but definitely her own once more. Abbie backed away as Eve's lips swelled until they split, her eyes rolled back, and the demon receded.

The coach came late in the morning. It would take them to the station to ride the Butterfield route all the way to California, but first they had to subdue Eve enough to get her there. So Abbie and Peter waited outside the medical closet within the church, hoping the priests kept something strong enough to keep Eve incapacitated for long periods of time.

"It's chloroform," the student priest said, handing a bottle to Abbie.

"Are you sure it will work?" Peter asked.

"We'll make do with it. Thank you," Abbie said and pushed Peter along back to Eve's room.

"She's been in a deep sleep for a long time. Maybe we can tie her up as she is and get her in the coach."

"We'll need this sooner or later. She won't sleep the whole trip. Do you think that thing inside her will let that happen?" Abbie asked.

"No, I suppose you're right," He said.

Abbie dowsed a cloth in chloroform and held it over Eve's nose and mouth. She didn't struggle or resist. Abbie removed it and nodded to Peter, "Let's go."

The coachman studied what looked like a priest and a nun. The priest had a young lady thrown over his shoulder while the nun struggled to carry three bags.

"She is in dire need of help. We aren't harming her," Peter said after lying Eve in the seat of the coach.

"I'm not paid to ask questions," the driver said.

"Good, then we'll be on our way."

Abbie handed Peter the bags one at a time and took her seat inside next to him. The coach lurched forward and bounced on the rough street outside the church.

Eve was unconscious most of the day but twitched and fidgeted the whole time. Peter instructed the driver to continue as quickly as the horses could manage; he and Abbie didn't wish to stop anywhere. They ate in the coach, small bites of food, though neither of them had much of an appetite.

They passed into Texas as evening stained the sky, and they still wouldn't make it to the station until well after dark.

"Texas territory!" the driver hollered. "Good to be home!"

"We just have to make it to Franklin, and from there we'll hop on the Butterfield and head to California," Peter said.

"You make it sound so easy. We have to keep her alive for more than two weeks." Abbie sounded disgusted and anxious. She had a strange feeling in her gut riding into Texas again. A dread only the past could conjure, memories beat into her brain like a hammer.

"We'll make it," Peter said.

"We're lookin' at almost twenty days on the trail, all the while keeping her from killing herself or someone else."

"I just hope Father Connor receives our message quickly and readies Father Glover."

"Peter, how do we even know if Father Glover won't be dead by then?"

"We have to have faith, Sister. Father Connor told me Father Glover was the greatest demon slayer he had ever seen. Is it true?"

Abbie nodded, trying to banish the negativity. "I have met him, only once. It was a bad case, one I'll never forget. That's how I knew what you felt like when you spoke of nightmares. There is only one other incident which plagues me more..." her eyes passed over Peter, recalling the face of his mother. "He told us possessions can take some time, sometimes months for a demon to fully take control. That was the case for a young boy we saved. It didn't take him over completely for weeks, giving Father Glover time to coax the boy into fighting back. We were successful in the end. Father Glover is far more advanced at exorcisms than, you, me, and Father Connor combined. If he is alive, he will cure Eve of what's inside her. You'll see."

Peter smiled, his eyes tearing up.

"Yes, and he probably advises people not to open boxes when they're told not to." Peter's words hung in the air between them. His guilt was still torturing him. Abbie placed her hand softly on top of Peter's.

"Do not blame yourself."

"How can I not?" his voice broke as tears run down his cheeks. He wiped them away and ran his hands through his hair.

"We need to focus. Eve needs us strong to defend her," Abbie said.

As if on cue, Eve lurched forward, sitting up in her seat. Her wrists were bound, and she pushed away the blanket Abbie draped over her while she slept. Peter lunged forward and grabbed Eve's bindings, and holding her in her seat.

"What's happening? Where am I?" she asked.

"Calm down, Evey Bee," Abbie said, using a nickname she called Eve when she was just a little girl smelling all the flowers in the garden.

She smiled assuringly, grabbing a canteen. "Here, have something to drink," Abbie said.

Eve took the canteen in trembling hands and brought it to her dry mouth. She reclined back against the seat, gulping the water down.

"You haven't called me that in years!" Eve said.

"You'll always be my little Bee. Soon this will be over and you can go back to picking roses."

"I hope so," Eve said.

"I brought some bread from the kitchen. Are you hungry?"

"Yes, I'm starving," Eve answered and traded the canteen for a small piece of bread.

Peter was on edge, praying the demon would allow Eve to eat. It needed to stay lost somewhere inside her long enough for her to nourish herself or she would die before making it to their destination.

Eve nibbled bread and motioned for another drink. Abbie helped her drink and took a seat beside Eve, who stared at the ropes on her wrists.

"Stay calm, they're for your own good," Abbie said.

"What's wrong with me?" Eve asked. "I feel so tired, so sick."

Peter realized he would have to tell her what happened sooner or later, that something evil was trying to steal her body and soul.

"Shhh, try to rest now. We'll talk about it later," Abbie said and smoothed Eve's hair down. There was a long streak of white hair at her temple. Peter didn't even know how they would tell her when the time came. How could he possibly scare her so badly with the truth? She would crumble, mentally and physically.

The coach lurched forward, startling Peter, but then it halted. The sudden stop sent dust floating by the window.

"Why are we stopping? We're supposed to ride through. That's what we paid him for."

"Driver? What's going on?" Abbie yelled.

A muffled voice beyond the coach window and the harsh bark of the driver told them he was speaking to someone. Peter opened the window and stuck his head out to see a young man standing next to a big trunk. It hung out into the road, and the coach couldn't get around it.

"Bless you! I need a ride badly!"

"I ain't got room! Get your ass outta my way!" the driver ordered.

"Oh please! Please! I can't be left out here in the night this close to the cemetery!"

After a few minutes of silence from the driver he said, "If you don't pay, you don't ride."

"Oh, yes, I can pay! Look, look, here take all of it;just let me ride with you!"

"Driver," Peter said, his voice betraying his aggravation, "we agreed this would be a private coach."

"Oh, are you a priest? Please, Father, give me a ride. I walked by the cemetery up the road and I don't want to get stuck by it in the dark. You understand, right?" the young man pressed his palms together, pleading with Peter.

Peter sighed and climbed out of the coach. He came close to the young man and opened his mouth to speak, trying to think of an excuse to leave him out in the dark but halted when the man on the road stuck a gun against his stomach.

"Oh thank you! It must have been your godly presence that saved me from getting stuck out here at night!" the man said with a chuckle. He winked and jammed the gun harder against Peter.

"Wait, you can't..." Peter tried to reason with him but couldn't say he had a possessed girl tied up inside the coach.

"It'll only be a short ride, and if you refuse I'll shoot you and then the driver and have my way with whatever little nuns you got inside," the man whispered.

Peter nodded and stepped aside, allowing the man to pass by him.

"Would you mind helpin' me with my trunk, Father?" the gunman asked, his voice and demeanor spelling out to Peter that if he didn't there would be bloodshed. Peter was shaking, franticly trying to think of a way out of letting him in the coach, but he was stuck allowing the man to ride along with them. He prayed it was for only a short distance because he didn't want them all shot dead before they ever made it out of Louisiana.

Peter climbed over to sit beside Eve, keeping her between him and Sister Abbie who pulled the blanket up to cover Eve's bound hands. Abbie's face spoke to her concern about another passenger, but Peter shook his head and silenced her.

"It's only for a little ways." His voice was unconvincing even to himself, but he couldn't tell her the truth or they would all be shot.

The trunk was wedged into the coach allowing barely any foot room, and the gunman sat across from them with his hand inside his jacket and a grin on his face.

Peter could see he was rather short but stout. He was maybe the same age as Eve and Peter, early twenties, and had a patchy haircut. He wore a long jacket that wasn't unusual with it being nearly winter, but it was dirty and Peter felt nothing but repulsion for him.

"My name is Merrel. What's yours Father?" the gunman said, keeping his charade going.

"Peter."

"Thank you, Father Peter. I really needed a ride."

Peter shifted nervously in his seat and whistled to the driver. The coach leaped forward, and they were on their way again. They hadn't sat in silence for more than a few minutes when Merrel started talking and wouldn't shut up. Each time he addressed either Peter or Abbie, he scooted in his seat and peeped around the side of his trunk. A wicked game of peekaboo, Peter knew it. He swallowed a lump in his throat each time Merrel spoke and cursed himself for stepping out of the coach in the first place. Had he stayed seated, the driver may have been able to scare Merrel away with his own shotgun he undoubtedly kept at his side.

Merrel was obviously amused by thinking at any second he could appear around the side of the trunk with his gun drawn and murder them all.

"Sorry, I have to be lookin' at you when I talk to you. Otherwise, I feel strange," he said to Abbie as he leaned around the side of the trunk to talk to her.

She smiled at him politely, but he knew in her mind she called him every dirty word she'd heard in her life.

"A priest and a nun. I got really lucky! Nothin' bad'll happen to me while you two are here."

The trunk creaked, and Merrel held it with filthy hands. His nails were black and chipped. Abbie studied him; his eyes weren't as friendly as his mouth pretended he was. She wasn't sure if it was Merrel or his cargo, but there was a smell like dead flowers permeating the inside of the coach.

"What're ya'll doin' with the girl? Is she sick or somethin'?"

"Yes, she's ill," Abbie answered.

"What's wrong with her? Hopefully not the consumption."

"No, another ailment. We're taking her west to where the sun will do her some good," Abbie said.

"That's good. My mama had it, the consumption, coughed her lungs up and died."

"What are you doing out here?" Abbie asked.

"Visitin' my mama's grave," Merrel said, his smile fading.

The hours passed; night bore down on the quiet desert outside the coach, and Merrel continued to barrage them with senseless conversation all the while gripping his trunk. Luckily, Eve slept so there was no way for Merrel to discover the truth about her.

He kept looking out the coach window, which didn't slip by Abbie. She also noticed how tense Peter was each time the man spoke, and she got the feeling Peter wasn't just concerned about Eve waking up. There was something strange about the way he allowed Merrel to hitch a ride with them. The young man had promised he only needed a short lift, but hours later he still sat across from her stinking like moldy earth. And he kept glancing out the window like he was expecting something.

"Looking for something?" she asked.

"No, it's just we're getting close to the cemetery."

"I thought you said the cemetery was close to where we picked you up?"

Merrel turned his eyes to Sister Abbie, but he didn't answer. She could see the gears grinding in his mind.

"We're almost to Franklin!" the driver shouted.

"Looks like my stop!" Merrel grinned, his teeth just as filthy as his hands.

He drew a pistol from his jacket, his face shifting to a callous stare.

"Give me all your valuables, and I'll let you live. See Father, I did my part; now do yours. Gimme all you got in here!"

Peter tried to speak, but Merrel lifted the gun and leveled it at his forehead. Each bump in the road his hand jerked, and Abbie prayed his finger didn't pull the trigger.

"I said give me all you got, or you gonna meet God sooner than you thought."

A wheezing laughter issued from Eve, and she sat forward.

"Shoot'em in the eyes!" the demon laughed.

"What the fuck? Are you tryin' to test me, bitch?" Merrel asked, popping his head around the side of the trunk to look at the sick girl.

He scooted to the side and aimed the gun at Eve instead of Peter. "I'll blow yer brains out first. I don't like women makin' fun of me."

Eve's mouth opened wide, and the sound of multiple voices giggling filled the coach.

"What the fuck? What's wrong with her? You said she was sick!'"

"There's somethin' else wrong with her." The demon finished Merrel's sentence, mocking his voice. "What's wrong with you? Dragging around a trunk with a corpse in it!"

"I'll shoot yer ass! You better shut your mouth!"

Eve leaned forward, eyes black pools, staring into Merrel's. "That's what you did to your mama, right? Blew her brains out, let her corpse get all dry out by the woodpile until you almost got caught. Now, she's crammed in a trunk."

"No, I...she was sick. I couldn't let her suffer."

"Horse shit! You got tired of her refusing to share her money. You leech. You killed her and took what you wanted. Did the money run out? Now you gotta rob coaches?"

"I'll kill you, you crazy bitch!"

"I don't think so," the demon said, deathly serious.

Merrel's arm trembled as he held the gun out. His hand cracked. His trigger finger bent backwards, but he didn't drop the gun. The demon in Eve growled, and in a crunch, Merrel's arm went sideways, bending unnaturally until his elbow joint bent inward. He screamed and nearly fainted.

"You brought her up here to bury her in the cemetery because you felt guilty for fucking her corpse in the ass, but your stupid ass forgot the shovel. Did you stick flowers in her asshole too or just her mouth and eyes?"

The coach jumped over the rough road. The trunk fell sideways, knocking the gun from Merrel's useless grip. It hit the floor and went off, blowing a hole through the wall of the coach beside Peter's head.

The trunk lid popped open, and a desiccated body fell from it. There were hundreds of dead flowers inside of it and shoved into the corpse's gaping mouth and empty eyes sockets. Maggots fell from its mouth after the flowers rained down onto Abbie and Peter. They squirmed in Abbie's lap, writhing angrily at being forced out of their feeding grounds. She screamed and slapped them away. The coach came to a stop. Eve lunged forward, and even with bound wrists she managed to grab Merrel's gun first. She brought it up and stuck it in his mouth.

"Say hello to mama."

The demon in Eve pulled the trigger as the coach door was flung open, decorating the driver with Merrel's brains. He wiped them away and shoved the barrel of his rifle into the coach.

"What the hell is happening in here?"

"He tried to rob us, and there's a dead body in his trunk," Peter stuttered.

"Drop the gun, little girl. Everything is okay now," the driver ordered.

Eve turned to him, the demon receding enough to make her appear like a frightened young woman, but it was still pulling the strings. Tears ran down her pale cheeks. "I was so scared. I thought I was going to die."

"It's okay now, honey. We'll just drag his ass and that trunk out here and leave it by the cemetery. I'll send a lawman back this way whenever I see one," the driver said.

Eve nodded and trembled as she went to sit back down between Peter and Abbie, but she didn't drop the gun.

"Help me drag that piece of shit out of here," the driver said to Peter.

Peter looked to Abbie who was shaking her head.

"Help him, Peter. I don't want to see that anymore," Eve said and winked at Abbie who didn't take her eyes off the pistol in Eve's hands.

"Not so tough now are you, Sister?" she whispered to Abbie, her breath reeking of sulfur and rot.

"Come on now. The quicker it's done the quicker we can get the hell away from it," the driver urged.

Peter stood and hesitated before shoving the dead woman back into the trunk and shutting its lid. He pushed the trunk to the door, and the driver, who left his rifle propped up against the coach, grabbed it by one end and pulled it outside.

Maggots fell from it and squirmed on the floor. The driver grunted as he struggled to get it off the road and left it lying beside the cemetery gates beneath the light of the moon. He returned as Peter was fighting to get the corpse of Merrel to the coach door. Blood stained Peter's hands and stuck to his black coat, soaking into it and leaving its stench behind.

The smell of gunpowder and Merrel's blasted open skull hung in the air, leaving Peter nauseated. The driver grabbed Merrel under his armpits and hauled him out to prop him up next to the trunk. He stopped to cross himself and went back to close the coach door, stopping for a moment to light the coach lantern and hanging it inside. With its glow, the blood, brains, and maggots were too visible. Abbie was nauseated and still warily looking at Eve who gripped the dead man's gun.

"We'll be on our way shortly. Just let me clean my hands a little bit and take a leak."

He closed the door and went to the front of the stage-coach.

"Eve, please. Listen! If you're in there, give me the gun!" Peter pleaded.

Eve gasped and gripped her stomach. She looked around and kicked at the squirming pile of maggots, panicking at the bloody chunks falling from the ceiling of the coach.

"Eve?!"

"What's happening? Why is there blood everywhere?" she whimpered.

"What am I doing?" she looked at the gun and shook her hands frantically but couldn't release it.

"Peter!" she cried.

"Peter!" the demon screamed from inside of her.

Eve rocked backwards and choked, as if something was stuck in her throat.

Abbie grabbed the barrel of the gun and tried to yank it away, but the demon wouldn't let go of it. It pressed it to Eve's temple. They could see in her eyes the terror and confusion; her body was not her own, but she was fighting with all she had.

"Abbie, why don't you tell them both the truth? You're a lyin' bitch! Do it, or I'll kill this little whore! Come on, Sister! Tell them...I can see into your mind, your heart, I know what you hide from them both. Tell them!"

"What does it mean?" Peter asked.

"Don't listen to it. It's lying to you!"

"Did I lie about what was in the trunk?" the demon asked.

It slid the gun down along Eve's cheek and jammed it into her mouth. Forcing it in deep until she almost choked on it.

"Abbie!" Peter said.

"Okay..." Abbie swallowed and looked to Peter.

Her throat was as dry as cotton; she didn't know how to begin.

"Peter, it's true your mother died during an exorcism performed by myself and Father Connor, but you don't know how."

"How did she die?" he asked.

"I shot her."

"You shot her? You shot my mother?"

The demon pulled the gun from Eve's mouth and left it pressed to her cheek but slid it up until it was jamming in her left eye. "Shot her through the eye, right?"

Peter's memory flashed the exorcism of Elizabeth. He saw her eye bleeding.

"You watched her fall down like a little snowflake into the river of flood water," the demon teased.

"What's happening?" Eve's voice suddenly broke through,

The driver knocked on the door, "Almost ready to go. Everybody okay?"

Eve looked to the door with the eye without the barrel of a gun stuck against it by her own hand. Abbie lunged for the gun. She wrenched it away from Eve's face, but the demon roared and fought. It was too powerful. It turned the gun and put it against Sister Abbie's right eye and pulled the trigger.

Abbie's left eye was wide, but she could no longer see in this world. The right was a smoking hole. She fell backward against the wall and her own brains and skull fragments, her habit soaking up blood.

Peter fell on Eve and wrenched the gun from her hands.

"What the fuck! Put the gun down!" the driver had opened the door.

Peter watched the driver run to his seat and retrieve his rifle.

"I should have never done this run on my own. I should have brought Ricky!" he cursed to himself until he came back armed.

His arms shook as he pointed the gun at Peter.

"Help! He wants to kill me," Eve's voice was angelic again;the demon had a plan.

"Come on over here, girl."

The driver kept his finger on the trigger while Eve scurried out of the coach behind him to hide.

"Drop the gun or die, you sonofabitch. I should have known you were strange. I should have saved this girl back in Louisiana, but you came from the church."

The driver meant business, shouting, "Drop it or die, Padre!"

Peter nodded and slowly put the gun on the bloody coach floor.

"Kick it this way."

Peter did as he was told, his heart thundering in his chest as he kicked the gun to the driver. The demon was waiting like a serpent about to strike. The driver took the gun from the coach and stuck it in the back of his pants.

Eve was weeping, "Thank you so much. He was going to kill me."

"It's okay. He won't hurt you because I'm gonna kill him and leave him with that other piece of shit and his trunk."

Peter looked beyond the window at the cemetery in the dark. A cold wind blew in from outside. The driver stood still, but his hand still trembled, his finger itching to pull the trigger.

"You don't understand," Peter said.

"Shut your damn mouth!"

"She's not sick, she's..."

A roaring blast split the driver's head from behind. He dropped to the ground, and Eve stood behind him, holding Merrel's gun. She had retrieved it from the back of the driver's pants.

"Go ahead, Peter. Say it. She's possessed!" the demon laughed.

Peter glanced at Sister Abbie. His heart nearly burst seeing her with blood running from a hole where her eye used to be. He was upset he never knew the truth until the end, but many of his childhood years were spent in her care. She was like a mother to him.

He reached over and grabbed the bottle of holy water on the seat beside her. He palmed it, hoping he could get Eve under control again. California was still their only hope.

"Come out here, Peter. The night is beautiful." It was Eve's voice again, sweet and soothing. "I didn't mean to kill her, Peter. Please come out and talk to me."

Peter didn't trust her, even if he needed to so badly. He only got out because he needed to find a way to subdue her again.

The night was cold; it was already December

"That's a good boy."

"Don't shoot me, Eve," Peter said, trying to get through to her.

"I won't as long as you're nice."

He could see her grinning widely in the moonlight, her eyes like a predator's shining.

He cautiously approached her

"Let's take a walk through the tombstones, but first, drop what's in your hand."

"What?"

"Don't play coy with me. I know you got Sister Abbie's little bottle of shit water!" She raised the gun and pointed it at him.

"Okay, okay! Don't shoot!" He dropped the bottle into the dust on the roadside.

"Good boy. Now, come here and walk with me."

Peter approached Eve who held up her hands for him to untie her wrists. As he did so, she grabbed him by the arm. Together, they took a few steps before Eve tossed the gun into the dying brush.

"Don't get mean. You know I can kill you with my hands if I have to and it will be much more painful. I'd rather us be gentle with each other, like we used to be." Her voice was soft, Eve's voice.

AMONG THE DEAD

SHE LED THEM THROUGH the cemetery gates and down a path between the headstones.

"This is how I always wanted to be, Peter. You and me, man and woman. We never really had a choice, did we?"

He didn't know if it was the demon reading Eve's memories or if she had come through again.

It made him long for days before demons and boxes, when they gazed at the stars in secret and their love was an unspoken promise between them.

She pulled him to a stop and guided him to sit on the ground at a grave with a grand stone cross at its head. There were dead flowers placed on top of it, wafting their sickly-sweet smell up his nose.

"Let's stay here and look up at the stars for a while," Eve said as she lay down on the ground.

Peter was overcome with the need to feel normal again, to tell her he would always love her. He settled down beside her and let her snuggle up against his shoulder.

"I'll always love you, Peter," she whispered.

"And I you, Eve."

His head swam with the smell of flowers and dirt and with her warmth against him. His heart would burst if ever lost her.

"Eve, you have to fight. I need you to be..."

She shushed him and kissed his neck.

"I'll always be yours, Peter. Always."

His breathing deepened as she continued to kiss him, her warm, wet mouth on the softness of his neck. He couldn't resist her, and he was too tired to fight what he wanted.

"Kiss me, Peter," she whispered.

He did, and with all the longing built up inside of him. He spilled it all into her in that kiss and felt her sigh. Lightheaded and shaking, he rolled onto his back and she straddled him. Her kisses awakening the desire he tried to keep in check. She grabbed his hands and guided them to her breasts. He squeezed them and admired the vision of her on top of him, smiling down at him with bliss in her eyes. She bent down over him, and her mouth found his. He felt like they were sharing one breath; he was in her and she was in him, joined forever.

She slid out of her dirty dress and let him look at her naked body beneath the moon and stars. He sighed as she knelt beside him and helped him remove his pants, jacket, and shirt. He stared down at himself, nude and erect for her. She straddled him again, and he could hardly contain his excitement. Her hand slid down his stomach until she gripped his cock. She positioned herself over it and slid it into her. He moaned and she did it intentionally slow so he could feel how badly she wanted him.

Eve began sliding up and down, rolling her hips slightly. He gripped her hips and bit his lip. His eyes rolled back as she quickened her pace. She leaned over and kissed him, grabbing his shoulders to motion him over to be on top of her. He moved fluidly, never pulling out. He thrust into her, feeling her slick wetness, taking him in, all of him. Her moans sent a thrill through him, and he moved faster until he came hard inside of her. She sighed and held him there, feeling him spilling his seed deep within her.

"Peter! You're mine!" Eve cried out, her voice growing deep and guttural. "Forever!!"

Peter panicked and looked down at her; her hair was frazzled, and the white strip at her temple was bright in the moonlight. Her eyes went black, and he pulled out and fell back on his ass in the graveyard. His mind cleared. What was he doing? She had seduced him. The demon had seduced him.

"You're mine!"

Peter grabbed his pants and fought to get them on. Eve rose from the dirt and stood naked, laughing at him. Thunder rumbled overhead, a storm was gathering, covering the moon and stars. He ran through the rows of tombstones, ashamed, disgusted, panic stricken. She danced between the graves, nude and cackling.

"You're mine, boy!" the demon's voice echoed behind him.

His head spun and his vision went black. He recalled hitting the ground. In a daze he opened his eyes to the stars wheeling above him. He had no idea how much time had passed, a minute, an hour? His skin crawled knowing the demon had him at its mercy.

Eve straddled his chest, her weight constricting his lungs. He couldn't scream. His mouth filled with the taste of copper as Eve whispered, the demon whispered, in a tongue he knew only the denizens of Hell spoke. His eyes popped open wider when his mouth was pried open and something round and sticky was stuck inside. Peter panicked. His limbs finally reacted to his brain urging them to move.

He threw Eve off his chest and gagged out the obstruction in his mouth. Vomit followed it when he realized it was an eyeball. Voices all about him swallowed him up. He looked around frantically to see spirits among the gravestones, some weeping and others pointing at him and laughing.

A flash of lightning crossed the sky, illuminating the dead brighter, pitiful voyeurs to the blasphemy he committed in their final resting place. He got to his feet and shook his head. He wanted them to disappear. His mind couldn't take seeing them in their states of decay.

"You can see now, Peter. Like Eve could see. They made fun of her being so afraid of storms, but they had no idea what Eve could see in them. You can hear them too, can't you?" the rasping voice of the demon spoke.

The voices of the dead assaulted his ears and his mind. Among them he could hear a tiny voice weeping, "What have you done to Eve?"

He ran for the coach and knelt in the dirt, running his hands through it blindly in the darkness of the storm clouds stealing the moonlight.

"You can never resist me!" the voice rasped right behind him.

Peter's finger ran over a smooth glass bottle. He gripped it, opened it, and spun. The holy water splashed across Eve's bare breasts, and she screamed. She fell to the ground, and Peter jumped on top of her. The demon in her wrestled with him, its strength almost too much for him to handle alone, but he managed to grab her by the jaw. He dumped the holy water into her mouth and the demon cried out. Peter emptied the bottle into Eve's mouth, and finally she fell silent.

She was subdued, but for how long Peter wasn't sure. Peter searched until he found the restraints and tied them back around her wrists. He left her naked as he gathered up their clothing and searched for a way to keep her from killing anyone again. In the darkness his gaze fell on the trunk. The sky opened up and rain began to fall. He had no other choice.

Peter opened the trunk and pitched the dried corpse of Merrel's mother out on the dirt beside her son. He dragged Eve's unconscious body over and laid her inside of the trunk, closing the lid. He hauled the body of the stagecoach driver over and deposited it next to the other two corpses carefully carrying Sister Abbie from the coach.

She had always seemed so strong, hard as stone when she needed to be, and on occasions let her foul mouth slip, but now she felt as light as a feather. He marveled at how much easier it was to carry her than the other bodies. He could hear Father Connor's voice in his mind saying it was because their earthly sins had weighed them down where Sister Abbie had nearly zero when she departed. She was a good woman, a precious soul. He didn't think he could bear telling Father Connor of her death once they met.

Peter found a broken slat of wood from the low fence hemming the burial grounds and dug into the earth. He refused to leave Abbie out in the open where the vultures and coyotes could feast on her. The earth was hard, but he managed to dig a shallow grave for her.

He wiped the blood from her face and that's when he noticed her other eye was gone. Eve had plucked it from her skull while he was unconscious and shoved it into his mouth. He slid her into the hole. Her empty eye sockets stared up to heaven as he covered her up.

Then, he stopped to pray over all of them, but his memory couldn't hang on to the words he had learned to recite over the dead. He mumbled and stuttered his way through a few sentences until he gave up. He felt like a hypocrite, an abomination, filthy right down to his soul. He felt like an infection was festering somewhere in his body. The air was cool but his face was hot; his muscles ached and his stomach churned with acid. He looked around in the dark. It was just him and the trunk, not knowing whether what was inside was really Eve anymore or ever would be again.

Thunder rolled overhead as Peter fought until he got the trunk back into the coach and took up the reigns himself, hoping he would find Franklin and the station to head westward where his last hope remained.

HEART'S DESIRE

EVE WAS SURROUNDED IN darkness. Her body ached, and her tongue felt thick and dry in her mouth. She lifted a weak hand to feel rough wood inches from her face. Panicking, she felt around to find she was inside of something, a wooden box, a coffin? She tried to scream but it came out more like a strangled whisper from her sore throat.

Claustrophobia gripped her chest, and a smell like old dirt and rotten flesh choked her. The sound of thunder sent a shock through her. If a storm came and she was trapped, then she would have no escape from the spirits and their shrieking demands.

Calm down, girl.

The voice was so close to her, right beside her...no, it was inside of her ears. She slapped her dirty wooden prison and clawed at it to no avail.

I said calm down. I made an agreement with your lover. Peter agreed to take us to California. Aren't you excited? You always wanted to travel.

She recognized the voice now. It was the same that spoke to her and told her to unleash her inner desires for Peter.

"Who are you?!" she whispered trying not to make herself known to any dead souls seeking one with her abilities to hear them.

Not one of those other spirits who liked to torment you, that's for certain. They're weak little human souls who flit around like sad shadows. I'm much more than them.

"Leave me alone!" Eve tried to be forceful but sounded shrill and exhausted instead.

We're much too close now. Besides, why would you want me to go away? I gave you something much more exciting than what you had inside the church. Look at you going on an adventure to the West, and I gave you your heart's desire.

Eve fell silent, her brain flooding with memories of the past days. The feeling of Peter's hands on her body, his mouth on hers. She was terrified but consumed by the overwhelming sense of feeling complete. Peter was all she dreamed of, even more so than the vows she promised to take. It was then she remembered calling him her hero after they made love in the wild roses and he carried her inside away from the storm. There was an ounce of shame, but that burned away with the memory of his embrace and the smell of his skin. Eve felt her mouth turning up in a smile even when tears stung her eyes.

Oh yes, you're remembering now, right? I gave him to you, let you feel what it means to actually live, to be a woman completely. When I spoke to you, I gave you courage and strength. Did you notice what else I can do for you? Listen...

Eve didn't hear a single spirit among the storm winds whipping up outside of the wooden box she was in. It was freeing, but also it made her wary.

"Who...what are you?"

Why do you ask when you already know? Let's say I'm merely a passenger in your body for a time. You give me what I want, and I'll continue to give you what you want. Peter, freedom from those pesky ghosts that cry your name at night, a chance to see how people live outside of the prison you've grown up in.

"That sounds too good to be true. Only the devil makes deals like those."

And if I was? Who else is offering you all the treasures I have? God? Don't make me vomit, child. He's the liar. He's the thumb on your head, keeping you chaste until you're dried out and covered in dust and only dreaming of having a normal life. Do you want to end up like Mother Marie? An old shrew with a crucifix jammed up her ass. Or maybe you'd like to end up like Sister Abbie who died never being able to pursue the man she loved?

"Sister Abbie is dead?"

You killed her...or we did.

"No! I didn't kill her!"

"We did, but she was going to take Peter from you. She would have made him keep his promise to become a priest, and you would have only repeated her same sad history. Is that what you wanted?"

"I can't make any deals with you. You killed Abbie!"

"What if I promised from now on our only prey will be people who deserve it? Peter already agreed to it."

"Peter agreed to that?"

"Yes...because he loves you and wants a future with you."

"You're lying. I can tell when I'm lied to!"

Pain gripped Eve's skull, and her thoughts flooded with the cemetery and her voice saying, "I'll always love you, Peter."

And him responding, "And I you, Eve."

Tears streamed down her cheeks; her heart ached. He had spoken his love out loud to her. She couldn't take losing that love, his love. She couldn't imagine walking away from it to devote her life to a convent. If this was the only way to have him, so be it.

"Only those who deserve it."

I wouldn't dream of anything else, dear girl. And I promise you're gonna live the lives of three while I'm inside you. It will never be a dull moment!

"And I want him, to feel his love again. He completes me. He always has. I won't accept this without him."

"You'll have him all you want. I swear it."

And the pact was made. Eve accepted her damnation in exchange for living like she would never die at the side of Peter. Even though, in her heart, she felt she would die, and far sooner than if she had stayed trapped within the dull walls of a convent languishing from loneliness and haunted by dreams of a life she never had the guts to live.

OF BLOOD AND FIRE

ALEJANDRA WATCHED THE COACH approaching slowly for the third time that day. The driver slumped down even more this time. She wondered if he was drunk. Why else would he be driving around in circles in the middle of nowhere? Or maybe he was hurt?

"That stupid bastard has passed by a few times, hasn't he?" Mr. Drake asked.

"Yes, sir. He has."

"We'll stop him, make sure he finds his way. Tell Ricardo to get his rifle just in case things get hairy out there."

Alejandra stepped out the kitchen door and hurried to her brother who was tending the horses. She halted on one side of the corral fence and waved him down.

"Patron needs you. Bring a gun."

Ricardo nodded.

Alejandra spun on her heels and raced back inside to take cover behind the thick adobe walls. She had grown up in the Texas territory and was accustomed to shoot outs. She lost her parents to a few stray bullets. Her father took one in the head and her mother, racing to cradle her husband, was shot through the stomach.

Alejandra's father died instantly, but her mother hung on for three days; gut shot was a terrible way to go. She and her brother were lucky the rancher, Mr. Drake, took them in. He always said he owed it to Alejandra's father for being such a great friend, but she often wondered if he hadn't really done it for her mother.

She crouched down by the window to listen and peek out occasionally at her brother and Mr. Drake as they stepped out into the road leading to and winding around the ranch. Ricardo kept his rifle in full view to prevent any violence from taking place.

Ricardo was older than Alejandra by four years. He had smile that broke many girl's hearts, but he had a mean streak in him strangers didn't want to test. The slow-moving coach came inching up to them and stopped a few feet away. The man at the reigns lifted his hands and pointed his face skyward as if in thankful prayer. He nearly fell from the coach as he climbed down to speak to Mr. Drake. The stranger's hair, dark as coal, fluttered in the wind. He looked like he was usually clean cut and well kept, but his clothes were dusty from sitting behind the horses. He wore mostly black, which could have killed him in the desert if it wasn't December. At his throat there was a line of white beneath his collar.

"A priest?"

Alejandra stood up completely, feeling a little more comfortable to be seen in the window. She watched as Ricardo climbed up to the driver's seat and urged the horses towards the ranch entrance while the priest walked beside Mr. Drake toward the house. Her heart fluttered a bit; the priest, if he was one, was handsome. She smoothed her apron and hair and went to the door to greet them.

Mr. Drake opened the door, and the stranger followed him inside.

"Alejandra, this is Father Peter."

She shook Peter's hand. "Please just call me Peter."

She felt her cheeks flush uncontrollably.

"Sorry, son. You dressed the part, ya know."

"I can see where there might be confusion," Peter said.

"Why don't you fix Peter something to eat? He got lost out there on the road to Franklin and he's tuckered out. Been trackin' around for two days with nothin' in his belly."

Mr. Drake clapped his hand on Peter's back. "She's a good cook, and her food'll fix you right up."

"Yes, sir," Alejandra said and excused herself.

She went to the kitchen where she already had a pot of stew cooking and lifted the lid. She stirred it and took a taste. It wasn't how her mother used to make it, but it would do just fine for a man who hadn't eaten in days.

She looked out the window to Ricardo who had unhitched Peter's horses and was feeding them by hand and running his hand over their coats. They seemed a little skittish, but she knew many of the coach horses could be, especially if they were tired and thirsty. She wondered where Peter had come from and why he hadn't used mules instead; they were faster and heartier. She grabbed a bowl and ladled it full of stew, filled a cup with fresh water, and carried everything to a table in Mr. Drake's sitting room.

Peter sat in a comfortable chair at the table, and Mr. Drake was lighting the fireplace. Alejandra placed the bowl before him and smiled.

"That smells delicious. Thank you."

She got to study his face closer without Mr. Drake or her brother watching her. His dark hair was streaked with silver at his temple, but his features appeared to be of someone very young. She was only nineteen and guessed he could only be a few years older.

"You're welcome, Peter."

His name felt nice rolling off her tongue. She knew her brother would have preferred her to set her eyes on someone rougher than Peter, a rancher or cowboy, but his gentle smile made her stomach flutter. Mr. Drake and Ricardo were always trying to look for what they considered a suitable husband for her too, but they also let her heart lead her. Too many times they suggested callous handed, sunburned, cowhands, but to her they all smelled like sweat and dirt. She imagined Peter would smell fresh and his hands would feel smooth against her skin.

"That's all for now," Mr. Drake interrupted the fantasy only beginning in her mind. "Get the guest room ready for Peter. He can sleep here tonight, and we'll get him on the right road in the mornin'."

"Yes, of course." Alejandra almost skipped from the room. It had been years since any company had stayed overnight at the ranch, and never had anyone as good looking as the student priest stayed there for even a minute. She went about tidying the room and making the bed with clean blankets.

Ricardo loved horses. Ever since he was a boy he couldn't stay away from them, even when his mother was frightened he'd get trampled. The team of four draft horses was uneasy when he first set them free in the corral, but the gentle giants calmed the farther they got from the stagecoach.

Ricardo fed and watered them and took a moment to take a look at their hooves. They seemed in good shape despite wandering the desert for days. He turned his attention to the coach, but before he could open the door his sister called him inside to eat dinner. He didn't see any luggage attached to the top of it and guessed the stranger only had a bag inside of it. He figured he would run back out and grab it once he filled his stomach. It would give him a chance to check on the horses again and bring them into the barn for the night. He knew Mr. Drake thought it was luck to hail the priest down and offer him shelter, but Ricardo thought it was odd that a priest would be driving a stagecoach himself and have not a single passenger.

"Ricardo! Are you deaf?" Alejandra yelled from the back kitchen door.

He dusted off his hands and jogged in her direction.

"Come eat!"

"Okay, I'm coming!"

"You better wash your hands!" she complained as he walked past her.

"I will. Stop your nagging."

"Mr. Drake and Peter are taking dinner in the sitting room. Go on and I'll bring your food."

Ricardo didn't argue with his sister, not when she sounded excited. He hoped it was because she hadn't had any guests in more than a year and was anxious to hear of their travels and not because she had taken a shining to the priest.

He entered the sitting room to hear Mr. Drake telling one his tales of the ranch, the same he told everyone when he first met them about how he shot a rattlesnake in mid-air before it could strike him. The old man liked to brag about his prowess with a gun, but it wasn't exaggeration. Ricardo had witnessed Mr. Drake's sharp shooting skills first hand.

"In the blink of an eye I blew its head clean off. Only a second before it could get its fangs in me."

"Impressive," Peter said with a smile.

"It's true, right, Ricardo?" Mr. Drake looked over his shoulder.

"Every word of it," Ricardo said.

"See, now this young man is like my son, but he would never lie about it." Mr. Drake smiled.

"Where'd you say you was from?" Mr. Drake asked.

"Louisiana but I was born here in Texas."

"You don't say. Where about?"

"I'm not sure. I'm an orphan so I can't really say," Peter said.

"An orphan?" Alejandra said coming in from the kitchen with Ricardo's dinner.

"Yes, but I was taken in by the church."

"We are orphans, too. We were blessed that Mr. Drake took us in," Ricardo said and looked to the old rancher.

"Now, you both became the children I never had. Your folks were good people, the best kind. I would do it all over again in a heartbeat," Mr. Drake said.

"You are a wonderful soul, Mr. Drake, Peter said.

In his mind a nagging call kept trying to break through.

The trunk, Eve, she was waiting. He felt a stab of regret in his heart. How could he leave her alone in the darkness of a box while he ate dinner and enjoyed conversations? At the same time he felt a freedom he hadn't felt in weeks. It was like his life was normal again, like before he witnessed the true evil the night of Elizabeth's exorcism.

"Peter?" Mr. Drake stared at him.

"Oh, I'm sorry my mind drifted on me."

"No problem, son. I asked where you're headed. You told me west but where abouts in the west?"

"California. There's a new church being built in San Francisco, and I promised my mentor I would come to see it."

"You won't make it before Christmas."

"Christmas?" Peter asked.

"Sure, son. Are you tryin' to make before then? It's only a little more than a few weeks away."

"No, the church opening doesn't have an exact date. I had no idea Christmas was so soon. Peter marveled at how quickly time had passed him by, as if he'd been riding around the doomed stagecoach lost to time. Ordinarily, he would be helping Father Joshua prepare the gifts for the orphans.

"That's quite a journey to make all alone. You should have a gun with you," Mr. Drake said seriously.

"I am supposed to join another group in Franklin, but I got lost." Peter blushed, hoping his lie wasn't easily picked apart.

Mr. Drake was focused on his food, probably trying to soak up some of the whiskey running loose in his blood stream.

"Where did you get the coach? Didn't you have a driver?" Ricardo asked the question Peter was hoping no one would.

He took a long drink from his cup, his mind spinning, looking for an excuse. "Yes, unfortunately my driver died miles back. A heart attack I believe, but I'm no doctor. I buried him at the cemetery,and before he succumbed to his ailment, he just said to follow the road. You are the first people I have come across to inform of his death."

"That's too bad. Was he an older gentleman?" Mr. Drake asked, but Peter could feel Ricardo's eyes hadn't left him.

"Yes, he was."

"Too old for that job. It can be taxing on the body. He should've retired and went West just like you."

"Yes, he should have." Peter felt a wave of dizziness. He sat back in his chair and loosened the collar at his neck.

"You feelin' alright, son?"

"Oh, yes. Just exhausted," Peter said.

"Alejandra has a bed ready for you whenever you need to sleep."

A whisper in his mind reminded him of the cemetery and how Eve or the demon inside her proclaimed him as hers until the end of time. He feared their sexual connection was like a thread keeping her bound to him even when she was out of his sight. He could still taste Sister Abbie's blood in his mouth. Nothing was normal, and it never would be again.

"I think I'll turn in, too. I just gotta put the horses away and grab Peter's bags." Ricardo said.

"No, that won't be necessary," Peter said. Again, the voice spoke to him, bidding him not to come out the door after the moon rose.

"Suit yourself," Ricardo said.

Peter watched Ricardo leave, his heart thundering, hoping Ricardo would stay out of the stagecoach. He didn't bother praying. Why would God answer such a devious prayer?

"It's an old man's bedtime, too. I'll see you in the mornin', Peter." Mr. Drake clapped him on the shoulder and disappeared down a dark hallway.

Peter stayed in his seat. His eyes turned to the flames in the fireplace. He envisioned himself in Hell, his flesh consumed by the Devil's creatures. His mind drifted into those nightmare realms where he was sure a spot was secured for him.

He kept thinking he should just go out and make sure the trunk was not disturbed, but the voices warned him to stay put. He feared what they meant to do. The rancher and his adopted children were far too kind to let anything terrible happento them, but he had no idea what to do.

"Aren't you tired?" Alejandra's voice spoke from the same hallway Mr. Drake had sauntered down.

"Oh, yes. I think I shall go to bed," Peter said.

The energy coming from Alejandra was too much like Eve, innocent and flirtatious. He wouldn't know what to do if she came on to him. He quickly got to his feet, and she waved him to follow her. They came to the second door, and she stopped and pushed it open.

"This is your room tonight. If you need anything, mine is at the end of the hall," Alejandra said and winked at him.

"Alejandra, do you know how to get to Franklin?"

"Well, yes. The road you were on, there's a smaller trail on the east that leads to Franklin. You probably just missed it because you were so exhausted."

"I think you're right," he smiled.

"Well, if you need anything you know where to find me."

"Alright, thank you. Good night." Peter said and shut the door behind her.

He went to the window and pulled the curtains aside. He had a good view of the yard between the house and the barn where the stagecoach sat outside. The moon flooded the terrain in its white light. He could see very well and, though he needed to sleep, resigned himself to sitting up and keeping watch over it. He pulled a chair up beside the window and sat down. His eyes burned; his eyelids felt heavy.

He fought hard to stay awake but drifted off into a dreamless sleep.

Ricardo waited for a few hours in his room before slipping his boots back on. He stayed fully dressed because he had a plan in mind. It was cemented when he saw how oddly the supposed priest acted when he mentioned opening the stagecoach.

He knew Peter was hiding something, and he meant to find out what it was. There was no way he would let a bank robber or murderer sleep in the same house as his sister and Mr. Drake; he wouldn't lose another family member to the hands of a criminal.

He's probably not even a priest.

When he felt confident their guest was asleep, Ricardo slipped out of his room and across the kitchen floor to the back door. The moon was damn near full, and the light blanketing the stagecoach was enough to see no one else was out there. He grabbed a pistol he kept sitting on top of the kitchen cabinet for emergencies and then snuck out the back door.

Winter was upon them, and the breeze chilled Ricardo's skin as he made his way closer to the coach. He held his breath and opened the door. The inside reeked. It was a familiar smell that conjured memories of his mother's deathbed, blood. He looked around but only found a few bags and a large trunk sitting in the middle of the floor, taking up most of the leg room inside.

Ricardo climbed inside and opened the bags. The first was full of men's clothing and things he knew must belong to Peter. The second and third sent a chill through him because they contained women's clothing, more specifically the contents looked like things nuns would wear and hairbrushes. He shoved the items back in the bags and turned to the trunk. The lid faced him with the latch just within inches of his hand. He leaned forward and for a second, he thought he heard a faint sound coming from within it, a scraping or scratching noise.

"What the fuck?" he whispered.

He wondered if he should open it, then a voice inside prompted him to do it. It was a muffled crying. A woman was inside.

"This sick bastard." He said to himself. Ricardo pressed his ear against the lid to be sure he had actually heard what he thought he did, and that his nerves weren't playing tricks on him.

"Help me," the voice pleaded from within the trunk.

"Don't worry. I'm here. I'll get you out of there!" Ricardo said.

He tried to flip the latch open, but it was filthy and rusted. He leaned back and gave it a kick, and it sprang loose. He quickly undid the latch and pulled the door open. The smell inside was a mixture of rot and withered plants. His eyes could hardly see with the darkness of the coach and the absolute blackness of the inside of the trunk, but a pale hand came out and he grabbed it.

"I'm here. You're okay now."

The young woman inside came out slowly, falling into Ricardo's lap. She laid her head on him and wept.

"What did he do to you?"

"Help me. He's sick!"

"He won't do it again. I'll protect you!"

Ricardo helped the girl out of the coach. She was a frail, pale skinned young woman, dressed in a filthy night dress. She was bruised and disoriented, and he had no idea how long she had been locked up in the trunk. His mind suddenly went to his sister and how she was sleeping just down the hall from a complete mad man.

"Stay here. I'll go inside and drag him out."

"No, don't leave me out here!" she cried, gripping his wrist in a surprisingly strong grasp.

"My sister is in there and Mr. Drake. I can't leave them in there. Just hide in the barn. He won't find you in there."

Ricardo rushed her to the barn and showed her to a ladder inside that lead up to a loft piled with straw.

"Hide up there. I'll be back."

He left her there and rushed back to the door to the kitchen. His heartbeat pounded in his ears as he made his way through the dark house.

He would be a hero this time, not like when his mother and father were shot before his eyes. He was a child then but now he was grown, and he wouldn't let anything happen to his sister or adopted father. He gripped the pistol in one hand and halted outside the door to the guest room. He took one deep breath and kicked the door in. All that greeted him was an empty room and an open window, the curtains billowing in the wind.

"Sonofabitch!" Ricardo cursed.

A scream ripped through the darkness from outside, and he ran to the window. The barn door was open, and the silhouette of a man was slipping inside.

"What's goin' on?" Mr. Drake was in the doorway, rubbing sleep from his eyes.

"Your priest is not who he says he is. He had a girl locked in a trunk inside the coach."

"What? Get my damn gun!"

"Wake up Alejandra and tell her to hide!" Ricardo said.

He went to climb through the window, but Mr. Drake stopped him. "Hold it. We're goin' out there together."

Ricardo nodded and followed Mr. Drake down the hallway. They opened Alejandra's door, and Mr. Drake shook her awake in the darkness. She was startled, but he put his hand over her mouth.

"Get in the attic and don't come out until we tell you!"

She didn't say a word, only followed his instructions. It was their emergency plan if the ranch was ever raided; she would hide while Ricardo and Mr. Drake defended the land until their last breaths.

He pushed by Ricardo and went to his bedroom. He came back wielding pistols in both hands.

"I'm ready. Let's go."

Another scream sent them running through the house. They stopped at the back door.

"She's in the barn!"

"Guns a blazin' understand, son. We don't stop until we cut him to pieces with lead."

Ricardo nodded.

"And if this is my last night on earth," Mr. Drake gripped Ricardo's shoulders, "I'm happy you came to be my son."

Ricardo hugged the old man, and they pushed the door open.

Peter was jarred awake by an awful feeling. He opened the window and crept across the yard. He snuck into the barn, and a shriek from above sent a shock of horror through him.

"Please, Eve. These are good people. They only wanted to help me!"

He looked up at the dark loft to where she stood in a single beam of moonlight filtering in through a dusty window. He fell back against the wooden door and gripped his chest. She no longer looked like the fragile young woman, but a beast. Her night dress had been shredded and her body was contorting, her arms stretching long and spidery. Her face was monstrous and spider-like, grinning down at him. The creature opened its mouth and screamed, high pitched, bone chilling, the cry of a woman in danger. Peter shook his head, "NO. PLEASE."

A heavy thud hit the barn door at his back and cursing from the other side confirmed his worst fear. Mr. Drake and Ricardo had come to Eve's rescue not realizing her cries were a trap and they were running to their deaths.

"Please, don't come in!" Peter screamed.

"Open the door!" It was Ricardo.

The demand was followed by a clicking, the hammer of a gun being drawn back. Peter jumped to the ground as a bullet blew through the rickety wooden door. He crawled on his stomach through dirt and horse shit to take cover in a stall beside his team of horses. The door was kicked open, and Peter could see two sets of feet run into the barn.

"Where are you, you little bastard?" Mr. Drake hollered.

Peter put his shaking hand over his mouth and cried. He knew what would come next.

"Come out you bast..."

A screeching cut Ricardo off mid-sentence.

"What the Hell is that?" Mr. Drake said.

Gun fire deafened Peter; even at the distance he was his ears split. He put his hands over them and screamed. He opened his eyes to see elongated feet standing before two pairs of boots.

More gunfire and screaming, the sounds of a nightmare coming to life only feet away. Peter didn't want to watch, but he couldn't look away. Blood and entrails fell at the feet of one of the men. The gurgling cursing that followed told him it was Mr. Drake. The old man fell to his knees and slumped over sideways, his dying eyes fixed on Peter.

The booming report of a pistol followed by a screeching from the beast, it was clear to Peter that Ricardo refused to let Mr. Drake die in vain and had hit his mark.

Peter watched the monstrous clawed feet lunge forward, and a thud against the stall wall sent him scooting back farther into the darkness. He could see Ricardo plainly, bleeding profusely from a gaping wound and a stump where the rest of his left arm should have been. The severed arm was thrown against the side of his head, but his eyes didn't even blink. Screeching cries outside the barn signaled the beast was running toward the house.

Peter hadn't heard or seen Alejandra. His heart stuttered. He couldn't allow her to die. He couldn't be so much of a coward as to lie there anymore. He forced himself to climb out of the stall. He looked down to Ricardo and the pool of blood beside him.

"I'm sorry," Peter whispered.

He made the sign of the cross over Ricardo and ran to the barn door just in time to see the beast breaking through the back kitchen door.

"EVE! STOP!"

Peter chased her inside, not knowing if she would eat him or spare him.

The arachnid creature went through the house smashing everything it could, ripping the doors from their hinges. Peter slunk up behind it as it sniffed the air. It was looking for the last living member of Mr. Drake's makeshift family.

"Leave her alone!" he demanded.

The beast spun to face him, its mouth dripping blood and saliva.

"Let's go. Leave her alone. Please!"

The face of the beast twisted into a snarled grin and laughed.

Its eyes darted up to the ceiling. Peter looked up, and he could hear a faint gasp. Alejandra was hiding in the attic, and the beast knew.

"Please, leave her alone," he pleaded. "I'll do anything you say, just don't kill her."

The beast's features and skin turned almost to jelly, and its bones began to shift. Peter backed away in disgust watching as it morphed back into the form of Eve. She grinned at him as he fell to his knees.

"I beg you. Please spare her."

"Eve and I are slowly becoming one. I whispered to her there was a girl in this house trying to fuck you. I could feel her jealousy of this bitch. I know I torture her, but I have to give her what she wants once in a while, right?"

"Please. I didn't do anything with Alejandra. I only love Eve."

The demon laughed, "It's too late."

It went to the fireplace where the embers were still hot and red. It scooped up handfuls and threw them on the curtains. They smoldered and caught fire. Eve went to a lantern hanging on the wall by the front door. Peter got to his feet and lunged to grab it, but Eve stiff armed him in the face; his nose crunched and his vision went black.

He awoke in the dirt. Eve was wearing a new dress and hitching the horses to the stagecoach. They danced and kicked, nervous of the evil inside of her, but she managed to get them to mind her. Heat on his back and a blazing glow behind made him roll over and see the ranch house was burning. It's adobe walls looked like a screaming skull, fire erupting from the top of its head and dancing in its empty window eyes. The flames were so high it looked like they were touching the stars.

"She screamed your name as she burned to death. Do you think she minded I took a few of her things?"

"Fuck you," Peter wept.

"I'll get in the trunk if you promise to keep heading toward California," the demon said.

"California?"

"I know why you're taking me there. You want me to see Father Connor again. Do you think I fear him or any other old motherfucker he brings along? We have unfinished business, he and I, before I move on to better things."

Peter didn't say a word but cursed himself inside. How could he have possibly thought he could keep California a secret from a demon?

"Take me there or I'll twist Eve's head around on her neck and take your body as my own. I can do it; we have a link now. Remember the cemetery? Our little union, you let me touch your soul. I could use that to creep inside you. It would be fun to dwell inside a man, have a cock, and priest's skin. Imagine all the things I could do."

Peter wasn't frightened by the demon taking him over; he was scared for Eve. He couldn't let her die. Too many had already died: Father Joshua, Abbie, the driver, Mr. Drake, Ricardo, and Alejandra, their deaths could not be for nothing.

His only hope was when they reached Father Connor he was stronger than Peter, and he alone or with Father Glover's assistance could banish it forever from the earth.

"Take the deal, Peter. Your sweet little Eve accepted it already when I told her this would be the only way she could ever be with you. Her love for you is stronger than her disgust of murdering sinners, isn't that sweet?"

The demon with its trickery and threats had fooled them both and now it had Peter by the balls. The mention of Eve's love was something it knew Peter couldn't turn away from.

"She damned herself for me?"

"Without hesitation."

Peter nodded and ran his hand over his face in resignation.

"Okay. Get in the trunk!"

"No funny business, Peter. Or little Eve will suffer a thousand deaths before I let her perish. Oh and once in a while you'll let me out to play. If not I'll rip this bitch apart from the inside out. You have my word that we'll only go after the sinners...how does that sound, *Father*?" the Demon laughed at calling Peter that.

"Only the sinners," Peter repeated, feeling cold sweat on his back, sick with the agreement. He knew even the criminals and drunks and whores deserved better than "playing" with the demon inside Eve, but he hoped maybe if it was distracted with its debauchery he and Father Connor could rid the earth of it once and for all.

Peter got to his feet and shakily walked over to the coach. The demon slunk inside and climbed into the trunk. Peter threw the latch closed and turned back to watch the house burn for a few more seconds. It hurt, but he needed to see it. He needed it seared into his memory. He needed the anger to grow within him in order to destroy the thing hiding in Eve's skin.

Days passed by. Peter existed in a nightmare world. Getting on the coach at the Butterfield line was a blur of lies and paranoia. He found himself sitting across from an older white woman and a black girl who was maybe twelve years old. The woman smiled warmly and nudged the girl.

She spoke, "My name's Jessie and this is Miss Cassandra. She's mute, but she can hear just fine. I do the talkin' for her. We're going all the way to California. And you?"

"Me too." Peter said.

"Are you a preacher? Looks like we'll have a blessed trip if you are. Miss Cassandra said she's gonna buy me a new dress when we get there."

Peter's heart ached. It was obvious Miss Cassandra was taking the child to give her a better life far from any brewing war over race. He hoped they would be safe in his presence. He didn't think he could take watching anymore innocent people die.

"What happened to your nose?" the girl asked.

"I fell down trying to kill a spider, Peter lied, his hand straying to his broken nose. He knew he must look like a corpse.

Peter's exhaustion and anguish were a nightmare but nothing compared to Eve's. She remained in the trunk, and in the darkness there was no company but for the demon in her skin. It crawled over her brain like a maggot picking it for all the rotten things she had lived through, the memories she tried to suppress, and all her feelings of inadequacy. In the beginning it taunted and teased her for the secrets it discovered in her psyche, but as the miles passed beneath the hooves of the stagecoach horses, its commentary turned and its tone grew to more of a mentor of sorts.

"When you were a girl, your father beat you. He called you a little, worthless bitch. A mistake. He beat your mama too, left her looking black and blue on a regular basis. Once, you tried to stop him and he split your lip and made you sleep in the outhouse. You began to equate him with the smell of festering shit. In that dark, stinking place, I can see you becoming feral almost...and you dreamed of cutting his throat. So why, dear girl, did you weep at his burial? Was it to appease the small crowd of folks gathered to look over his pine box and lie about him, pretending his was a good man? Let me tell you a little secret. Death don't change what a man was in life, and your father went to the earth as a rotten piece of shit. You covered those ugly parts of your life with memories of when he wasn't drinking and brought you a basket of apples. But don't you remember he only did to apologize to your mother because he whipped her across her back with his belt and left bleeding lines in her skin? You saw them when she bathed them with clean water in the morning when he was still passed out on the front porch. The drunken bastard."

"Why tell me things I already know? Things I want to forget!"

Because, you need to see what life really is. It is full of suffering and degradation, yet humans pretend they aren't swine with thumbs. What makes you better than an animal, my girl? Why hide from what gives you pleasure?

"You're going to teach me about life, that's rich!"

Don't get disrespectful or I'll twist your ovaries until they burst!

Pain erupted like a set of knives in Eve's abdomen, a show of force.

"No. Please! I, I won't do that again. I'll be good."

"Promise?"

"Yes," wept Eve.

The pain subsided.

"Are we going to work together, or do want to do this the painful way?"

"Yes. We'll work together."

"Good, I'd hate to have to hurt you like that again, like your father did...but I will."

"I won't do it again. I won't fight you."

"I'm giving you Peter, but I want to give you more. I want to give you pleasure and power. What good would this arrangement be if we didn't get to have a little fun together?"

Eve nodded her head weakly. She wanted nothing more than to be free of the box for a while and to be with Peter. She could feel death was close, and if any day could be her last she decided to enjoy all she could and cling to the precious minutes as man and woman she and Peter had left in the world.

ONLY SINNERS

"PETER? PETER? WHY DON'T you let me out for a little while?"

The voice was smooth and calm and dangerous. The soft hiss of a coiled serpent. He knew it wasn't really Eve talking at all.

"Peter, please, my dear. It gets so stuffy in here. And lonely too. You know how much I love your company."

The last part was drawn out a bit, hinting at what the young man sitting across the room was both ashamed of and longing for.

"It's barely dusk, Eve!"

He was trying to calm himself and be ready for what was coming. What he had done in these last few weeks made him unsure of whom he was anymore; a half-empty bottle of whiskey by the bed spoke to that.

His palms were clammy and cold. The sun falling outside the window stirred something in his gut and sent a wave down to his crotch. He wondered if he wasn't possessed too. Possessed by Eve.

"Open up. I can feel the darkness setting in. It's time to play."

Her words were like a blanket falling over him, her voice warming him, soothing him into obedience. He rose from the rickety bed, dust motes floating in the dying sunlight, drunkards' dead skin and whores' spittle forming snowflakes of sin.

"Remember our agreement."

"Yes, I know. Only sinners."

He flipped the latch, and the trunk lid slowly opened.

She was still wearing a night gown taken from Alejandra's closet, a pale shade of blue now mottled with blood spatter. He opened a bag and threw a dress at her, another item stolen from the dead girl. He didn't feel right holding Alejandra's clothing, like a traitorous jackal that came in from the night to tear her throat out only to keep it as some sick reminder of her.

"Such a pretty dress. The ones Eve had were so plain, didn't hug her curves. After your reaction to sweet Alejandra, I knew I needed these. Do they bring up bad memories for you, *padre*?" the demon scoffed, standing naked for a moment before sliding into Alejandra's dress.

Peter had spent countless hours staying up into the early morning to scrub crimson stains from the soft and slightly tattered dresses she had worn in life, every second thinking of the girl and imagining her cooking in them or sweeping the wooden floors of the now torched ranch house.

"Leave me be!" Peter nearly wept

Peter was so exhausted. Every day, he walked around in a daze from getting only a few hours of sleep a night. If it wasn't from chasing Eve down to make sure the demons kept its word about its prey choices, it was the hours of seduction she'd put him through before he gave in and let her ride him. He couldn't deny he enjoyed the moments of lust they shared but watching her deteriorate and slowly meld with the demon was agonizing.

He couldn't believe how far he had fallen, but if he didn't placate the demon it would surely go for Cassandra and Jessie. It had teased him about conversations he had with the woman and the child on the longer stretches of the trail, reminding him of what it was capable of.

There were small moments here and there when the true Eve showed through but she was in worse shape than him mentally and physically. She didn't question what was wrong with her, and Peter guessed that she knew since she had accepted the deal with the demon. It sickened Peter how the demon was so deeply embedded inside of her that she'd taken to calling it her passenger? As if she was no more than a stagecoach for the demonic.

He held little hope Father Connor or Father Glover could even separate them anymore, but he still had to try. It would be his only redemption. Peter had snuck a second telegram to Father Connor, letting him know they were nearing California, beseeching him to meet them on the road if Father Glover could handle the journey. He knew the demon suspected his treason and didn't stop him only because it was ready to wage war with his mentor.

Peter gave in to her and was left drained by Eve's sexual appetite. It seemed to be growing by the day. Every second the demon dwelled inside of her, whispered to her, showed her the seedy parts human existence Peter felt like he was becoming less appealing. He almost couldn't keep her satisfied, and it ate him alive with jealousy and shame. His night would pass, like the last few weeks had been spent with him praying internally that she/it wouldn't go overboard or draw too much attention. They had to get back on the stagecoach in the morning and continue through the Arizona territory to the next little town and so on until they got where he desperately needed them to. He hoped Eve would not be completely consumed by the filth that hid inside her and lost to it forever before they made it to redemption.

The demon didn't trust Peter; it knew better. He was only a dog at its feet. The demon knew Peter loved his little nun but would he truly be willing to do anything to save her? Would he bring them to the hands of the priest who may kill Eve in the process of waging war with her passenger? It still was unsure, but at the moment it was going to enjoy the hunt and spend the dark hours inside the trunk rooting itself deeper into Eve and preparing to wield her as both a shield and a weapon against Peter and his mentors.

She was already coming around to its twisted way of existence, and she really didn't have to be pushed very hard to step over the line of becoming a wanton woman and a cold blooded murderer. The key to controlling her was keeping Peter alive, and the demon could give that to her as long as the wannabe priest kept them on the road toward California. The creature within awaited the day it was met by the old priest again, it being an ageless evil, and the holy man of course being only a man had aged, grown weak of body, it would be too sweet.

The night was in full swing now, streets emptying out. The families had gone home, and the only ones left out and about were grown men looking to have fun either with grown women or playing cards. Drinking and revelry would start, for even in small cattle towns or mining communities there was always a saloon, always singing girls and soiled doves. Always, there were men ready and willing to drop gold for the pleasures of the flesh and drink. There were plenty of sinners for Eve and her passenger to play with and to devour.

Eve could smell it around her; her dark passenger yearned for release. Down the lane, a saloon was lively and beckoning them to it like a moths to flames. The demon's whispering became full of demands in her mind, instructions and blueprints to the madness it craved.

All around men and women drank and laughed. They cheered singers and played piano. Many were upstairs making other kinds of transactions by candlelight. The demon had so much sin to choose from and wondered if it shouldn't take the body of one of the cowboys and ride off into the bloody sunset to enjoy days of bloodshed and nights of whoring.

"First let Peter take you to Father Conner, then find a new home in some cowboy and burn down California."

No one noticed the young woman talking to herself or when she bumped into a drunken gentleman and pick pocketed a velvet pouch from his coat. The demonic passenger decided on the gambling first and turned their attention to a card shark in the corner.

The men eyed Eve strangely as she approached like a slinking cat, smiling shyly...seductively. The table was quite, but the man in the corner smiled and said, “So, little lady, you want to play cards?”

Eve coyly smiled and said, “Yes,” in a mousey sort of way and added, “I love to play cards. I’m just a lady, but I don’t think you big men would mind if I sat in for a few hands?”

They were leering now, smiling at her body and the jingle of gold in a velvet pouch pulled from her bodice. It was soft velvet, and she stole it from a prostitute in a previous small town because it accentuated her breasts and men are hypnotized by tits. She sat down in a chair offered by a large smelly man with white whiskers.

“Now, little miss, I assume you know the rules? And that you wouldn’t try anything stupid?” the dealer asked with a gapped grin.

“Of course,” she said in her best lady voice.

The demon loved the cat and mouse games of humans. It also loved damn near everything else about the human world, the booze, the sex, the depravity, all of it besides the actual humans. There were too many laws and pleasantries, too many morals. Of course it had no intentions of following any of mankind’s rules.

“We’ll only let you play if you’re nude,” A stinking, hairy man said. He looked like he just crawled out a mountain’s asshole, a miner.

The demon in Eve thought about opening his throat like the gill of a fish. It enjoyed humiliating Eve but only when it chose to and not when some toothless worm of a man demanded it.

"Your mother plays nude for coppers."

"What'd you say?" the mountain man asked.

The demon wasn't easily disgusted, it had eaten corpses for fun, but his breath slithered up Eve's nose like a serpent made of pig shit.

The demon forced a grin and remembered the man's face; he would die at Eve's hands. The demon made Eve stand up and took its stolen gold with it.

"Pretty lady, don't go running off! I can teach you a few things about pokin'!" the tall, grizzled man said as Eve walked away from the card table.

Eve's passenger had no care for coin or gold or anything really. What the demon sought was more suffering and chaos, a night of debauchery and death, one the demon was setting up any moment now. While poor Eve, she was a puppet of flesh, carrying out the thing's demands.

The stinking mountain man excused himself from the table as well and followed the beautiful lady to the bar.

"Hey there, little lady, I never got your name!" he called, but she kept walking away as if she didn't hear. The demon loved this old game. The chase was always better than the catch, and old shit breath was about to find out.

"Hey, little lady! I'm talking to you! Don't act hard of hearing now. You weren't when I told you to get naked at the card table!"

He was getting flustered, and it was wonderful. When planned just right, this move had started a thousand barroom brawls. The demon was slowly reeling the man in, leading him to catch a glimpse of Hell.

Eve couldn't control it. She was like a sleepwalker witnessing and feeling her living nightmare. Even if she wanted to stop this game she couldn't, but after seeing the real world these last few weeks with the demon in control, it showed her a side of man that she was almost a willing accomplice to the games the demon dealt out to the pigs of every shit hole town on the trail westward.

She and her passenger continued past a table of more finely dressed men who looked to be military, possibly from the fort near the border of California. They grinned, and Eve slowed just enough to cast a worried mousey glance at one of the well-dressed men. His eyes caught Eve, and he was trapped. The demon was greedily awaiting the outcome.

This is going to be good, just watch girl.

The tall grizzled man was now right behind her, and he grabbed her shoulder spinning her around. He spat as he talked. "Look here, you bitch. When a man is talkin' you listen!"

"Well, sir. I think you are mistaking me for a prostitute. I'm not a girl for sale, and I don't take orders from you, you drunk bastard. Maybe you should go to your hotel room and sleep this off."

Eve put her hand on her chest and poured on the glances to the table of well-dressed men.

"If I go to a room, bitch, you're going with me."

The table of finely dressed men stood up, pleasing Eve's demon passenger.

"Listen, you vulgar horse's ass, the lady isn't going anywhere with you! And you had best be making your way out of this establishment right away! We are here for a fine, relaxing evening, but if we must we will take your sorry ass outside! Excuse my language miss." The gentleman said.

The mountain man laughed, "You and what damn army, pretty boy?"

"The National Army!"

The mountain man realized he was speaking to actual military men. From behind him, a few tough types stood up in his defense and shouted a chorus of insults back at the soldiers. This went back and forth for a few minutes before a fist fight erupted. The mountain man and his gang of toothless cavemen battled the finely dressed military officers. Both groups were equally brutal in their tactics, and in the midst of it all Eve had squeezed her way past the ruckus and up to the fine staircase that led up into the "ladies' quarters." The demon in her halted her for a moment and stood there smiling with glee as hell was unleashed on the bottom floor. Blood flew as fists connected and men howled curses while the room erupted into chaos. The demon passenger took this as a sign to go find more fun before they were locked up in the dark trunk again. And glancing up into the landing above, fun was spotted. Two saloon girls seemed to have had a bit too much opium for the night.

"We can't possibly leave them unattended?" the demon said to Eve smiling up to them in the haze of smoke.

The prostitutes grinned back, and in their eyes she seemed just a friendly girl; perhaps she was lost or in need of employment.

"Hello, ladies." She called to them.

They waved to her. She seemed nothing to worry about with the ruckus coming from the bottom floor. Eve made her way up the last few steps, smiling warmly and holding the cold darkness that moved her just behind her pale eyes at bay as she ascended. Eve's passenger was urging her on.

She protested inwardly, unwilling to hurt the poor women, but she was too weak to physically hold the demon back. Excitement for the kill made the demon feel jittery, and Eve's heart pumped like a piston inside her chest. It took control, guiding her toward its desires as it always did. That was the agreement, wasn't it?

"I'm scared of the fight going on down there. Can I seek shelter from the unease up here with you two?" Eve asked the working girls.

With the breaking glass and sound of men tussling all over the dance floor and beyond and the sounds of the brawl seeming to spill out into the dusty streets as well, they agreed.

"Of course, sweetheart!" a redhead called over the profanity drifting up the stairs. "Hell, let's get into my room just in case! Shelly, get the keys. We may need to lock ourselves in!"

Shelly, the other woman, was blonde and from a closer standpoint, older than she appeared.

"Yes, please, let's hurry!" Eve cried as a glass shattered near her head.

The blonde retrieved the key ring, and they ran past following the red head into a room to the left. Shelly followed them in and did as the redhead said, locking the door from the inside. The room was dim and smelled of cheap perfume. Straightening her skirts, the redhead smiled, "I'm Gretchen."

Eve was happy to hear her name for some reason. She knew it was silly and the demon chided her in her mind over it, but she wanted to know the names of all who were kind to her.

I just want to know.

She'll be dead soon so who gives a shit.

Because I care, you filthy beast.

Eve surprised herself when she got so rough with her demon. Never had she stood up so much for herself. *So sorry, little nun. I just figured why does it matter? You know what happens next.*

Eve almost replied out loud, but she could see her face must have caught Gretchen's attention.

"You okay, honey? I know these little dirty towns can get rough. Where are you from? You have an accent."

Eve looked into the redhead's eyes and smiled a warm weak grin like a child, a defenseless girl. The demon laughed inside.

Nice touch and you pretend not to be my accomplice.

"Yes, it got rough out there! I am from New Orleans. My name is Evelyn." She looked between the women, and for a moment she actually felt a little bit defenseless as to what she knew was coming next. How would she, or they, overtake both of them? The last few were lonely drunks or men too old to fight her off. These were two women in good shape and obviously not alone.

Her passenger pushed the doubt away.

No, don't ever second guess what we're capable of, girl! We could've taken on that entire room of men down there! It's just best to not make our strength so damn apparent to a whole town! Just relax. This is going to be a hoot! Just go with it! I haven't gotten us into anything we can't handle!

Again, the redhead picked up on Eve's strange demeanor.

"Don't be scared."

Eve smiled and nodded.

The silence was momentary but seemed an age as Eve stood with her other half screaming in her skull. It liked to tell her what it wanted to do before actually doing it, and this time it felt different, as if it was trying to teach her how to take another human's life.

At first, she didn't understand, but then it was like a curtain was pulled back. Her passenger took over, and the demon was in control of her every muscle. Eve was moving quickly toward Shelly who was standing near the locked bedroom door. The poor woman was completely taken unaware by the sudden attack. Eve had her by the throat, and was crushing it before Shelly realized it. Shelly grabbed at her wrist to try and pry her hand away.

"You crazy, little bitch!" she choked.

The demon laughed through Eve and squeezed harder. From across the room, rage erupted from Gretchen. The big redhead wouldn't be easy to take down.

She'll kill us! Eve exclaimed to the demon,

That will make it more fun, you stupid child! The entertainment is this mouse in our paws!

And to Eve's new terror, she could see her hands were forming into what looked like clawed appendages. In her mind Eve was screaming in horror as much as Gretchen was in real life. The demon had changed her before in the barn at Alejandra's ranch, but Eve couldn't remember it completely. The fire and destruction of that night only came in short glimpses of nightmares while being stuck in the suffocating darkness of the trunk.

The tall red-haired woman was throwing chairs and figurines against what was once Eve. Somehow the student nun was now an eight-foot creature like something from a campfire story. She spied a glimpse of herself in a mirror as she turned to howl at the screaming combatant who was now stabbing at her with a knife that came from a desk drawer. The glance showed Eve she was a huge growling beast, a wolf.

The demon howled again, loving every second of it. They dropped Shelly's crumpled form to the wood floor. Her neck nearly squeezed in two, her head wobbly like a broken doll, blood pouring from her mouth and nose. Gretchen wouldn't be so easy. As she was already breaking out a window to try and run, Eve leapt the room's space in a single bound and easily dragged its prey back to the floor, cutting her deeply on broken glass. Red fluid and piss flowed onto a floral rug.

A growling laugh escaped her drooling mouth, and Eve was sent hiding in her own self; she would no longer be a wary student. The demon, fully in control, gripped Gretchen by her long red hair and lifted her into the air. She tried to cry out to God, to anyone for help, for salvation. A long claw dragged across her milky throat pouring blood down her chest, stopping her cries for help and prayers and replacing them with a gurgle. With a throaty chuckle from the beast, it dropped Gretchen to the carpet. Eve came forward but clenched her eyes, trying not to see the scene of red mayhem before her.

The night is young, little nun, and I'm not done so go hide if you can't stomach what's coming!

The creature climbed out onto the roof through the broken window that Gretchen tried to escape from. Returning to Eve's delicate form and slipping into clean clothes taken from the brothel closet, she looked like everything a man could desire. And that's just what the passenger wanted.

Tonight is going to be a real shindig! Don't be such a prude!

Before dropping to the dusty street below, she/it pushed over an oil lamp. They would watch from across the street as the fight they had started would finally wind down, only to turn into a raging inferno from the blaze on the second floor.

From their hotel window, Cassandra and Jessie watched the beast drag Gretchen back through the window and then emerge as a frail, pale-eyed young woman. Cassandra tried to put her hand over Jessie's eyes, unwilling to let the child watch the brutality, but she pulled it away.

"That girl, I see her sometimes come out of Peter's room. I don't know how she's ended up in the same places we have been, but I've seen her three or four times."

HELL'S HIGHWAY

In countless nameless towns the madames were very weary, not even trusting of the frail form of Eve or her pouch of gold. Their reputation was spreading just like the many fires they set and throats they slit. Word was going around saloons and brothels were doomed all across Texas. Many whores refused to service anyone they didn't routinely see.

It made the demon and Eve's nightly escapades more dangerous. In the end, the demon always got what it wanted from the skittish ladies of the night. It was always some real magic to finally catch them unaware by becoming the shadows creeping through their windows to leave them eviscerated on their silken sheets.

One in particular was a real good time, and the demon admired its work for a long time before slipping into the darkness, leaving the madame strung up from the ceiling with her rib cage spread open and her insides nestled on her bed. It left Eve's body weak and shaking, but the demon urged her to liven up before it set the whore's curtains on fire with her fine candles.

Eve finally fainted from exhaustion, leaving the demon's human vessel in danger of being burned alive. It twisted her kidney until she awoke in agony. She got to her feet, her hair catching fire before she scurried out the window and leapt into a trough of horse water.

Eve crouched beside a building in the dark. She couldn't breathe. The smoke rising from the saloon was choking the streets and burning her lungs. She fought momentarily to push the demon back and take control of her body. She just wanted to sleep, but the demon still held the spirits at bay when she behaved so it called upon the worst of them to torment her if she didn't do as it commanded. Luckily for her, there hadn't been many storms during their time in Texas; it would have amplified the strength of the ghosts and their wailing voices.

I'll let them have you. You better get your ass up and get ready to play!

Eve's mind swarmed with the shrill cries of approaching entities, and she did as she was told.

"No. I'll do what you want."

The voices were banished and her head cleared. She coughed as she backed down the alleyway to let the demon continue its voyeurism in a less conspicuous location.

You've been a good girl, even enjoyed many of our escapades but don't get cocky with me. I'll show you who calls the shots!

"I'm sorry. I'm just so tired."

"You ain't seen nothing yet."

The demon didn't notice the stranger sneaking toward her with the smoke hanging in the air. Before it knew it, a stinky body was pressed into her.

"Get up, bitch! Get up and get to moving! You're coming with me!"

It was the mountain man. The demon was delighted and sent Eve forward; her true fear would be its bait. Eve was shocked and tried to stammer out a sentence but was slammed hard into the wall behind her. She couldn't handle the sudden switch to actually being alone in herself.

"You deserve this after the shit you pulled. Are you going to make this hard on yourself?! Stupid cunt, stand up!"

Stinking breath crawled up her nose, slapping her face again without a hand. His mouth reeked of rotten teeth and tobacco.

"No you don't want me! Leave me alone. I'm not well!" Eve pleaded.

"Shut up, you whore, and get to doing what you do!" The man spat and shoved her skirts up.

"I'm not a whore!" she cried.

He ignored her, ripping her under garments off and pushing her legs apart.

I can help you! Just say you need me, the demon said.

Eve was tired of its games, one minute torturing her and the next treating her like a protégé while it killed and offering her help.

"Stop!" Eve screamed. The man smacked her again.

"I didn't say talk, whore!" he said with his filthy hands fondling her.

Yes, help me! she pleaded in her head.

Ok then but this will change things....

Eve was awakened by Peter crying and holding her, wiping something from her face. In a daze she glanced around to see him over her with blood covering his hands.

"What happened? Was I stabbed?" she cried.

"No, no, you're fine. It's just this man is not. What happened?"

Eve sat up to see the body of what must have been her attacker. He was dead, and his breaches were around his ankles. His member was torn from him and lay beside her in the bloody mud. Peter looked dumbfounded.

"Things have changed," she said.

In those few days following the killing of Abbie and having her eyes shoved in his mouth, Peter tried praying with Eve in an attempt to keep the demon at bay. But it only seemed to irritate it, and she suffered for it once it surfaced. With each holy verse she would begin to feel violent and then try to punch Peter in the mouth. She'd cuss him and spit on him so he stopped. He was forced to keep her locked in the trunk most days. She'd whimper and claw at the wood, but he'd leave her there.

When night fell she became the demon's toy again, like clockwork. Just as sure as the sun would set, it pushed forward and took control of her. It's not like it couldn't do it during the day, but even the demon knew its vessel needed to sleep if it didn't want to run her into the ground like a hysterical horse, frothing at the mouth and having her heart burst in her chest. It needed to preserve her until it met its grizzly needs. What those were Peter wasn't exactly sure, but he knew the creature threatened to do battle with Father Connor again.

Now, he puzzled over the change Eve spoke of. His hopeful side clung to her possibly growing stronger and fighting back against the passenger within her, but he knew hope was about as useless as tits on a bull. His more realistic side told him she had come to a new arrangement with the demon.

Peter boarded the stagecoach but only after he watched the trunk getting secured safely to the top. He took his seat across from Cassandra and Jessie.

"Good morning," he said politely.

Cassandra nodded and smiled but Jessie only stared out the window.

"Did you have a good night?" he asked.

Cassandra nudged Jessie who turned to look at Peter. She kept her hands clasped tightly in her lap.

"Yes. We slept fine."

"Well, that's good." He felt a little awkward trying to pull conversation from the child so he fell silent and followed her lead by watching out the stagecoach window and letting his mind drift.

"Did you hear about what happened in the other towns we passed through?" Jessie asked.

"Um, no. What happened?" Peter's hair rose on the back of his neck, and though it was creeping close to Christmas and the air was cold, sweat broke out on his forehead.

"Hear tell there was quite a few tragedies. Fires, like the one last night, people murdered in the night in every town."

"Goodness...that is horrible. You know this is dangerous territory out here," he said.

"It is, but folks are callin' this Hell's highway, now. They say the trail west is cursed by evil," Jessie said, studying him with her dark eyes.

"Rest assured that I will protect you both. I have God on my side. I won't let anything evil hurt you while I'm with you," Peter said.

"I sure hope so," Jessie said.

Cassandra put her hand on the girl's shoulder and shook her head. Jessie nodded and went quiet.

Peter looked up to the roof of the stagecoach and prayed the demon hadn't heard the girl. He got a strange feeling she was watching him, and his gut knotted. Suspicion was a very dangerous game, and he prayed Cassandra and Jessie wouldn't venture to spy on him.

"It's gonna be a long ride, Father Peter. I can't believe you didn't bring anyone to keep you company."

Peter's face flushed, "I have someone waiting for my arrival."

"A girl?"

Cassandra grabbed Jessie by the wrist, and the girl shut up.

"No, not a girl, a priest," Peter answered flatly, "and with any luck he'll catch up to me before we get to California."

Peter didn't need to be told the horror stories spread from town to town; he had his hand to play in all of them. The demon used Eve's body to murder and pillage as it pleased, setting fires and leaving a trail of blood and death in its wake. He wished he didn't empty the rest of the holy water down her throat by the cemetery; he might have used it to keep Eve incapacitated. Chloroform may have helped, but Peter worried if he used too much of it he'd end up killing Eve, so he avoided it.

"There was a man who said he worked for the Pony Express back in town. He told me all the stories he heard on the trail. Horrible things...scary things."

Peter didn't want to look too obvious. He had to keep up his polite façade at least until the next town. He figured he could feign illness and stay on an extra day in whatever shit hole they stopped in and let Cassandra and Jessie go on ahead of him before their mouths got them killed.

"You like stories?" he asked.

"I don't really like them type. When I hear them I have nightmares, but I thought we could talk about them since we have a few more stops before reaching our destination."

"Alright, let's talk about them," Peter said.

"The man who told me, he said something evil is on this road. It ain't a highwayman, but a monster," she whispered.

"A monster? Did he see it?"

"Yes, the old boy only had one arm. He said it ripped it clean off."

Peter swallowed and his mouth went dry. He was certain the demon in Eve could rip a man's arm off, witnessed it with his own eyes.

"What else did the man say?" he asked.

"He told me when he found it, he was gonna blow its head off."

Cassandra pulled a notebook from her bag and a pencil. She jotted a note to Jessie.

"That's enough!"

Peter eyed the notebook. He reached over and held his hand out. Smiling, Cassandra placed it in his hand. He worried he would regret it, but he couldn't think of anything else to do.

"Ride through and leave me at the next stop. DO NOT STAY OVER NIGHT. Please. The monster is real."

He handed it back to Cassandra and held a finger over his lips to keep them from speaking. He pointed up to the roof, to his trunk nestled on top.

Jessie grabbed the notebook and wrote, "The girl is the monster?"

She handed it to Peter, and he nodded with tears in his eyes and motioned for the paper once more, "I need the other priest. He is our only hope."

Cassandra and Jessie read his message and nodded.

The hours after the exchange of written messages dragged by; it felt like an eternity of sitting in anticipatory silence, staring out at miles of cactus and sand. Each second he prayed the demon hadn't read his thoughts.

Ricardo gripped the reigns in his only hand. The stump of his other arm hurt constantly. If he hadn't burned the wound close with the embers of his former home, he would be dead just like his sister. It wasn't a miracle he didn't bleed to death.

He didn't believe in miracles anymore. He survived solely to avenge his family, and he didn't care if he lost his other arm or life trying. He found the coach of death burned outside of Franklin and knew the priest was looking for the station to hop on the Butterfield route to California so he followed in that direction.

Each town he rode into had been left a mess, burned saloons, piles of dead bodies, and he knew he was on the right track. Speaking to the girl was pure luck. He lied and told her he rode for Pony Express. She told him she was on the Butterfield route and she shared a stagecoach with a priest. The look in her eyes told him she wanted to say more, but the old woman with her dragged her away.

Ricardo didn't need to hear anymore; he was sure he found the man he sought and the trunk he carried along with him. He would take his time, stalk them, and take his revenge. Mr. Drake had taught him many things in their years together and one of them was how to shoot. He only needed the pistol on his hip and the horse beneath him to fulfill his task. Once it was done, if he survived, he'd lay down somewhere in the quiet desert and let death take him.

The trail stretched out long ahead of him. Hell's highway it was called now. The saguaros on both sides reached up like hands to the sky asking God for mercy. The wind was cold and painful on the bandage bound stump where his arm used to be. His body hadn't recovered from the trauma it suffered, and neither had his mind.

He slipped a chunk of hardtack in his mouth and sucked on it. It felt like a rock in his mouth and didn't taste any good, but it was all he could find in the barn when he abandoned his home in search of blood.

"Our stop!" the driver yelled, and Peter looked to Cassandra in desperation. She nodded to him, the agreement stood. The tiny town rose from the desert to greet the coach and its passengers. Ordinarily, it would have been a welcomed sight, but Jessie and Cassandra just wanted to put it behind them as quickly as possible. The coach came to a stop, and the door was pulled open.

"Are you all overnighting here?" a young boy asked.

"No, only myself," Peter answered.

"Very well, mister. We'll get your luggage and get you in a room for the night. You ladies are riding on?"

"Yes," Jessie said and Cassandra nodded.

"We're gonna switch out the horses and get a new driver and send you on your way."

Peter helped them both from the coach and whispered to Jessie, "Get on the next coach. Don't wait here. Please."

"We won't, and Peter, if I see another priest, I'll send him this way."

"You're an angel. Thank you."

The exchange was only a few seconds, but it made Peter's gut turn. Cassandra hugged him, and they left him there waiting for the doomed trunk to be unloaded.

Peter watched from his hotel window as their coach departed and finally was able to breathe again. The winter sun was still shining in the sky. It gave him hope they would make it far away from him and the curse he carried with him.

He turned to look at the trunk in the corner of the room. Anxiety gripped his heart and restricted his lungs as he flipped its latch open. He'd set her free as he always did and wait until morning to hear what destruction was wrought by the hands of his beloved. If Jessie had noticed

Eve coming out of his room at night, then others surely had, too. He would warn her to be more cautious.

Their infamy was spreading like wildfire, and they couldn't afford to get burned before they even made it to California. The demon may or may not understand they couldn't outrun the law if they were fingered for any crime, but he figured surely Eve would and with whatever secret changes had taken place maybe *she* could make it see they needed to be more conspicuous.

He opened his bag and pulled out a bottle of whiskey. Peter needed to sleep before night fell and alcohol was the only thing to stop his mind from turning. If he didn't get some rest he'd feel like the walking dead, and he needed to keep at least half his wits about him in order to keep Eve hidden and complete the journey toward Father Connor. He lay on the bed and opened the bottle. He took a deep swig and let it burn him alive inside. He kept drinking until his mind went blank and his eyes closed.

They didn't open until the next morning before the sun rose. He never got the chance to speak with Eve or the demon inside her, to warn them to make their bloody debauchery not so noticeable. He glanced over frantically to the trunk. Its lid hung open, and there was nothing inside but the smell of death.

Before dawn Eve and her passenger wandered down a dusty alley. They had hunted after their fun in another saloon, and they didn't anticipate the fire they set this time to raise so many people to help put it out.

The streets were crowded, and she was covered in blood.

"Damn it!" the demon moaned, its voice falling from Eve's mouth.

It wanted to have a bit more fun before Peter locked them away; now they'd have to hide.

"We must find our way back to our room before we are noticed by the sheriff or anyone," Eve said, this time without fear of angering it.

The demon knew this. Already, folks were trying to figure out how the upper rooms went up in such a blaze at the saloon. There had been a massive brawl, but most couldn't see how it ended up burning down the upper levels when most brawlers were tossed out in the street moments after the fists started flying. This time the word was the fight started over a girl dumping a glass of whiskey over the piano player's head. The locals didn't take kindly to it, but she was defended by a handful of men riding through.

"We weren't seen. I'm sure of it! As far as anyone could tell, the whores accidentally knocked over a lamp while intoxicated," the demon said.

Eve's passenger always had an answer. No wonder the devil was blamed for man's tendency to lie. Eve sighed. She was tired and needed to rest. She was not ready to see Peter. She knew he might have heard about the brawl and subsequently the fire, and he would ask a million questions.

The demon loathed hearing Peter go on and on to Eve about fighting the evil side and keeping God close to her and all his hypocritical bullshit. It was all mostly drunken blabbering now, and his days of being a true priest were slipping away from him.

The tall oak doors of their boarding house loomed before them.

"Well, here we are, girl! Let's go up and be pestered to no end!" it said.

Making a point Eve started really dragging her heels.

"Ah ha you know it! You hate it, too!"

"I love Peter. I'm just so tired of being trapped between you both."

Eve looked down at her filthy dress, the blood of a drunkard and his mule soaked into it. Her hair smelled like smoke perpetually from setting just about every saloon ablaze for the last thousand miles.

"It will all end soon, child." The demon's words were like a death sentence.

She knew it would only use her to cause chaos, and once it met up with Father Connor, she would be sacrificed just to kill Peter's faith in God and man. She would be nothing more than a tool but the exhaustion she felt, so strong it felt like it was eating into her bones, made her almost welcome it. At least then she would be free and maybe find peace in death.

Cautiously, she halted and once again she slid along the wall taking a last glance at the crowd. They were too occupied with putting the fire out to notice her in her bloody dress. She ran for it.

Eve slipped into the room and saw Peter on the bed. His eyes were hollow and dark circles rimmed them. He stared out the window at the smoke.

"Every town it's the same," he said.

"You know I can't fight it."

"Get in the damn trunk," he said.

"Peter," she said.

It was all Eve; she managed to hold the demon back with the last of her strength, "I'm so sorry."

"I said get in the trunk and shut your mouth."

Her head swam as she slipped back into herself. The demon laughed at her, "Romeo ain't so in love anymore, is he?"

Ricardo crested a hill and watched the smoke rising black against the morning sky. He knew he was in the right place. He headed toward it and rode down the center of the main thoroughfare. The calamity of men with buckets of water and women crying, tears running down soot covered faces, marked this place as another stop on Hell's highway. His mostly empty jacket sleeve lay across his lap, and his pistol felt heavy on his hip.

"Virgil's dead!" a woman screamed running in the direction of the crowd dowsing a smoldering saloon.

"What?" an older man wearing a sheriff's badge said.

"I found him over on the hill by the cemetery, lookin' like something ate him up. His mule is torn open, too!" The woman was hysterical and fell to her knees in the dirt trying to catch her breath.

"I'm gonna take a look," he spoke to another man. "Marvin, you keep at this. I'll be back shortly."

Marvin threw his hands up, "This place has gone to shit in just one night. What's goin' on?"

"I'll tell you what it is," the woman said and got to her feet. "This is Hell's highway now. There's evil out there huntin' all of us."

"Settle down, Mamie," the sheriff said.

"You know it's true," she said and hurried away, not looking back.

Ricardo climbed from his horse and moved to the very perimeter of the scene. Across from him walking up an alleyway was a disheveled woman in a filthy dress. She looked to be having a conversation with herself. She halted and pressed herself flat against a wall to look at the ruins of the saloon.

He squinted and studied her face. Though she was far away, she looked vaguely familiar. A pang of terror hit his gut. She was the monster in the barn. His hand went to his gun, but he halted at the voice of Mr. Drake in his memory.

"A good hunter knows when to take his prey. Don't jump too quick or you'll end up with nothin' but a handful of feathers, son."

He rounded his horse and used it to cover himself. He watched her run into a boarding house.

"I got you, bitch. I bet that priest is in there, too."

Peter prayed for hours. He could hear muffled noises in the big coffin-like box he kept Eve in. Even though he put many holes in it he knew it was claustrophobic. He also worried he had been too harsh to her, fearing he would push her closer to the demon with his hurtful words. Regret filled his hollow heart, and he let himself cry.

Eve had strong faith once, but Peter knew he was her first fall from grace. He led her astray before any box was opened, with his smiling eyes and compliments, his hidden flirtations that bloomed into love.

"You're my hero, Peter." Her voice echoed in his memories and brought a wave of nauseating shame. She had called him her hero after he had taken her in the mud amongst the wild roses, defiling her innocence with his greedy lust for her. Tears stung his eyes as they streamed freely down his cheeks. What had they become?

He felt great sorrow for her, but he was sick bending to Eve's will and ultimately to the demon. He had lain with her too many times; she was his weakness, a sickness he needed to cure or kill. Peter took his leather belt and gripped it in his hand. He prayed fervently as he pulled his trousers down. Father Connor had spoken to him about self-flagellation. It wasn't really sanctioned by the diocese, but some older priests thought it was helpful to purge one's self of sin.

"Oh, Lord God, my sins of the flesh I destroy mine flesh!"

He whipped himself, a quick snap against his groin, and sweat gathered on his upper lip.

"Oh Lord, my God, no one is above you. I'm sorry, Lord! I give you my blood as penance!"

He flogged himself again and a trickle of blood flowed down his leg from an open welt left behind.

"Lord God, my sin of the flesh. I will destroy mine own flesh!"

He then took the belt and in a swift whip of his wrist he brought it down onto the head of his member. Crying out and falling onto the floor gasping and almost losing consciousness completely, he moaned, "That will keep me from wanting Eve. If I do so much as think of her in that way, I will know great pain. The pain I deserve for getting the one I love so deeply into this!"

Laughter issued from the trunk and a drawn out sniffing noise.

"Is that priest's blood I smell?" the demon mocked Peter's suffering.

"Be silent." Peter's voice was weak.

"Do you think that will keep this wild cat from having you? Foolish little man! You want her so terribly, even with a mangled cock, I give it a few days and you'll be begging her to put it in her mouth. We'll see how long your celibacy lasts!" the demon threatened and then broke into a shrieking laughter once more.

The cackling, it drove Peter mad and sickened him because he worried the demon would try to break his resolve. He didn't know if he could truly withstand it. Tears of anger and shame streamed down his cheeks and raced to the dusty floorboards he laid on. A thud from within the trunk and a short, strangled cry told Peter his self-punishment had finally sunk through the hold of the demon to Eve and it broke her heart.

After what felt like hours of lying on the floor, he finally sat up and cleaned himself up. Then he blotted his welts with a damp cloth and called for the hotels handy man to help him move his huge box headed for California.

"Only a few more days," he mumbled to himself.

The handy man turned to look at him questioningly, confusion on his face.

"Oh no, friend. I'm sorry that wasn't meant for you."

He smiled and gave the man a nice tip from a pouch he was sure Eve stole from some drunk or prostitute. When the helper left to gather more luggage for the long stage coach ride to Colorado City or whatever the small spot would be next, Peter sat down in a chair at the stage coach station to rest his sore body. He saw the sheriff walk by, who tipped his hat and said, "Good morning, Father."

"Good morning."

Peter was no true priest, and never would be; he was a sham and a disgrace. He watched the sheriff as he started questioning the new folks in town waiting at the station. He went on about some god-awful thing happening, and Peter knew it was all Eve and the demon's doing.

Lucky for him, no one ever questioned a priest very much. He watched the men trying to put out any smoldering pieces of the saloon. Every now and then, they hauled out pieces of charred bodies. The other times, he never stopped to look much at what the demon did at night to "sinners." He couldn't bring himself to do it. This time he saw the carnage; he made himself look.

The whorehouse on the top floor was burnt completely, only black bones of the women left behind. There was hushed talk between two older women not far from Peter of a brawl started over a young woman.

He didn't want to uphold his bargain with the demon anymore, but he knew Eve would suffer if he didn't. He couldn't keep her in that box all the way to California or she'd surely die; possessed or not, she had to eat and drink. Something ate at him when he wasn't drunk. It was a tiny voice in the back of his head telling him Eve was starting to like what she and her passenger did together. Maybe that was what she meant about things changing?

The stagecoach was ready. It pulled up before the station, and Peter took a deep breath. The miles between there and California was getting shorter. Hope was in sight; he just had to convince himself to keep looking for it. A rumbling in the sky drew his attention. A storm was gathering on the horizon.

" Sir? Sir? It's time! Get on in the coach, Father. We don't want to be running behind. There's powerful storms that have been hitting California! Floods are a comin'," a station assistant said.

"Flooding?"

Peter felt like a knife was plunged into his heart. His hopes of reaching Father Connor were slipping away.

"Father?" The young man was staring at Peter, holding the stagecoach door open. The driver had leaned around the side and was looking at him with exasperation.

Peter nodded and climbed in, grateful that he was the only passenger for this stretch.

The stagecoach pulled away from the station. The burnt saloon passed by its window like a silent victim watching its attacker sauntering away. Peter looked away from it.

The trunk thumped against the roof of the coach as it bounced over a rut in the road. They weren't on the trail for more than a few miles when the rain started. Peter could feel a static charge running up his arms. Thunder boomed over the coach, and after it he heard the driver and his guard cursing the storm. There was another voice, fainter, but it was there, whispering his name.

"Eve?" Peter worried out loud and gazed out the window in dismay at the torrential downpour sweeping over the coach.

"Try again, Peter," the voice came from the seat across from him.

He knew he boarded alone. His skin rose in goose bumps. He turned slowly to see a pale, eyeless apparition. It was Sister Abbie, sitting with her hands folded in her lap. Her image wavered in and out of view.

"Abbie?"

"You look terrible," she said.

"I'm so sorry I couldn't save you."

"I knew what could happen to me when I insisted on leaving Louisiana," Abbie said.

"I need Father Connor and Father Glover. I can't do it on my own. I'm not strong enough. I'm not fit to be called a priest after all I have done."

"Forget trying to save her as a priest. Just save her as the man who loves her."

A bright flash beyond the coach window and a crashing boom startled him. Lightning struck something nearby. The coach jarred and jumped as the driver tried to right the frightened horses. Peter looked back and the ghost of Abbie was gone.

"I am the man who loves her. It is my duty to save her."

BETWEEN THE LIVING AND THE DEAD

FATHER CONNOR FIDGETED IN the seat, his jaw clenched, his hands wringing a crinkled letter in his lap. His patience was about gone, but he didn't dare speak his concern to the man next to him. Father Glover was nearly a ghost already and couldn't be urged to move any faster than they already were. The never ending rain had made it impossible to push the horses much faster anyway, and the journey had been agonizingly slow going, Father Connor could only guess as to the trials Peter and Abbie had been through in their Hail Mary journey to reach him.

The ailing Priest looked more like a skeleton than the supreme fighter of evil he used to be. Cancer steals from everyone, and priests are not immune to it and its ravages. It had robbed Father Glover of his bodily strength...but not the fire in his heart. Father Connor was surprised his mentor even dared make the trip to meet Peter and to do battle with the force of evil they both had experience fighting. Both priests had waged war against its master and its creed since the day they both devoted their lives to the service of God, and Father Glover had become an expert in sending them back to Hell years before Father Connor ever donned the stole and collar.

Even as the carriage bounced along through the gathering storms, Father Connor prayed his mentor would not die on the road. Lightning scored the horizon in two outside the thin window, illuminating the countenance of Father Glover. He looked like a corpse in the bright burst. Father Connor felt a chill run up his spine and the cab of the carriage took on the scent of roses. For just a moment he imagined he was in New Orleans alongside sister Abbie, with the rain whipping around the courtyard between the dormitories and the church.

"She's here with us," Father Glover spoke, his voice labored.

"Pardon?"

"Your Abbie is here," Father Glover said but didn't turn his eyes from the window and the storm.

Father Connor opened his mouth to speak but couldn't find any words, his heart aching at the possibility of his mentor losing his sanity as his sickness took root in his brain.

"I'm dying, I'm not insane."

"I'm sorry, father...I just," Father Connor began but fell silent.

"You're in the presence of the dying and the dead, an unusual crossroads. If you close your eyes and listen, she'll impart to you secrets only a spirit would know."

"Father Glover, Abbie isn't dead," Father Connor said, feeling tears sting his eyes, thinking for sure his old friend was now lost to the madness of the sickness eating him.

Father Glover weakly shifted, his eyes falling on Father Connor, "Close your eyes and listen. Only God could allow such spiritual contact...if the Devil can send his army here to do evil, our Lord will certainly send his own to even the odds."

Father Connor was once again overcome by the scent of blooming roses and a warmth he hadn't felt in months, not since long before he and Peter had exorcised Lady Elizabeth. No, the last he experienced such an encompassing feeling of contentment and safety was when he sat beside Sister Abbie in the courtyard and spoke of San Francisco. He nodded and closed his eyes, as a swell of euphoria welled up inside of him and his head fell back on his seat. He didn't see the courtyard or the church, only blackness and in its center a pinprick of light. The small white orb grew until it filled his vision and joy filled his heart.

"Hello again." Abbie's voice filled his head.

Father Connor was struck with sudden fear; something wasn't right. The joy wrapping around him like a warm blanket had an underlying sadness to it, and he realized he had felt something like it when he was comforting his dying mother.

"Abbie?!" he spoke.

"I don't have much time." Her face became clear in his mind. Her skin was smooth and without a wrinkle after all she had endured in life, and her eyes were bright and fearless as they always were, but the color of her skin was so pale.

"What's happening?"

"Father Glover is telling you the truth. I'm no longer alive."

For a moment he heard nothing else. The shock and disbelief of her possibly being dead was too much for him to comprehend.

"No, Abbie. No!"

"Listen to me! Peter needs you!"

"I know. We're on our way to help him, to stand beside you."

"Things have gotten worse since his message...the evil we fought many years ago, it has taken over Eve."

"Abbie, how did you..."

"I'm going to show you. It will be horrible but much faster...don't let go of my hands."

Father Connor felt the soft, strong grip of Abbie; he squeezed her hands and felt his heart stutter at how cold they were. Her eyes were staring into his as her soft skin began to split, her bright eyes turned to black holes, and a gunshot opened in her forehead.

"ABBIE!" Father Connor screamed.

"Don't look away! This is important!"

Father Connor sat forward, startled out of his sleep. Father Glover patted his knee and asked, "Did you see the truth?"

"How did you know?"

"The link between the living and the dead has been made. I've seen and heard things, especially when the storms are bad; the spirits are telling me their secrets. I could hear Abbie calling your name."

"I can't believe the horror she showed me. It was like a nightmare," Father Connor said.

"She only wanted to prepare you, to strengthen you. I don't have much time. You know that. We must end this; I can't leave this earth until I end this."

"We will," Father Connor promised.

The coach powered through the storm and stopped outside a cantina. Father Glover laid his head against the window, his breath steaming up the pane of glass.

"Get out here, and wait...look for a girl and a woman who doesn't speak," Father Glover said softly.

COLORADO CITY

"AUDREY, GODDAMN IT!" JIM spat through clenched teeth.

This woman had turned him into the scum he used to gun down. He loved her too much not to have her, but the plans she laid out to him were nearly unthinkable.

"The only reason you would never agree to this before is because of Cletus. Well, here we are! He will be out of the way for weeks or months, Jim! He can't work with a busted leg! It will be just you, and you have never given any reason to doubt your words. Well's Cargo won't miss the money, and they will get more pay roll sent out to the miners in a few weeks; they won't go without. Please Jim; it's the only way that we can run away together. The only way I can retire from the saloon and be with just you! You're getting older...how long will you keep riding the trail like this? Will you be like Cletus, a sixty-year-old with nothing? He could've died last week and for what? No one would've even mourned him. If you weren't there no one would've even helped him out of that ditch. He would've been buzzard meat and for what? A nice reputation? Can anyone retire on that? You know for damn sure I won't! I can't do this much longer Jim! I'm thirty-eight. That's old for this business. If not for you and a few others I would starve."

A few others, she liked to throw that in his face when she was upset about working, like he didn't already feel as low as cow shit thinking about her sleeping with other men for money. Jim listened to Audrey and stared at his hands. The arthritis had started in his fingers, and his grip was weakening from long hours of holding reins and rifle. In his mind, he knew he wouldn't have the speed it required to stay alive much longer when slinging a pistol. One day, some kid would lay him low because his hands and shoulders were going to be sore and stiff.

But still, Jim was never a thief and had always preached that thieves were the lowest next to people who hurt children and women. Yet, at that moment, he was torn. Audrey was the one woman that he couldn't resist. And she was the only person ever to know the darker corners of his heart and mind. He told her more than once all the mistakes these highway men made. Late at night by the fire wrapped in blankets he whispered how easily he could become a highway man himself, just once because that's all it would take if a man were smart.

"Just once...take a shipment from Well's Cargo and disappear into Mexico. That's it! No messing around, no getting cocky and going for more."

If there's one thing he saw was that if those young men would take the money and run down across the border they would be kings for the rest of their days. "Never get too many involved!" he whispered to Audrey.

Too often there would be a gang of ten men for a job that took two. Then those men would turn on each other like starved dogs. And eventually if the law didn't catch up then they would kill each other in the end. The idiots would always brag, too. If only they let sleeping dogs lay they wouldn't be caught up to.

"No, I say just get a good sack of gold and run off, and keep quiet and live a nice restful life somewhere."

He had told her all these things. He had placed the thoughts in her head, and he'd have to deal with the consequences.

"Also don't be flashy with it, you know. Don't go buy a brand new suit the second you get into a town down the way. Some of these guys go and immediately buy their favorite whore five new silk dresses like no one in the small cattle town would notice that!?" he said.

Jim had all the right ideas, but Audrey would roll her eyes and sit up out of his arms.

"Why go on and on like this, Jim? You have the whole thing planned out, but you don't have the spine to do it!?" she said combing her hair back into place.

Jim sat up and stared. "What, you think I should actually do this? I should really go out there and rob my employer of ten years?"

"Yeah, I do! I think you should've done it years ago!"

They stared at each other in the dim light. Jim knew by the look in her eyes that his life was done. Whatever he thought about being a good guy that could live a normal fulfilled life with his job and a sweet wife was done. He loved this woman in spite of where she was leading him. Jim knew in that moment he would do the stupid, risky thing she asked. He just prayed to God it went as easily as he always bragged it could.

"Ok," he whispered.

Aubrey hugged him and stared at her own reflection in a dusty mirror with a grin.

"You mean it? " Audrey asked. Jim nodded his head as he swallowed a shot of whiskey.

She danced around the room with joy like a child would when getting a new toy.

"How much?"

"Well, since its goin' to the bank...about forty-five in gold."

"Forty-five thousand? Forty-five thousand?" she whispered.

"Yes! Damn it! Calm down. I said let me look into it really well! Ok? I'm not going to rush into it and be stupid!" Jim hissed.

She just smiled and kissed his cheeks and danced around his room.

He had a rotten gut over all this. He knew if he didn't do this just right all hell would break loose. There couldn't be anything here overlooked or anything that could go sideways. If any part of this plan got cockeyed, they would not proceed. Jim told her the rule five times, and he meant it. Audrey smiled so wide her face was almost terrifying! Jim took another shot. The sky opened up outside the window and the smell of rain filled the room.

"Cletus! Cletus!? You there, old man?" Jim yelled through the door to the small wooden home his oldest work partner lived in. The sky was gray, and clouds gathered overhead, storms were rolling through again.

Cletus had no wife or kids and preferred to only go to town to visit the saloon when he felt the need for company. Aside from that and his job with Jim, Cletus kept to himself.

It was just him and his stagecoach and of course the "girls," which is what he called his prized mules used to pull the coach for Well's Cargo. The girls consisted of Becky, June, Rita, and Cindy. All were strong, fantastic animals. They were dependable and trustworthy through the worst of times. All were gentle and easy going except...Cindy.

She was known as a three bell mule. The bells were the shape their tale was trimmed into so that anyone could see right away if they had any "issues" a coach man needed to know about. Each bell signaled that they were a bucker, a biter, or a kicker. Cindy was all three. Cletus knew this but loved Cindy anyways. He knew just by the look in her eyes whether or not she was going to act up. And before the fateful day of the incident, Cletus didn't have too much of a problem with Cindy.

However, the day came and he didn't notice the subtle change in her eyes. He was a little hung over when Jim was busy harnessing the other three girls. Cletus made the mistake to approach Cindy from behind. In a split second, she kicked back launching the older man five feet into a stall wall. Luckily for Cletus, Jim was there to get him up and away from the cranky mule. Cletus was rushed into the nearest doctor, which happened to be the town veterinarian, and got his broken leg set quickly enough. Unfortunately, Cletus and Jim could see he wouldn't be driving the coach for weeks.

Jim promised to come out and check in on him every few days to be sure he wanted for nothing and was resting up. Both men knew keeping Cletus in bed for weeks on end would be the hardest part.

Jim could handle the next few weeks of coach runs alone. He knew the routes like the back of his hand, and the mules and equipment were no problem either. Cletus did worry about the random stagecoach robberies, but he was hoping it wouldn't happen while Jim was alone. It hadn't happened to them in many years so the likelihood of it taking place was slim to none.

"Get your old ass yup, Cletus! I think this vacation has got you lazy!" Jim yelled jokingly because he knew he would likely find Cletus up doing something the doctor had warned against.

Cletus dropped the ax he was awkwardly trying to chop small logs with and tried to make his way through the back door of his old wooden home and into his bed before Jim found him up and about. Jim pushed the cabin door open just as Cletus sat down on a chair by the hearth.

"Just what were you up to, old man? Leavin' my ass out there in the rain." Jim asked winking.

"Oh nothin', Jim. Just takin' her easy," Cletus responded wiping his brow of sweat and newly falling rain drops.

"And that strange sound was nothing? Certainly not you, up and trying to sneak back in here before I could see you doing some dumb shit that I could do for you!?"

"Maybe it was thunder?"

The friends looked at each other then and shared a laugh. Jim needed to ask a few questions of his old friend just to be sure he was clear to pull off his heist plan. Like he told Audrey, Jim wouldn't do anything unless he was sure that the deed could be done without any clues leading back to him.

"You sure you can make the run all by your lonesome?" Cletus asked.

"I'm sure I can. They don't plan on sending someone to fill in for ya?"

"No," Cletus laughed. "They promised they could send someone down in another week or two, but you know how short they are, not enough tough men like us."

"Don't worry, old man. I can do it on my own."

"I know you can, too...just stay away from Cindy's backend!"

Jim decided it would be the time to make it happen before Cletus got up and around anymore and decided he wanted to return to work. The old bustard was pushing himself to get well as quickly as possible. Cletus was as stubborn as his damn mules and wouldn't stay home long.

"The first run, it'll be light. The second one, though, if any highwaymen catch a whiff of it, they'll try to jump your ass!"

"Don't worry, old man. I'll be packin' somethin' just in case."

Jim made up his mind then. The run taking place in two days was the run when he would be alone for sure, and it would be the run that would conveniently be held up. Jim could imagine the look on Audrey's pretty face, and he could imagine the way she would reward him for the good news.

"The storm sound like it's gettin' worse. You better keep your ass inside," Jim warned and left Cletus.

Jim walked out of Cletus' shack and into the stable. He needed to take Old Red out for a ride. That was the best way for him to clear his mind and get his plan in order.

He had gone on a few short runs without Cletus that went well, so this showed the big wigs in charge of Well's Cargo that he was fine to make the larger payroll delivery. They didn't know it would end up being his retirement. The main issue he had was deciding whether to flee directly after the robbery and make it seem as though he was killed in the process or pretend to have survived somehow and save his good name. After all, Jim had never ever had a bad day at work, never a report of misconduct, never a cross word said about him. He hoped that alone would quell any suspicions.

He felt guilty already and would rather not be found out to be the outlaw thief. If he were to make the robbery seem like he was taken by surprise and out manned or if he pretended to bravely live through the attack and hid the money until weeks after people stopped looking for it, then he could still be seen as the same great man. He would feel better about himself; his pride would remain intact but Audrey wouldn't like it. She'd want to run away immediately to start spending the money. Jim knew she could be bought, which was the other kink in the plan that bothered him a bit. There were questions eating at him at night when he laid his head down to sleep. Could she stay true? Could she ultimately be trusted? His life depended on it.

He rode the big roan over the hills outside of town, letting the rain soak them both. Colorado City was a good sized town with plenty of gold going in and out. Many crooks already had their eyes on it, he was sure of it. Jim would need a good hiding place to take the loot to in order to hide it for a few days.

He knew a few miles away in the tiny sleepy mining town of Bodi there was several old run-down mines that he could use as a great hiding spot. Also there was not a full time sheriff there so at least there wouldn't be a permanent law man he would have to steer clear of. The plan was coming together. The payroll coming down from Freshwater had been delayed by a week or else he would've already rushed head long into something foolish. As long as Cletus didn't make a sudden recovery, Jim would be all set.

On the clouded horizon he watched a stagecoach racing through the storm, rain pelting it and lightning tracing through the sky. It looked like the coach was leading it, dragging in the nasty weather. He hoped it wasn't a bad omen for the plans he had. Old Red jumped and snorted at the sudden clap of thunder.

"Easy, boy," Jim said.

Audrey wouldn't be excited about the way Jim was going about it. She had begged him months ago to just kill Cletus and run off with the gold. But Jim wasn't that kind of man. He may become a robber, bandit, or whatever you may call it, but he wasn't looking to murder his oldest buddy in the process.

Jim sat silently by a small stream near the old mines as the rain fell steadily down on his head. This place would do fine. It was on the way to where he would drop off payroll and it had the perfect set up to create a fake ambush. He had several old pairs of boots he found under Audrey's bed from men who had to make quick getaways when their wives had come to beat down Audrey's door. All of various sizes and some with different types of heels and widths in case Well's Cargo hired good trackers to investigate the robbery. It would appear to be a gang of men in on the job, instead of just one man hiding the payroll away in the mine and making all seem like he had been jumped.

He hid a mask in a creosote bush to wear in case a passenger was sent along in the stagecoach. He'd slip it on and subdue them and leave them tied up in the coach while he pretended to fight to protect them outside. Though it wasn't likely anyone would book passage to the tiny shit hole Bodi where he'd be hauling the gold on the way to his next stop. He would even use old Apache tricks to hide his tracks into the mine, dragging tree branches behind his horse to cover the hoof prints. Once things settled down after a week or so, he and Audrey would leave one day after he made a public showing of asking for her hand in marriage. Who would think anything of him aside from him being a man who saw the light in a near death experience and asked for his lady's company for life?

He would keep his good name in case he ever came around these parts again. He wouldn't have trouble, and above all else, Well's Cargo wouldn't suspect him and send the law after him. He couldn't have them hunting him for the rest of his days. The Well's Cargo company had the money and means to have him tracked for the next hundred years if they chose, chase him down like a dog and shoot him in the back. Jim was hoping Audrey understood that part, too. They could be hanged for such a heist.

Peter awoke to the driver calling to him.

"Sir? Hello, father? We are at the last stop today, Colorado City. This is Blue Sky Inn. You can stay here tonight," the driver said. "Your luggage will be taken inside, and your larger box will be kept in the stables just for tonight."

Peter nodded and thanked the man, handing a few coins over to a kid that was helping carry his suitcase up to his room. He would go out in a few minutes to check on the trunk to make sure no one opened it, as Ricardo had back at the ranch. He couldn't stand much more tragedy.

He made his way up to his small room and set his belongings out for the short stay. He would have to go out and let Eve out for the night. He couldn't spend time with her, not sexually, after his flagellation; his body hardly would allow it, but he could warn her again to try to hunt away from the town. His heart stuttered in his chest at the rolling thunder outside, and he worried about seeing or hearing any spirits traveling on the electrical energy gathering in the air. Would Abbie visit him again and see what a failure he was?

After washing up a bit and eating a small meal, he gathered up some leftovers and tucked them into his jacket and made his way to the stable in the guise of checking on his cargo. There he made sure to be alone and opened the lid of the trunk.

Eve popped up immediately saying, "Didn't we stop an hour ago!? I can't be locked in this box any longer than need be, Peter! It's driving me crazy, and I can't keep from wanting to claw my way out! The storm, riding through it, was a nightmare!"

He saw she was having great anxiety and tried to calm her, "I'm so sorry, dear one! I won't tarry next time. I simply needed to be sure we aren't interrupted. Here, have a meal and try to calm down. You are free for a while more, but I must implore you this. We are in a small town; you cannot go around setting fire to the whore house! And you must stop hurting folks who are so noticeable! Plus, there's a storm rolling in, a big one."

He tried to speak to her calmly because he felt terrible for being harsh with her in the previous town. His drunkenness had worn off, and now he was just sick with pity and fear. They were getting so close to California, their redemption, and he couldn't afford for them to have a showdown with a sheriff. He didn't even mention what Jessie told him of the rumors going around about a monster killing people along the westward trail.

Eve glared as he spoke. Peter saw a feral anger in her, and he feared what the next morning would bring. The sky yawned open beyond the barn and dumped rain down into the dusty streets, turning them to mud.

Eve could feel the passenger stir in her, and she didn't think the demon would let Peter's words go easy. He sounded sweet but accusatory, and the beast never took that well.

With the energy from the storm outside she knew it would gather any wayward spirit into its army to torment her if she didn't do exactly as it demanded. Her heart was exhausted; she was tired down to her bones of being a prisoner, stuck between a desperate Peter and the vile thing inside of her. She would end it all soon.

I would hate to let Peter meet the other side of you! What would old Petey think of such a creature? Would he still long to fuck you when you're seven feet tall and covered in hair? Because that's what he will see if he thinks of any stupid plans!

Eve cried out into her mind, *No, no! I will get him under control. Just please don't hurt Peter. He is only looking to help!*

The demon hissed, *Help who, girl? Yes, you better get him under control! Since he beat his cock to pieces, you can't even seduce him. If you can get him to stop his incessant bitching, then I will promise not to rip his face off, but if he tries something stupid...he's dinner. That I swear!*

Peter noticed her growing quiet and he could see she had a look about her, one that people have when they are inside themselves thinking or, in this case, he knew she was talking to the dark one.

He wondered if it was the storm. He was given a glimpse of what she saw when the rains came; he couldn't imagine dealing with that on top of being possessed. She looked like a caged animal for a long while but then shook her head as if casting aside a hood. She looked a little more like herself again, and it eased Peter a bit.

"Do you remember when Sister Abbie started calling you Evey Bee?" he asked.

She looked him in the eyes and nodded sadly. He knew it must sting to hear him mention the happier times in their lives. They seemed so long ago now after all the horror they'd lived through.

"We were in the garden, and I was running between the flowers, sniffing them. She said I buzzed around like a little bee."

"Like an Evey Bee," Peter said.

"And you fell in the manure she used to feed the flowers," Eve added to the memory.

"And everyone laughed at me...but not you."

"That's because," Eve said and patted the back of his hand, "you never made fun of me about the storms, never called me a chicken. You accepted me as I am."

"Accepted you and loved you, and I always will," Peter said, his voice cracked as if he might cry.

"And I you."

Eve smiled faintly, and Peter handed her the small loaf of bread and cheese he had brought out. He gave her a bit of fresh water from the well outside the stable. For a moment they both pretended all was well and things were still on track. Peter assured himself they would meet with Connor and this would all end happily. Neither one of them was stupid enough to believe it would be so easy. They both could feel things shifting, but he needed to at least pretend. They both loved one another, but it wasn't enough to stop whatever fate had in store for them. Lightning struck a tree out beyond the stable. Peter fell away from the stable window, but Eve only watched wide-eyed.

"Are you okay?"

"No. Leave me now, Peter. And don't come back until the dawn."

"Peter...Peter??" Her voice was so soft in his dream.

Eve's voice came from the elaborately carved box, the same he had peeked into once but could never remember what he saw inside. His hands shook as he opened it. It opened like a doorway, and he stepped into it.

Eve stood on a staircase of dark oak. He could smell flowers perfuming the air, and she wore a beautiful white gown of silk. Wedding tunes played from some band in the distance and Peter was shaking. There stood his only love and the woman he had wished for so badly. She put out her lily white hand and beckoned to him. He walked in a haze to her outstretched hand and grasped it, intertwining their fingers. She led him up a few more steps to a massive set of dark doors.

"This is it, my love. Are you ready? Together we shall be finally and forever!" Eve spoke.

Peter could feel the dream state washing over him, warm and dizzying. He wanted to cry for it to be real, for this to be the end of their horror story.

They walked side by side, hands held tight; the huge doors opened before them. The room was dark, and he could feel a rush of cold damp air blow past them. Entering, he heard his feet splash in small pools. Water? He wondered and as he tried to look down Eve caught his gaze.

"Never you mind that, my love, it awaits us now... "

He thought she said more but the rest escaped him. Suddenly before him something was looming.

"Eve, what is this? Are we to be married?" he asked.

"No and yes," she said. "But first, we must be buried."

He turned to her; did he hear that?

He pulled her to face him, and the beauty of her countenance was gone. All that remained was sunken and dead, like one of her flowers in the garden, withering away. All he saw was no longer his lively and beautiful young woman but a skull with skin stretching over it.

She screamed and dark fluid poured down her once smooth chest. No longer full and inviting, just a shrunken skeleton and bruised looking flesh. Peter fell back from Eve trying to cry out, but his throat was being strangled by an invisible force. He couldn't breath, He couldn't speak. Her beauty was wasting before him. Her head leaned far to the side and toppled off her neck. Her body collapsed in on itself.

"Eve!" he choked. "No! No! No!" He barely got words out; they were startled gasps as his throat was still being constricted. Her corpse lay in a heap before him. He fell to his knees, gagging and crying and crawling to see how she had crumbled into nothing. He fell over on top of what was once her and held what was left. He looked to his hands; the flesh was drying and peeling away in gray sheaths. His breathing stopped and his heart was slowing. He too was nearly dead; he could feel it. Words in his head echoed, "First, we must be buried."

Peter woke up crying. His stomach spasmed, and he leaned to his bedside in time to wretch. Peter shook and vomited again. All the stress and fear were eating him alive. The keeping of secrets, and most of all it was seeing his pretty Eve becoming something different.

"We only need a few more days, Lord. Please keep her on the right path! Or at the very least, Lord, please help her to resist the dark one enough to not kill anyone again!"

He prayed and laid down in the dark staring at a cross hanging on the wall.

Eve slipped from the stables side door and into the night. The demon had an itch Eve would have to scratch or she knew the consequences.

Chaos and blood it craved, and she would fulfill it. Even though it occasionally spoke to her like she was more than a captive, even saved her being raped, she knew better than to cross it.

She physically could feel the demon's desire to be unleashed, a twisting in her bones so strong she found herself almost needing those horrific things as well. Her muscle memory had already determined that killing meant she would be left alone for a while and she could almost be in control of herself even if only for a few hours. Eve was thinking on Peter's warning in the way that it would only hurt her when the morning came.

The smell of manure and livestock, familiar scents, meant there were plenty of barn animals around somewhere they could take their frustration out on. And then Peter couldn't use this night as ammunition against them, or chide them to no end. After all it was only cows and pigs! They wouldn't kill everyone in town. They would just kill all their stupid animals! Eve was relating all of this to the demon through her mind. At first the demon laughed. "Childish," it spoke through her. "We are beyond such things!"

But Eve persisted, "Peter is right. If you want to kill Father Connor, we can't get caught gutting whores and drunks."

"What fun is killing cows?"

"We could let the wolf out and slaughter all their food for months. They'd talk about the beast of Colorado City for decades," Eve reasoned trying to make her idea seem even better.

"Yes, infamy! Now you're tempting me."

The demon was giving in. Eve could feel the balance of power shifting, her true self gaining a little more control. They heard and smelled the cows before coming upon the pasture.

"Well, here we are! Why not give these cows the night of their lives?" Eve said aloud. The demon chuckled, turning her voice guttural, "You may want to leave your clothes here, girl. We won't be shopping at the brothel tonight."

Eve took that as a good sign and began to unlace her gown. She laid it beside a wild rose bush thinking she could find it easier once the night was over. The fragrant brush reminded her of home; it felt right somehow. Her naked skin tingled in the falling rain and about them she could see a gathering of spirits. One of them was only a child who shyly hid his eyes at her nudity.

"We have an audience tonight. The storm brought them in. I guess you knew they'd come, didn't you?" the demon asked.

"They have always come to me, ever since I was a girl, to frighten me, demand things of me, paw at me."

"Well, why don't you show them you're nothin' to be trifled with?"

It was so moody, one moment wrenching her insides into a knot and an hour later it's teaching her to defend herself. She had no idea why the demon would sometimes treat her like a student, but she didn't question it; her survival depended on it.

"The night air and rain feel so nice on my skin," she said.

Eve started to feel a warmth racing from her gut and tingling all over her body. For a moment she was afraid to feel the pain that accompanied the change, but she pushed it from her mind.

The air was crisp, the downpour eased a bit, and the small wild roses smelled sweet. She thought of years passed, back before she was orphaned, before she was forced to take the vow to be fed. She had a good life with her mama, her daddy not so much, but he was rarely home. She lived wild and free in the country with muddy feet and a dirty face, but she did as she pleased. Eve realized she didn't want to truly be a nun. After all she had been through she could fend for herself, and California would free her in more ways than one if she survived

The passenger chuckled, "Have you forgotten I can read your thoughts? If you survive what's to come, I think you'd do better to leave the church behind you. If anything else I've taught you that death is waiting for all humans, one heartbeat away from taking you. Why waste it in a black dress and no cock to please you? If I don't end up killing you, I've taught you to live, child. Now, give me a chance to feel that life. Step aside."

In the distance cattle roamed and mooed.Eve let the passenger take over. Her body, cold and wet with rain, began to stretch and move in the moon light. Her form changed quickly into the beast again with hardly any discomfort this time. Eve felt strong and invincible. She was massive but also could move on four feet nimbly. In the moonlight she saw she was covered in fur of the darkest shade that blew in the wind as she ran.

Eve had an exhilarating feeling of complete freedom. No Peter, no mother Marie, or Sister Abbie to tell her how to feel or what to do. All there was in the moment was life, beating hearts, pulsing with blood, lungs filling with winter air. The dead watched from the shadows, envious of her strength and grace. She cocked a large black and furry muzzle and cried to the moon.

We'll hunt them all, shed their blood, and feel the power of the kill! The demon's voice spoke in her mind.

Checking on the edge of the clearing the beast watched a group of cows as they stood under the arms of mesquite trees and dozed in the night's stormy breezes.

Eve was feeling more primitive and cared nothing about the farmer who would need these cows. No human thoughts entered into this. It was time to feed.

Through the tree cover that hid the massive wolf's approach, the cattle were unaware of the monster watching them. The wind carried their scent away from them and to the nose of the beast. Dark patches of brush hid her approach as Eve and her passenger closed in on her prey. Before the wind changed direction, she sprang from the bushes taking down the only bull sleepily standing watch. He was young and not experienced with more than small coyotes. Eve sank her teeth into his neck and sprayed blood across the wet grass. With huge clawed hands, she raked his sides, laying them open. She tore into his throat, and his blood filled his mouth. He couldn't send out a warning to the rest of the cattle.

With hot blood pooling around the bull, Eve ran to the next, an older milk cow that spied her shadow racing in on the group. It let out a warning. The others, sleeping and deafened by the storm, barely began to flee as Eve came down upon them with slashing and tearing claws. One was gutted, spilling its innards across the yellow grass. Another had its head twisted around backwards, snapping its neck like dry firewood. A calf was ripped in two separate pieces by Eve's powerful claws. The field was becoming a blood bath of mud and gore.

The demon urged Eve to start rolling in it, enjoying the warmth of the guts and blood before death and the storm cooled them forever. She killed more than she could ever eat, but they didn't come here hungry for food; they sought only violence and destruction. She strolled over to the bull and wrenched the head the rest of the way from it. She placed its head on the fence post for the farmer to find and heard a cackling from her mind. The demon passenger was pleased.

Further up the road was a barn full of chickens and pigs. She could smell their foul stench. With her human-like hands she couldn't be kept out of places other night predators would be. She simply slid the latch open and walked into the barn to have some fun. She popped heads off of chickens and sows. She used her incredible strength to throw the dead pigs into the hay loft. In the corner stood a half-blind mare shaking in fear; it wasn't strong enough to fight the beast. Eve rubbed her huge hands into pig's blood and left the farmer a surprise of giant clawed handprints all over his horse, which fainted in fear.

Kicking a hole through the splintered wooden barn wall, she walked out into the early dawn. Sniffing her way back to her clothes, she decided she and the passenger better make a getaway before the famously early rising farmers were awake.

Her body shrank back to that of her human self. She was exhausted and filthy so she found a trough of water and washed up. Putting her dress back on, they walked back to where the trunk was stored.

"Well, Peter didn't want to hear of any dead people, but he didn't say anything about cows and chickens," she said, the demon laughing heartily in her mind.

She lay down in the box and pulled the lid closed. She waited to see if Peter said anything when he came to visit before their next coach arrived, but after a few hours, through the trunk she could hear a commotion.

"The sheriff said no coach can leave today, not after the slaughter that happened last night!"

Peter threw the lid open and glared down at Eve.

"I told you not to cause trouble and now we're fucked!" he screamed.

"Yes, you both are," Father Connor's voice spoke from the doorway of the stables.

Peter looked to Father Connor, the priest who had taken him under his wing, and beside him stood the frail frame of Father Glover. Tears streamed from his eyes, and he nearly fell to his knees.

THE HEIST

JIM RODE OUT EARLY through the rain, manning the Well's Cargo coach on his own. The exchange happened in town, and without any questions he was sent on his way without any passengers. Even if someone wanted a ride to Bodi, the sheriff ordered no one new to town could leave. Apparently, there had been a slaughter on a ranch; all the animals killed. Jim couldn't believe his luck. The dead livestock would keep the lawman busy and out of his hair for most of the day. The trail was rutted and muddy from the unending storm, but it still held so much promise.

Fortunately for him, Well's Cargo didn't accept excuses for late deliveries. No rain would halt his plans. He kept repeating in his mind he had to make this work. No messing around. This would end with his neck in a rope or a bag full of gold in his hand. Every part of his plan had been thought through; it was now or never.

After looking around and scanning the hillsides for trouble, he drove the stagecoach to where the "robbery" would take place. He checked around the small creek and made sure he had plenty of tree limbs there to wipe out any tracks that he didn't want seen. He neatly bundled the sets of large and small shoes and made fake tracks. He even silenced a few pistols and fired into a tree here and there to set up the gun battle that was supposed to take place. He had several old handkerchiefs and a shredded old work shirt he bloodied up and tossed aside to seem as though he clipped a bandit with either gun or Bowie knife. He had planned it all so carefully he wondered why he hadn't done it years ago. He and Audrey could already be living in Mexico like a king and a queen. He laughed to himself then chided himself in the same breath.

Ain't outta the shit yet, keep going.

If he got too cocky it could be the end of him. So he set about hiding his loot in a hole, which was a deep gouge in the ground next to an old mine entrance. He covered it with branches until it could hardly be discernible.

The rain hadn't let up, and he hoped a downpour would keep nosey people away until he got his chance to come back and claim it. He knew folks would come a looking sooner or later. With a finder's fee and of course the good old reward sure to be hanging in the air, people would be searching the mountains like bloodhounds on the scent, but he hoped they would assume the robbers had taken the strong box from under the coach driver's seat when they fled and that there wouldn't be anything to find out there.

He hiked back down a particular spot that was pretty rugged with sliding rocks and stabbing cactus. In the rain, he lost his footing and slid down the steep embankment on his back.

He could understand why this area was called breakneck pass because he did almost break his back in the drop, and his ass was torn up from rocks and shale. He lay at the bottom of the slide, coughing and wheezing. His whole body hurt.

He just wanted to lay back and try not to bust out crying when he heard something that nearly stopped his heart. A sound like this is one all cowboys, trailer riders, hustlers, hell, even school marms knew it, a distinct almost buzzing. The rattle sound, which made every person with a brain stop cold in their tracks, made him hold his breath, a rattlesnake.

The rattler was coiled up a few feet away. He must have nearly landed on it or it wouldn't have reacted so fiercely in the cold weather. Its cold blood should have been sluggish. It was probably looking for a nice place to hide and warm up when Jim's dumb ass came falling from the ridge above it. He wondered if he had enough time and space to roll away from it if it tried to strike. He racked his pounding head, which he realized probably got banged up to in the fall, too. If he managed to escape without getting bitten, he could blame his injuries on the fictional fight he would claim to have with bandits.

Rain ran into his eye as he tried to remain still. His back began to seize up a bit; he couldn't cry out from the pain unless he wanted rattler fangs adding to it. After what felt like an eternity of breathing softly and staying absolutely still, the rattle seemed to calm and he breathed a bit deeper.

It slithered away and in his peripheral vision he watched it go. Jim sat up all the way, but he felt his lower back screaming to him. Completely involuntary spasms racked him. His lower left side felt as though he was stabbed with red hot iron. In the split second he knew he had made a major mistake.

The snake had come back around and barely let out a warning rattle before it propelled its self at Jim. It missed the right side of his face. He screamed as it came at him again. This time he saw the snake lunging and barely scrambled away as it missed his arm by a hair.

His back screamed in pain and held him in place with agony. No, he couldn't move fast enough. Jim tried like hell as the snake rattled and wound around ready to go at him again. Jim knew this was it, it could mean certain death. Jim closed his eyes hoping it would be quick. The rattle grew in intensity and from behind a booming sound made everything go silent.

Jim was holding his breath until his chest hurt. His ears were ringing like the old bell his granny would ding to call him to supper. Jim fell over from pain and relief when he realized the snake bite was not coming. He lay face down on the dirt nearly crying; the sound he knew was the loud crack of a gunshot. Laying there he could only hope the snake was the true target and someone hadn't come for the gold. After a moment he decided to open his eyes and face whoever was there. Before him stood a man, grimy and dirty in the falling rain, Jim could see a smile on the stranger's filthy face. The man was speaking, but Jim still couldn't hear so he pointed to his ear and croaked he was not able to hear yet. The shot left him temporarily deafened.

The man nodded and put his large hands up showing Jim he meant no harm. Jim sighed in relief and nearly wept. He was in dire need of help. Still holding his hands up the man approached Jim and offered a canteen to the injured man. His ears were starting to clear up and he heard the man speak, "I'm Clive. I'll take you to rest up to see if you're needin' Doc Zahn in Colorado City."

Jim said, "Thank you," and tried to say more but he was out of breath.

The big guy put his hand on Jim's and said, "Don't talk, take it easy. It's okay. Let's get you laid down at my cabin. It's not far." He gently helped Jim up, his back cracking as he tried to stand.

"Let's see if old Mary can give you a ride. She should be helpful," the man said. Jim could see a mule grazing in a patch of grass nearby.

The man walked him slowly over to the old mule and helped him up to lay on her back. Jim couldn't help crying out in pain. If they had to go very far he wouldn't make the walk, so he grit his teeth and held on to her mane. With all the time Jim had put into his plans, he never seemed to notice the cabin nor the man living there. He was grateful now for overlooking the big man who had literally just saved his life.

As they plodded along, the stranger kept checking to see if Jim could hold on a little bit longer. Jim would hold on to the mule if it meant resting up a bit and hopefully not being completely crippled after this. Finally, they reached the cabin, and the man called Clive helped Jim get inside and lay down on a small bed. The cabin was not as small as it appeared from the outside. An old man sat staring out a back window and barely seemed to take note of the men struggling into the cabin.

From another room a man looked on. Jim could tell just by his appearance he might have been slow in his mind because while the man looked to be full grown and bigger than Clive, he held a small tattered blanket almost the way a young kid would. Jim could also see a kind of childlike innocence behind the grown up face.

Clive helped Jim get as comfortable as possible on the small bed with nearly no pillows or padding, but Jim was grateful for anything aside from hard rocky ground and rattlesnake.

"Sorry, bud. Well now we should get to know each other. My family, the old man over by the window is our father Goodman Marshall and the big fellow is my brother Caleb; he's a good man. Well, he is touched in the brain, so you know how that is, but he's a hard worker and always helpful. We have a little sister but she's away, and our dear mother is with God. I'm Clive. I work a ways up the mountain in the mine there."

Jim then thought the money he stole and stashed away was probably meant for this big man. The mines often paid in gold coins. Guilt hit him like a fist in the gut. Clive smiled at him and nodded. It was Jim's turn for introductions.

"I'm Jim Hardy. I'm a wagon man for Well's Cargo. I was just robbed!"

"Really? You drive for Well's Cargo? I bet you bring in our new equipment! Do you have my new shovel yet? My boss told me he would get me a new shovel," Caleb, the big "little" brother began, but Clive shushed him after a minute.

"Robbed? Oh, I hope that don't mean our pay will be late," Clive spoke but grew silent, his face taking on an interesting look. Jim didn't know if the look was of suspicion or something else, but he wanted to change the subject quick.

"I didn't get a good look at the bastards. Thank you again for saving me from the rattler, my friend. I owe you one or two. That would've been one terrible way to go."

Clive seemed to come out of whatever his mind was thinking on. "Hell, no problem. Jim, that thing was a giant. He was close to five feet! Haven't seen one of his size in many years. I would only hope that if I were in your position someone hopefully would be there to save me. With your back injury and that leg there would be no way to get away!"

Jim tried to sit up a bit and was able to prop up a little; his back and leg ached. Clive held a hand up to stop him and waved Caleb over. "Slowly, help him sit up a bit. Be gentle ok."

Caleb nodded and came over to help. Jim noticed his massive hands as Caleb slowly propped him up a bit on the little old bed.

"I really can't thank you enough! " Jim said. "If there is anything I can do to repay you I certainly will."

He could tell there was something that Clive wanted to say but held back. Caleb just smiled shyly. The old man in the corner spoke, "Well Clive, ask him, you want to ask him what the hell he's going out here by the old mines snooping around!"

The brothers looked to their father, embarrassed the old grump spoke to Jim so roughly. Jim could see the look; it was one he often gave his old man when he was being rude. A look of fright maybe, he sensed the brothers had to tread lightly around the old man.

Jim's heart pounded, and he wondered if these men noticed his activities in the area. How much had they noticed? He couldn't begin to say he was robbed on the road if there were witnesses.

"Dad, don't be talkin' rude! He hasn't been snooping around. I'm sure he's got official business for Well's Cargo up here and that's none of our business!" Clive said red-faced with embarrassment.

Caleb just stood with his eyes looking down at his boots, "No, really gentlemen, it's ok!" Jim said through pained breaths as sharp stabs ran through his lower back again.

"Really, it's fine, Clive. I don't take offense and yes, I have been around these parts a lot lately. It's just, well I work for Well's Cargo, and I'm sure you know I have to be careful with that information."

Jim was working it out as he went. "Well, I have several runs to make with payroll through these very hills soon in the coming weeks. I have to be so very careful. You see, my partner is injured as well and I just didn't want any surprises. But I guess with the robbery today, I wasn't careful enough." Jim twiddled the fabric on the old quilt he sat on.

"Mr. Jim, my brother and I are strong, and we live here in these hills. Could we be of help?" Caleb asked. "We sure would like to show those boys at Well's Cargo how helpful we can be." He spoke so much Jim was caught off guard, not figuring the boy was that bright.

Jim breathed a sigh of relief and decided he would make them an offer benefiting both them and him. If they accepted, he could claim they rescued him from the gang of highwaymen and a rattlesnake, then he could get them both jobs on the Well's Cargo line and then he wouldn't feel so bad for running off with their pay.

"You go along with what I say, and I can promise you both jobs on the Well's Cargo, that is if you'd be interested."

"We are!" Clive jumped to his feet and paced excitedly.

"When the rain came, I cursed out loud cuz we ain't allowed down in the hole when it rains like this. That meant we'd be missin' our pay until we was able to go back down, but God had you out here and we rescued you and now we got better jobs!"

"Do I get a gun?" Caleb asked.

"Oh, you sure do. Do you know how to shoot?"

Caleb said, "Daddy taught us how to shoot real good!"

"Sounds like ya'll better get cleaned up and take me into town. We'll tell the sheriff you rescued me from the thieves and from the rattle. You'll be heroes and I'll write a letter to my supervisor and ask him to hire you both."

Audrey sat beneath a tree, watching down the hillside as Jim was hauled into a small cabin. She gritted her teeth and cursed. He'd have to share the gold with the filthy miners or make up a good lie. Her palms itched at the thoughts of running her hands over the shimmering treasure from the strong box. She didn't know if she'd wait for Jim to spread his lies through town, proclaiming him the victim of a robbery while she was forced to work the saloon for months, sucking and fucking until he deemed it safe enough to run away together. She was damn near certain she was just going to leave his ass with nothing in Colorado City. She'd have much more to spend if she didn't have to share it with him.

"I told you, Jim. I'm sick of waiting around."

GET A ROPE

ERNIE STUMBLED INTO THE sheriff's office. He smelled as if he'd fallen face-first into a whiskey barrel and was forced to drink it all before he drowned.

"Is Dale around?"

The deputy, Bower, shook his head, "He's out at the Double R."

Ernie came closer to the deputy, "He's investigatin' all the dead animals ain't he?"

"He is, Ernie. Why?"

"Because I came to tell him I saw what, I saw who did it."

"Well, go on," Bower said.

"I want'im to hear this, it's important."

"I'm just as important as him. Spill the beans old man!"

"Hold yer horses, I wanted to ask if there'd be a..."

"A reward? Sure, there is, just get to talkin' damnit."

"Alright, now sit down for this."

Bower gestured to how he was indeed sitting already.

Ernie leaned over the desk and whispered, "T'was a monster, a Loup Garou."

"A what?"

"A werewolf."

"I think you need to sleep off last night. Just the smell of you is makin' me drunk."

"I'm bein' serious, ya little shit. Listen to me...after it killed every damn head of cattle, it turned into a woman and hid in the stable at the stagecoach station."

"What?"

"I watched, nekkid as a newborn, covered in blood. She put on her dress, washed off in the trough, and sneaked back into the stables around dawn."

"All that tells me is you climbed into a bottle and didn't come up for breath until the sun was a risin' and your pickled brain caused you to see naked monster women! Get in the cell and get to sleep, ya drunk."

"I'm not drunk, Bower. I'm tellin' you the God's honest truth!"

"You're not just drunk, yer drunk as a damn skunk and stinkin' even worse. Get in the cell and sleep off your whiskey madness before I throw you out in the rain to clear your mind."

Ernie hung his head and stumbled past the desk and into the cell behind Bower.

"I'm tellin' the truth, you'll see."

Ernie hadn't been snoring for more than fifteen minutes when Sheriff Dale came back into the sheriff's office. Behind him stomped the rancher from the Double R ranch, Mr. Danridge and his cattle hand, Shelby. The sheriff shooed Bower from his seat and turned to face the pissed off rancher,

"I told you, Danridge. We're gonna form a search party today. We'll kill whatever took your heifers down."

"Ya'll sure like to take yer damn time," Shelby said.

The sheriff glanced at the cattle hand, "I don't take orders from black boys."

"You watch yer damn mouth, Dale!" Danridge said.

"It's the truth. If his kind is lookin' for acceptance, he needs to keep headin' west, fall off in the ocean for all I care."

Shelby didn't speak a word; he just kept an icy gaze fixed on the sheriff.

"I'll show you, you sonofabitch!" Danridge cursed and Shelby grabbed his arm. He shook his head and slowly the old man regained his composure.

"What're you gonna do?" the sheriff asked, daring Mr. Danridge to keep threatening a man of the law.

"I'm gonna get a search party together and get to huntin,'" Danridge said, "and if you got any balls, you'll be in it."

"You don't need to question my balls."

"Hard to question somethin' that ain't ther," Danridge mumbled and turned to exit the office.

"Wait!" Ernie's voice echoed from the cell.

The men turned their attention to him. He was rubbing sleep from his eyes and drool from his chin.

"I saw her. I know what killed all of em'."

"Who? She?" Danridge said.

"I watched a monster turn into a woman. She was slick with blood. She had to do it!"

"Who is this bitch?" Shelby asked.

"She hid in the damn stables. Go look!" Ernie said.

"Oh hell," Bower said, "this drunk piece of horseshit has been babblin' about a woman monster all mornin'."

"I say we listen to him, go check it out." Shelby said to Mr. Danridge.

The old rancher agreed, and they headed out the door. "You comin' sheriff? I thought you had balls. he said.

Father Connor rushed forward and threw the trunk lid shut and sat on it. His anger subsided at the pitiful sight of Peter, the closest thing to a son he'd ever have.

"I received your first message, weeks back. I've been heading your way, but the storms and flooding have impeded my path." Father Connor said.

"Father Glover!" Peter said, helping the old priest to stand. "We need your wisdom! This is no ordinary possession." Peter said, stating the obvious.

"Most demons are linked to a name, and some are connected to objects...like boxes. This one in particular, I was there for the exorcism in a tiny German village many, many years ago. I was just a student then like you are now. My mentor chased it as it jumped bodies, until there was no one left but a rat. The demon leapt into its body and took refuge in a jewelry box. It is there it was trapped for weeks until the rat's earthly body died. The village's holy man carved runes of entrapment on the box, making it impossible for the demon to push open. The village was supposed to burn the box but as you can see, that never happened."

"It resurfaced here twenty years ago, entwining me and you in its fate. We got so close. We almost succeeded in banishing it to Hell," Father Connor said.

"But I opened the box," Peter said.

"Yes, you let it escape," Father Glover said.

"If I had never opened it, all this would never have happened," Peter said, eyes welling with tears, "Eve wouldn't be like she is..."

"Don't blame yourself. I wasn't honest with you from the beginning. If I had told you how your mother truly died, you would have never been tempted to look inside. I thought if you could handle this, this unintentional test, you'd be ready to be an exorcist and I could completely retire from it. I had such strong faith and pride in you, I was blinded by it," Father Connor said.

"You never told me Abbie shot my mother in the eye."

Father Connor nodded sadly, "I should have told you the whole story, but I was afraid to tell you what we did to your mother and...Abbie, my Abbie. She felt terrible for years. How I wish she was still here."

"That was my fault, too. I should never have let her come on this foolish mission," Peter wept.

"Come on. You can't fool me. There was no way you could stop her from coming if she put her mind to it." Father Connor said.

"You loved her, as I do Eve. Didn't you?"

"Not in a carnal sense, like you two. It never went that far. But we had a closeness priests and nuns are not supposed to have. She was going to come to San Francisco to retire with me."

"How did you know we...? I mean Eve and I...?"

"Abbie showed me."

"She wrote that in her letter?" Peter stared down at his shaking hands.

"No, she came to me as we made our way here. Her spirit told me when and how she died and your connection to Eve. She watched from the edge of the cemetery."

"Watched? She didn't have..."

"Spirits don't need eyes to see," Father Connor said.

"I'm so ashamed, Father. I have fallen so far. I'm not sure if I can ever be redeemed."

"You can and will be, both of you," Father Glover said.

A clawing at the trunk lid and a cackling laughter sent a chill through Peter. It had been waiting to see Father Connor again. As if to prove he too was anxious for a showdown, Father Connor stood up and cracked the lid open.

Eve's face shot up to the opening, her eyes rolling back in her head. The demon was in complete control. Father Connor pulled a bottle of holy water from his jacket pocket, opened it and jammed it into Eve's mouth. She choked as it flooded her mouth and went down her throat. She fell back into the trunk, unconscious for the moment.

"How can you be so sure we'll succeed? Look at what we're facing. It's already tainted us all."

"Listen, we travelled though some rough weather, rain for the last two weeks without end. The storms that have destroyed half of California are heading this way. We were one town away from here; it was nothing but a river. With Abbie dead, I didn't think you'd have the strength to make it this far, but then Father Glover bid me to stop...and to look for a girl. She was accompanied by a mute woman, Jessie was her name."

"Jessie? She found you?" Peter smiled.

"She did. She had no idea who I was, but she ran up to me and told me she knew a priest in need and when she described you, I knew God was speaking through her. She sent us this way. We left immediately, and here we are, ready to put an end to this!"

Peter knelt in the dirt before Father Connor and Father Glover. "Cleanse me of my sins, Father. For I have committed many. I have lain with Eve countless times, even knowing she housed a demon from Hell. I have set her free to let it commit atrocities at night. I am not worthy anymore."

Father Connor and Father Glover placed their hands on Peter's head. Father Glover studied the streak of white hair sprouting from his temple.

"I will pray over you, and you will be forgiven. You will be renewed, fortified for the battle to come," Father Glover spoke, his voice shaking.

They were lost in concentration, unaware of the crowd gathering outside the stables.

Word spread like wildfire throughout the small town of Colorado City. Even in the downpour, there was a hunting party gathering outside the stable at the stagecoach station and the prey was just inside.

Shelby stood next to Mr. Danridge, rough-faced men at their backs, waiting for a signal. An old woman came to the rancher, "Is it true? The monster who stalks Hell's highway has come to Colorado City?"

"Looks like it, and it killed every damn animal I owned."

"What does it look like?" she asked, eating up the gossip like a starved dog gnawing on a hambone.

"We was told it was woman, but she can turn into a monster," Shelby answered.

"A woman? A woman is the monster?"

"The perfect disguise, don't you think?" Mr. Danridge asked.

She nodded and wandered off through the growing crowd. A man stopped her, a stranger with one arm, "What is this crowd here for?"

"Didn't you hear?" she asked, excited to tell him the horror story as she knew it. "There's a woman in there, but she's not a woman, she's a beast. She killed all the rancher's cattle, and now he wants her blood."

The man grinned, "I'd like to join in on his justice."

"Just step forward, son. I'm sure he'll be happy to have you join him."

Ricardo pushed by her and came to the rancher's side, "If this is the thing I believe it is then I'm owed some of its blood."

"How so?" Mr. Danridge looked at him, glancing at his missing arm.

"Did she do that?"

"She took my arm...and the life of my sister and a man who was like my father."

"Then it's all true. She killed my herd. Stay by me, boy. You'll get your blood," the rancher promised.

"I'm the law around here!" Dale interjected, squinting against the rain.

"Unless you wanna hang with her, you better shut yer mouth," Mr. Danridge warned.

"You can't talk to me like..."

"Like what?" Shelby asked, sticking the barrel of his pistol against Dale's gut.

"You don't gotta be like that," The sheriff said.

"Then do your job and get that bitch out here."

A dark-haired cowboy carried out a noose from the saloon. His eyes were burning with the need for blood and the rain washing the perfume of a whore from his skin.

"That bitch left me without a job when she killed the cattle. Now, we're gonna string her ass up. Me and the boys just made this, Mr. Danridge." He handed the noose to the rancher.

Soon, nearly the whole town had gathered there outside the stables. No storm would stop them from putting an end to the monster and her bloody legacy.

"Well, sheriff? After you," Mr. Danridge said.

"Thank you," Dale said.

The crowd was far too large for him to disagree with their street justice.

The sheriff stepped forward and motioned to his deputy to follow him. They crept through the stable door and announced, "Colorado City sheriff. Bring the woman out or you're hangin' with her!"

Peter was startled, his frantic gaze shot to Father Connor then to Father Glover. He shook his head, "No, sheriff. You don't understand...she's sick."

"Sick? My ass!" Dale said and pointed a gun at Peter and the other two priests.

"I said get her out here, now!"

"Where is she?" Deputy Bower asked.

"I...I don't know. She jumped out the widow a while ago," Peter stammered.

"You lyin' little cocksucker!" Bower said.

"My deputy is right, you're hidin' somethin'. Get away from that trunk!"

"The trunk? No, only my clothes are in there."

"Like a priest hauls around a massive wardrobe? I'm tired of you feedin' me bullshit. Open the lid and step away!"

Peter pulled the lid open and moved quickly away. The sheriff rushed forward and looked inside. Eve was only half-conscious. The holy water scalded her mouth and knocked the demon back, forcing it to recede deep into her mind.

"That's the bitch, huh?"

"Looks like it," Deputy Bower said.

"Get her out of the box," the sheriff ordered his deputy.

Bower hesitated for a moment but pushed the story Ernie told him to the back of his mind. He didn't see a creature. He saw a frail young woman who appeared to be drugged and half-starved. He put his pistol in his holster and grabbed Eve by her wrists and dragged her to her feet. He lifted her out of the trunk and stood her up. Eve's head lulled to one side and her legs wobbled as he tried to get her to walk. Her eyes only opened slightly, and she mumbled unintelligible words.

"Is she on somethin'? Are you a sicko dressed up like a priest to drug girls, make'em sex slaves, or some nasty shit?" the sheriff asked.

"No, sir. She's sick, very sick, and I'm only trying to save her."

"How can a sick woman rip apart a whole barnyard of critters?"

"She, um, she..."

"She's possessed," Father Connor spoke the truth.

Deputy Bower nearly let her fall to the ground, "Possessed?"

"Don't let her go. They're full of shit and so is Ernie. She may be rat shit crazy but she ain't possessed. We're givin' her to Mr. Danridge before he burns this town to the ground."

"Tell him to get his ass in here and collect her then. I don't want anything to do with any devil shit!"

The sheriff hurried back to the door and motioned Mr. Danridge inside, "Come on, boys. She's in here!"

A mob flooded into the stable, shaking off rainwater from their angry faces. They pushed the priests away to tie up Eve's wrists. A noose was thrown over her head, and she was dragged outside into the waiting storm like a dog. A gun was pressed into Peter's temple and he froze, sticking his hands in the air.

"Nice to see you, father." The voice was familiar, but he didn't believe Ricardo could be alive.

"You're not...?"

"Dead?"

Peter's face went white as he stared at Ricardo's limp jacket sleeve, momentarily recalling the feet of the creature Eve had morphed into that night in Mr. Drake's barn.

"Go on outside, you're gonna hang with her," Ricardo said.

"Easy, son. Peter isn't responsible for..." Father Connor tried reasoning with him.

Ricardo pistol whipped Father Connor before he could finish his sentence. He wobbled on his feet and leaned forward to spit out a tooth. Father Glover gripped his chest and leaned against the wall, unable to put up any fight with Ricardo.

"You shut up. He knew he was bringing death to my family when we welcomed him in off the road and he didn't warn us. My sister burned alive!"

"You shouldn't have opened the trunk," Peter said.

"You act like it's my fault! This is your doing!" Ricardo said.

Father Connor looked to Peter who wept out of fear and shame. His heart sank, and he looked to Father Glover whose face was ashen. Peter wasn't exaggerating when he said he had his part to play in the atrocities Eve committed while in the throes of the demon.

"I said walk," Ricardo ordered.

Peter, Father Glover, and Father Connor were forced along at the back of the crowd as they walked down Main Street toward a massive Palo Verde tree at the edge of town. The citizens of Colorado City gathered under the eaves of houses and businesses to avoid the driving rain, watching the procession of cowboys, law men, and the damned they were leading to the hanging tree.

"This here tree is called Green Justice. It'll be where you take your last breath," Mr. Danridge said.

The men walked Eve beneath the hanging branches, olive colored and gnarled, and threw the end of the rope over the thickest one. A cowboy rode up on his horse and was tossed the end of the rope. He wrapped it around the pommel of his saddle and nodded. It would be a reverse hanging. Once the signal was given, he'd spur his horse forward and Eve would be lifted up off the ground until she was strangled to death. Eve still looked confused, in a daze, her eyelids fluttered and fell shut. Her body lurched forward, and she leaned against the taught rope.

"Please! Don't kill her!" Peter cried.

Deputy Bower silenced him with a few fists to the gut. Peter dropped to his knees in the mud puddles, fighting to breathe. Father Connor began to pray;he didn't know what else to do. Father Glover joined him, and their voices rang out in unison trying to reach the ears of God before Eve was strung up by her neck.

"She's the monster of Hell's highway!" the gossipy old woman shouted.

"Kill that bitch!" a man hollered.

The crowd was growing restless in the storm, cold rain beating down on them; they wanted Eve dead so they could celebrate with whiskey at the saloon.

Mr. Danridge stepped forward and lifted his hands to silence them.

"Do you have any last words?" he laughed and looked to Eve.

The crowd was hushed, staring holes into Eve, ready to watch her die. Eve opened her eyes and like the storm above their heads, they sent a static charge into the air.

Her mouth gaped open, and a red tide of gore spewed out, stomach bile and blood, a cow's ear, and then a gurgling moan escaped it, monstrously deep. A voice, speaking a language no one could identify issued forth. The crowd stepped back but continued to stare. Eve growled and brought her hands up to try to wrench the noose from her neck.

"I told you! She needs an exorcism!" Peter insisted.

"NOW!" Mr. Danridge shouted over the commotion Eve was starting.

The man on the horse dug his heels into its side. It jolted forward and took off. The rope around Eve's neck tightened and jerked her upward. Her feet dangled three feet above the ground. She kicked and struggled with her black eyes wide open. She brought her bound wrists out before her and with a single motion she yanked them apart breaking her restraints. Eve's mouth gaped and stretched outward into a muzzle. Her muscles rippled. Her body began to change, and her dress shredded and fell away. Her feet elongated, her knees shifted, her abdomen sank in, and her ribs bulged.

"Shoot her!" Mr. Danridge screamed.

Peter pushed away from Ricardo and darted out before the crowd. He shielded Eve with his own body.

"Please! No!"

His pleas were cut short by a hail of bullets tearing through his body.

He stood for a moment, breathless, staring out at his murderers before falling to the ground. The crowd watched him go down but turned their attention to the broken rope and the beast that tore free from it.

A massive wolf creature standing on two feet, it howled in rage and darted back toward the hangman and his horse. The beast ducked gunfire and lunged at the horse's legs. It shrieked as the creature hit it. The horse buckled, its hind legs and hips twisted and broken. The rider's leg got trapped under the fallen horse, his bone protruded through his thigh meat and stuck through his jeans like a bloody spike. The man screamed in agony but was silenced quickly when his throat was crushed in the jaws of the beast of Hell's Highway.

The crowd dispersed. Some stayed and opened fire, while others ran through the driving rain, seeking shelter from the rampaging monster. Father Connor ran towards the beast and fell on his knees at Peter's bleeding body. The rain was falling into his wounds, mixing with the crimson, diluting it as it raced down his pale flesh like watercolor. A bullet had torn through both his cheeks and destroyed most of his teeth. His speech was a mumbled, labored over coughing up blood.

"Please...save her," he begged Father Connor and Father Glover.

"We will, son. Don't try to talk. I promise, we'll save her but please just stay calm."

Peter gripped Connor's hand, squeezing it tightly. "Last rites," he wheezed.

Father Connor was searching the many bleeding holes in Peter, trying to decide which he should apply pressure to first, but he realized Peter was dying.

Father Glover leaned in close to Peter whose eyes were unblinking in the rain. His chest rose and fell slowly; he was waiting, listening. The bullets whizzed past Father Connor like angry bees, but the beast was howling from many yards away, plotting revenge of its own as it fled.

Father Glover placed his hand gently over Peter's eyes, closing them to the horror. He whispered the last rites into Peter's ear. He felt Peter's chest go still. He moved his hand until his palm was over where Peter's heart should have been beating. It was too is still.

Father Connor took off his jacket and draped it over Peter's face to guard it from being battered by the storm. The rain was freezing, soaking his black shirt in a matter of seconds. He turned to face Deputy Bower who was holding his pistol out, tracing the beast as it ran. He pulled the trigger until the gun was empty, but the monster didn't fall.

"GODDAMNIT!"

"Help me carry Peter inside somewhere and give Father Glover a dry place to rest," Father Connor said.

"I don't have time to play pallbearer. We gotta kill this fuckin' thing."

"I'm the only one who can stop it!" Father Connor raged.

The small group of gunmen looked to him.

"Carry Peter inside and get outta my damn way!"

"Do as he asks!" the sheriff ordered, and the men carefully gather Peter from the mud.

"What's your plan, Padre?" the sheriff asked.

"I need to get it trapped in something we don't mind killin', an animal, anything, and then burn it."

"We'll blast her ass, and you set her on fire."

"Not Eve. He said something else, a cat, a dog, a rat, anything but her!" Father Glover said.

"That's gonna be damn near impossible."

"I promised him, a dying man, my son, that I would not kill her. I will keep that promise. You can either help me or get the Hell outta my way!" Father Connor said.

Jim, Clive, and Caleb were cresting the hill outside of Colorado City when they saw the crowd walking down the center of town. They moved to the shelter of a tree to escape the rain and to get a better view.

"Look at that," Jim said.

"Looks like a hangin!" Clive said.

"I haven't seen one of them in years!" Jim smiled but his backside was in agony from sitting on the mule.

"Help me down a minute, boys, and let's watch from up here under this tree where the rain isn't drownin' us."

"Alright, Mr. Jim," Caleb said and helped him down from the mule.

"Looks like a woman they're hangin. I wonder what she did," Clive asked.

"Hard to tell, folks ain't hanged for no reason. Maybe she shot someone?"

"Could be."

They continued to watch the show unfolding down at the edge of town. When the horse took off and the rope was drawn tight around the woman's neck, hauling her off the ground, they snickered, but when the woman morphed into some kind of wolf monster they were speechless. When it rampaged away Clive and Caleb went to their mules, leaving Jim under the tree.

"Let's get the Hell back to the mines!" Clive said.

"Wait! Audrey, my woman, she's in town. I can't leave her down there with that thing loose!"

"Well, I ain't goin' down there!" Clive said.

"I'm all beat to shit. How can I go alone?" Jim asked.

Clive looked to Caleb, "What do you think, little brother?"

"I don't want to see the monster!"

"If you turn back now, you can forget the job with Well's Cargo." Jim said.

"Fuck! Alright, you got my nuts in a bind here."

"Help me get up on the mule," Jim said.

Caleb got down and hoisted Jim up on his mule. He felt a shockwave of pain shoot through him, and he wondered if he hadn't done permanent damage to his spine.

"How much ammo you got?" Clive asked.

"Six in my gun and a dozen in my belt," Jim said. "You?"

"Just six in my pistol, and Caleb, too."

Jim worried; it wasn't much in comparison to the creature, but it would have to do. He couldn't bear the thought of leaving Audrey to her luck in town with that creature running wild.

"We'll sneak in, get Audrey, and get out. We don't need to be heroes to everyone."

The brother's nodded in agreement, and Jim led the way.

HELL'S CARGO

Father Connor was surrounded in chaos. The storm was getting progressively worse, flooding the streets, and it only brought back memories of his time at the little hilltop church in Texas.

"Abbie, if you're with me. Give me strength. I need it!" Father Connor said, reaching into his pocket to find his bottle of holy water. It was halfway full, but he was an ordained priest. He could bless pig piss if he needed to.

Screaming erupted from the saloon, and he prepared himself for battle. He stepped into the street and made it halfway across when he heard a deafening roar. He looked to his right to see a wall of water heading for him. Father Connor had forgotten about the storms with all the drama of the lynch mob dragging them from the stables.

He didn't have the time to turn back. He ran forward and was washed away in a matter of seconds. The dirty water forced him along its murky current. Tree branches battered against him and forced him to the street below. Father Connor couldn't get his head above the water, so he held his breath. With each agonizing second, he prayed and waited for death. The branches were suddenly lifted, and a hand grabbed him by the hair and pulled him to the surface. He gulped air and dirty water, blinded momentarily, but he recognized a voice. It was the old rancher, Mr. Danridge.

"We got you. Breathe Goddamnit!"

Father Connor felt himself being dragged mercifully from the water. He was confused when he realized they were in the stables, sitting atop a tall wooden box luggage was stored in overnight. He looked over the edge. The flood waters were four feet high or deeper.

The rancher and his cattle hand, Shelby, were also soaked but hadn't been nearly drowned like Father Connor.

"We should have let you take care of the girl," Danridge said. "Now that thing is loose out there, probably tearin' everyone to pieces."

As if to punctuate his point, a head bobbed on the surface of the rushing flood. It was Deputy Bower's, his eyes and mouth wide open, stuck in the terror of his final moments.

"It'll keep killin' even in the flood," Shelby said.

"Father Glover is too weak, and Peter is dead. He would have helped me. Now I have to do it all on my own."

"What can we do?" the rancher asked.

"Originally, I wanted to trap the demon inside a rat and then seal it in a box, but with the storm, and Peter being gone, that's never going to happen. So, I need to find a place to isolate her, or the demon will just take over another body and it will get away. I need a place to bury her forever," Father Connor said.

Howling cries could be heard over the rushing flood water from the direction of the saloon.

"Where could we corral her that there would be no one around?" Shelby asked.

"Is there anywhere outside of town, somewhere if it all went to shit, we'll both die and no one would ever find us?" Father Connor asked.

"I know where," Mr. Danridge said. "The mines in Bodi, they're just over the hill from here. Two of 'em aren't in use anymore."

"That sounds a little risky. There could be holes she could escape through...but we have no other options it seems." Father Connor said.

"We're desperate, Father. It's all we can do. We can blast it closed, like a tomb. We just gotta get her to head that way, how? Bullets are like horseflies to her."

"How 'bout you say a prayer over our bullets. I bet they'd hurt the bitch," Shelby said.

Father Connor grinned, feeling hope blossom in him. "Yes, I believe that will work!"

Mr. Danridge and Shelby emptied their guns and handed the bullets to Father Connor.

The saloon was packed with a handful of citizens of Colorado City. They hid in there when they witnessed the girl turn into a monster. When the flood hit and the waters started to rise, most of them retreated to the second floor. A group sat on the stairs, watching the swinging doors of the saloon.

Upstairs, there were two locked rooms, one belonging to Audrey, the other to Madame Lucille who was hiding on the stairs to get a better look at the barroom. Two rooms weren't locked yet, but the remaining prostitutes ran for them. A whore named Melinda and her sister Kathy refused to let anyone into their rooms, barring the doors and not opening them even for their fellow prostitutes.

"Stay back! This is our hiding spots!"

"You bitches better open the doors!" a miner named Jones yelled.

Ricardo had taken shelter there too, but he kept to himself. He was there on purpose; he was hunting. There was a static feeling in the air, and he knew they too were already being stalked. He backed himself into a broom closet and slipped into its darkness, shutting the door.

Through a crack at the door frame, he watched the small crowd as they argued and shoved each other. Their raucous behavior was like blood in the water, a fly struggling in a spider's web. He knew it wouldn't be long before the beast was drawn to them.

He had already shot Peter, blew a hole through the side of his face. He watched the fake priest die. It only made him feel a bit better. He still wanted the bitch. He had to kill Eve. His arm ached, but it didn't match the pain he constantly felt in his heart. He hoped it would cease soon. The stairwell erupted in screaming and growling. He smiled in the dark and waited.

Jones stepped back from the door, lifted his heavy boot, and kicked it. It rattled on its hinges but didn't give. He was growing desperate. The thing running amok outside would certainly find its way into the saloon sooner or later.

He pulled his pistol and blew the doorknob off one of the doors. He kicked the door again and it broke in.

"You bastard!" Melinda screamed and came through the door swinging.

She punched Jones in the eye, but it didn't faze him. He grabbed her by the throat and slammed her against the wall so hard it busted the back of her head open.

"Get outta the fuckin' way!" he shoved her aside and ran into her room.

Behind him, the people on the staircase began screaming. Animalistic growls urged him to hide. He looked around frantically, and his eyes fell on the bed. He got on his belly and wedged his large body into the small space under it. Sounds like wet crunching and gurgling moans came from the doorway; the beast found Melinda. Jones could hardly breathe. His ribcage couldn't expand enough to get a good lungful of air. He bit his lip and watched a set of gnarled feet tread into the room, knowing it must have killed everyone in its path. He prayed it would find Kathy first, but she was next door and probably already crawling out a window. He heard a snuffling noise and a low gurgling voice spoke, "I can smell you in here, like pig shit and cum."

Jones felt his britches get warm and damp. He tried to crawl forward so he could get a good shot with the gun he gripped in a sweaty palm.

"You pissed yourself!" the demon wolf laughed.

Jones realized his decision to hide under the bed was a terrible idea, but he wasn't going down easily. He opened fire, blasting three bullets at the creature's feet. In a heartbeat they were nowhere to be seen. He knew Melinda had a dresser by the door and figured it had leaped on top of it.

"How many shots you got left? Two? Three?"

Jones forced himself forward, squeezing under the bed further until he stuck his head out the other side. He twisted his head awkwardly and tried to get his arm around to fire on the monster, but it was already mid-leap.

It landed on the bed with such force that it felt like it crushed Jones' ribs beneath its weight. He screamed and fired until his gun was empty. The wolf beast jumped up and down on the bed. Each time it fell, the bed smashed down on Jones who cried breathlessly. It was sick of playing games. The beast bounced off the bed and slashed Jones across the back of his neck with it claws, tearing his flesh away. It swiped again and broke his neck.

"We meet again, bitch!" Ricardo said from the door.

The demon beast was bent over, tearing at Jones' neck until his head was nearly free when the voice interrupted it.

It looked up to see a familiar man with a gun in one hand. The last time it saw his face, it ripped most of one of his arms off.

"Wanna give me a hand?" the demon cackled, a throating laugh as it ripped the miner's head off.

Ricardo lifted his pistol and aimed it for the beast's head. "I'll see you in Hell."

As he pulled the trigger, the monster wolf tossed the severed head. It hit Ricardo's gun, knocking it off its aim enough to have the bullet miss its mark and blow the creature's ear off. He pulled the trigger again as it bounded at him, hitting it in the chest but not stopping it from ramming him out the door and slamming him against the wall in the hallway. It lifted him by the throat, squeezing until his eyes bulged. He smiled and mouthed, "Fuck you."

He pulled the trigger and blasted a hole into the beast's gut. It howled in agony and crushed his throat. It dropped him and ran back into Melinda's room where it crashed through her window and plummeted into the flood waters below.

Jim and the brothers waded through the streets. Jim's whole body hurt so bad he could hardly make it to the saloon, but he refused to let himself give up. He had to find Audrey. They entered the flooded barroom. There were body parts floating atop the water. His heart stuttered when he saw the corpse of a woman bobbing by the stairwell. He rushed to her and rolled her over to see it was not Audrey.

"Thank God."

"Let's go upstairs," Clive whispered.

They climbed out of the water and ascended the steps. They were greeted by more dead bodies, men and women torn open. Entrails hanging from the banister, a scalp smeared across and stuck to the wall. Jim didn't know if he could handle finding Audrey dismembered. He got to the top step and looked down the hallway. There was a dead man against the wall and a woman he knew was Melinda on the floor, torn open.

"Audrey?" Jim called, his voice breaking, "Audrey, are you here?"

The door next to the dead man slid open, and Kathy burst into tears. Her sister was disemboweled, lifeless on the dingy floor.

"No!" she cried.

"Kathy, where's Audrey?"

She fell to her knees and tried to shove her sister's insides back into her open stomach cavity.

"Kathy!" Jim grabbed her by the arms.

"I don't know. She left hours ago," Kathy cried.

"Left? Where?"

"How the fuck should I know, Jim?"

"Well, where would she go?" he asked.

"I heard her askin' Jones and Miller about the old mines last night."

"Mines?" Jim's mind turned over and over with the information.

He didn't want to believe she'd ever betray him, but she only had one reason to ever go out to the old mines...she was going for the gold.

He turned back to Clive and Caleb, his face turning red with anger.

Father Connor and Shelby waded out the door first. Mr. Danridge came along behind them, cursing the cold water around his waist.

Shelby gripped Father Connor's shoulder and motioned to look at the saloon. The stable was facing the side of the bar and brothel. An upstairs window was broken and in the water below emerged the demon wolf. It was injured and pissed off.

"Kill it!" It was the voice of Dale the sheriff.

He and a group of four men came around the corner of the building. They opened fire, and the beast charged them. The sheriff stood his ground in the waist deep water, but his bullets didn't bring the beast down. She lifted a massive paw and slashed at his face. The impact of the blow tore his jaw off. He fell back into the water, and she fell onto him. His gang retreated, unwilling to fight the creature away from Dale's corpse.

"Are you ready?" Father Connor asked.

"Let's do this," Shelby said.

They trudged out into view, and Shelby whistled. The beast looked at them, its eyes burning into the priest's.

"Come get some, bitch!" Shelby shouted over the rain.

It charged at them through the water.

"I hope this works," Mr. Danridge said.

"So do I," Father Connor said.

Shelby and the old rancher opened fire on the overconfident creature. The blessed bullets impacted its chest and instantly it fell back, its flesh sizzling.

"Thank you, Lord!" Father Connor said looking up to the sky.

When they got within feet of it, they could see it had half-morphed back into the form of Eve. Her face was still monstrous, but her body was now a naked, frail woman,

"Tie her up," Father Connor said. "I'll get Father Glover ready."

Eve awoke to water hitting her face. Her body hurt so badly.

She became aware she was being floated along atop water in the same box she had been trapped in for weeks. The lid was open and above her the sky rained down on her. Lightning split the evening sky above her and she heard the whispering.

She struggled but found her arms and body were wrapped in thick ropes. Her old fear returned as the voices grew louder. Faces drifted in the wind above her, horrible decaying, eyeless spirits gazing down at her. Some laughed while others wept. Her heart thundered in her chest. A small voice spoke in her mind. The demon was weakened, but it still cried out for her to escape. She didn't want to. She wanted it all to end.

I told you it was all going to change.

You little bitch, don't just lay here. Get up, run!

No. This ends now.

A face broke through the spirits tormenting her, a familiar face smiling down at her. It was sister Abbie, now her eyes were in place. She looked placid, peaceful, loving.

"Don't fear, child. I'm here with you, Evey Bee."

Eve felt her heartbeat settle down. Her fear was replaced by contentment. Mingling with the voices of the dead were those of the living, saying things she didn't quite understand, but she didn't speak. She just allowed destiny to take over.

"Drag them up this way. We're almost there."

Father Connor's head popped over the side of the trunk. Eve smiled faintly up at him. She knew he would do what he had to save her soul. Her resolve was strengthened when an old man's face smiled down at her and in her mind she could feel the demon squirm, vaguely she knew it had to be Father Glover. All of her hope and Peter's hope had rested in him and Father Connor, and now she saw them both watching over her. Father Glover began to pray. She could feel the power in Father Glover's words and felt the demon writhe, could hear it howl in fear in her mind. She understood why Peter and Father Connor had spoken of him as such a force to be reckoned with. Even in his sickened state he spoke in a commanding voice, forcing the evil inside her to shrink back. The tendrils of darkness it had wound about her heart were loosening a bit. She was able to keep the demon in check for a moment, but her body felt so drained of life as if she were already dead.

"Peter?" she asked, her voice was hoarse in her ears.

"You'll see him soon," Father Glover promised.

Eve closed her eyes and cried. It's all she wanted, to be with Peter again.

Jim and the brothers rode up the hillside on the mules they left stashed on high ground, following in the path of the priest and his two companions. They dragged a trunk and a coffin along behind horses through the rain. Jim recognized Shelby and Mr. Danridge and hailed them.

"Shelby!"

The cattle hand turned his horse back around and came to meet up with Jim. "What do you need, Jim?"

"Where are you headed?"

"We're takin' the monster to the old mines."

"We live out that way. We can help," Clive offered.

"Yeah, go grab some dynamite and meet us there."

Jim turned to the brothers after Shelby rode away and said, "I'll be meetin' ya'll there. I got a little business to take care of."

He spurred his mule into a trot and took a path along the hilltop. He could see beside the old mine a figure in a rain soaked dress. Audrey was stealing his gold.

"Traitor bitch!" He rode toward her, and she turned.

Her face was filled with fear, and he could see in her eyes she was searching for an excuse.

"You're stealing from me, from us, from our future?"

"No, honey. I hadn't heard from you, and I came out to make sure you weren't robbed for real."

"You're lying."

"No, no. Look, we can run away now. It's the perfect chance with the flood."

"Did you happen to see what else happened in town?" he asked, walking toward her.

"No...what happened?"

"My God. I'm so happy to see you alive!" He was nearly crying, the joy of seeing her alive replaced the cold disappointment of thinking she had betrayed him.

She could see him easing; he was relieved to find her. She didn't know what happened back in Colorado City, but she had spent hours looking for the hole he left the gold in and finally found it. She wasn't about to let him take it from her, no matter what excuse he'd feed her.

Jim took a step closer, his eyes on Audrey's. He never looked down to see at her hip she held a gun. In a split second, he stood confused by the roaring blast of a pistol. A red hole between his eyes wept a line of blood down to his nose. He blinked once and fell to the ground.

"Sorry, but I don't need you anymore. I don't need anyone."

Clive and Caleb rode up to the three men outside the old mine. A good distance away, a shot rang out.

"That's comin' from the other old mine," Caleb said.

"Did you get the dynamite?" the priest asked.

"Sure did, Father," Clive said and handed him the sticks they had back at their cabin.

"I'm ready," he said to the rancher and his cattle hand.

They motioned for Clive and Caleb, and they climbed down from their mules.

Eve opened her eyes to her face burning.

She tried to sit up, but she was still bound in rope. There was a candle lit and she could see they were in a dark cavern. Over her stood Father Connor and Father Glover. She took a deep, labored breath. Father Connor was praying,harder than she had ever seen him pray before. He was crying as he recited his words and dowsing her with holy water. The demon in her writhed like a maggot, but it was still not strong enough to push her aside. The spirit of Abbie came into view again.

"Don't be afraid."

Eve looked to her side to see Peter's face. It was defiled by a bullet hole, but he had been cleaned of any blood.

"Oh, Peter. My love."

"I'm here," his ghostly voice whispered. "We'll be together forever, my love."

"This is the only way, Eve. I'm sorry," Father Connor said.

"Where are we?"

"The bottom of an old mine...and we're not leaving," Father Glover said.

The demon howled in her brain, its anger rising. Her insides writhed; it was growing powerful again. Her abdomen hurt. It bulged outward, and she screamed. It felt like it would tear her open from the inside. Father Glover lifted his voice and with the last of his strength he prayed.

"Hurry!" Eve screamed.

Father Connor held out a stick of dynamite in one hand and the candle in the other.

"No one will ever find you here, you bastard!"

The candle lit the fuse as Eve's gut burst open. A million flies filled the mine cavity. In seconds the blast buried them all.

Audrey rolled Jim's body off the side of a rise, and it splashed down in a deep puddle of gathering rain water. She ran back to the loot. She stuck her arms in the hole and felt the ground rumble. From the mine beside her a puff of dust blew out only to be swallowed by the rain. She hefted the bag onto her shoulder and struggled to get it over to her horse. She tied the sack to the saddle and climbed up to look around, wondering which way she should go, at what horizon her new life awaited.

There was a buzzing at her ear, and she swatted a fly away. It came back, persistent to escape the rain. It ran right into her face, and she opened her mouth to curse the damn thing, but it flew down her throat.

Audrey choked and gagged; vomit rose in her throat but she swallowed it back down. She could hear the voices of men approaching so she spurred her horse and retreated over a ridge. In the darkness and the rain, she watched a group of men come to where she shot Jim. They called Jim's name and searched for him, but they didn't see his corpse and wouldn't find it until the rain was gone and the wash dried up.

You'll be long gone by the time they find him.

She shook her head and looked around. No one was there. The voice had come from inside her head.

Don't be afraid. We're gonna have some fun!

Audrey nodded. She needed some fun. She frantically thought what to do next, and where to go.

I hear California is nice.

"California, yeah, that sounds exciting," she said.

Burt whipped the horses. He wanted to move quickly. There was a bandit gang nearby. Jim Hardy was murdered while running the route through Bodi and Colorado City a few weeks back, and they just recovered his corpse from the bottom of a wash after the flood waters finally dried up.

Burt looked to Caleb, the ex-miner who pulled Jim's body out of the mud. Poor old boy cried for days, saying they rescued him once, but they lost sight of him. The bandits must've come back to finish him off. Caleb was a crack shot with a rifle so Burt felt a little more at ease, but he told Burt there were things bullets couldn't kill. He'd seen something evil once and had taken to carrying a bible in his pocket. Burt would have laughed at the boy, but he seemed a little dumb, so he left the young man alone.

The strong box beneath Burt's ass had been loaded up with gold, so he hoped Caleb would keep his wits about him. He didn't appear to have too much wits, but he was a big, tough sumbitch, and that's all Burt required. His brother rode with old Cletus now and kept watch of those cursed roads where Jim fell, and every time they rode through there they'd say a prayer for the old boy, a hero taken too soon.

There was word someone or something was stalking the Well's Cargo routes; coaches had gone missing, drivers murdered along with whole teams of horses. It was a mystery, and the story was spreading like wildfire. People were calling the route Hell's Cargo now. Burt felt a chill run up his back. He hollered and gave the team hell. He'd run their legs off before finding himself gunned down by thieves or killed by some ghost or monster out in no man's land, Arizona.

"We're almost there, ma'am," he shouted over his shoulder to the passenger in the Well's Cargo coach.

She was beautiful but odd. He noticed she wouldn't show her face around Caleb, but he didn't ask her why. She was not very old at all, but there was a streak of white hair at her temple. She often held whole conversations with herself, but Burt pretended not to notice. He didn't get paid to ask passenger's their business, after all.

At their last stop, she came back carrying a fancy jewelry box under her arm. She had it specifically made just for her. She wouldn't let anyone touch it and when she thought she was alone Burt heard her call it a "just in case home."

After hearing that nonsense, Burt was sure she was as crazy as buzzard shit and wanted to ditch her right then and there but he took comfort knowing he didn't have to haul her much farther.

"Final stop, California!" he yelled and whipped the horses, eager to get rid of the strange passenger and her box.

ACKNOWLEDGEMENTS

A shout out to Jeremy and Steve at Dead Sky for letting us share our stories with the world—Keep it horror, Keep it Metal for life! And to Anna and Zoe for doing amazing edits—We are so thankful for all of your amazing work! So much love to all of our readers, fellow writers, and horror addicts!

ALSO BY THE SISTERS OF SLAUGHTER

Novels/Novellas

The Abyssal Plain: The R'lyeh Cycle - Journal Stone 01/29/2019

Tapetum Lucidum - Death's Head Press 10/01/2019

Isolation - Crossroad Press 01/18/2022

Mayan Blue - Crossroad Press 02/22/2022

Pandemonium, Arizona - Journal Stone 06/19/2022

Short stories

Wishful Thinking (wishes book 1) – Fireside Press 10/29/2014

Double Barrel Horror: Just a Few/Tenants rights - Pint Bottle Press 01/27/2016

Splatterpunk Forever - Splatterpunk Zine 11/23/2018

Other Voices, Other Tombs - Cemetery Gate Media 06/23/2019

Her Black Wings – Kandisha Press 01/12/2020

Splatterpunk Bloodstains - Splatterpunk Zine 12/06/2020

Were Tales: A Shapeshifter Anthology - Brigid's Gate Press 09/21/2021

ABOUT THE AUTHORS

Michelle Garza and Melissa Lason is a twin sister writing team from Arizona. Dubbed The Sisters of Slaughter for their horror and dark fantasy writing, their work has been published together and separately by Thunderstorm Books, Death's Head Press, Cemetery Gates Media, Crossroad Press, JournalStone, and Agora Books. Their debut novel, *Mayan Blue*, was nominated for a Bram Stoker Award. They are currently working on projects for Dead Sky Publishing and Thunderstorm Books.